**Praise for the Phoenix Chronicles by
LORI HANDELAND**

Doomsday Can Wait

"A striking series . . . with a decidedly sexy edge. Readers again view the world through the eyes of ex-cop-turned-humanity's-savior Liz Phoenix [in] this complex mythology."     —*RT Book Reviews* (4 stars)

"We really enjoyed i̶t̶ ̶ ̶ ̶ ̶ ̶ ̶ ̶ ̶ ̶ ̶ ̶ ̶ ̶ng forward to [more] i̶ ̶ ̶ ̶ ̶ ̶ ̶ ̶ ̶ ̶ ̶ ̶ ̶ ̶ ̶ ̶ ̶ ̶ ̶bots & Vamps

"Cool . . . ̶ ̶ ̶ ̶ ̶ ̶ ̶ ̶ ̶ ̶ ̶ ̶ ̶ ̶ ̶rv à la Mode

"Fascinat̶ ̶ ̶ ̶ ̶ ̶ ̶ ̶ ̶ ̶ ̶ ̶ ̶ ̶ ̶ ̶ ̶ ̶
                                —*Fallen Angel Reviews*

"Handeland does an amazing job of packing so much punch into the pages of this story without ever leaving the reader behind. *Doomsday Can Wait* ups the paranormal and emotional content of the series, adding strength to the heroine and a more human touch to one of her closest allies. This is an action-packed series that urban fantasy readers should thoroughly enjoy, and I'm looking forward to seeing where the author takes us next."     —*Darque Reviews*

"Handeland pens another tale that captured my heart . . . with captivating characters [and] an absorbing plot that will keep readers on the edge of their seats."
                                —*Romance Junkies*

## Any Given Doomsday

# Smoke on
# the Water

## Lori Handeland

St. Martin's Paperbacks

This is a work of fiction. All of the characters, organizations, and events portrayed in this novel are either products of the author's imagination or are used fictitiously.

SMOKE ON THE WATER

Copyright © 2015 by Lori Handeland.

For information address St. Martin's Press, 175 Fifth Avenue, New York, NY 10010.

ISBN: 978-1-250-02014-7

Printed in the United States of America

St. Martin's Paperbacks edition / August 2015

St. Martin's Paperbacks are published by St. Martin's Press, 175 Fifth Avenue, New York, NY 10010.

10  9  8  7  6  5  4  3  2  1

# Chapter 1

"Do I know you?"

I glanced up from the book I wasn't reading to find one of the inmates—I mean patients—of the Northern Wisconsin Mental Health Facility hovering at the edge of my personal space. In a place like this, people learn quickly not to get too close to anyone without warning them first. Bad things happen, and they happen quickly.

"I'm Willow," I said. "Willow Black. But I don't think we've met."

I'd seen the woman around. The others called her "Crazy Mary," which was very pot/kettle in my opinion, but no one had asked me. She was heroin-addict skinny. I gathered she'd done a lot of "self-medicating" on the outside. A lot of nutty people did. When you saw things, heard things that no one else did, you'd think you'd be more inclined *not* to take drugs that might make you see and hear more. The opposite was true. Trust me.

"Mary McAllister." She shuffled her feet, glanced at the empty chair next to me, and I nodded. She scurried over, sat, smiled.

She still had all of her teeth, which was an accomplishment around here. I had mine, sure, but I was only twenty-seven. Mary had to be . . . it was hard to say. I'd take a stab and guess between thirty and sixty. Give or take a few years.

Mary looked good today. Or as good as she got. Her

long, wavy graying hair had been brushed free of tangles. She'd had a shower recently, but she still wore the tan jumpsuit issued to problem patients. The more you behaved like a human being, the more you were allowed to dress like one. I, myself, was wearing hot-pink scrub pants and a white T-shirt that read NWMHF, which placed me somewhere between Mary's solitary-confinement jumpsuit and the jeans and Green Bay Packer designer wear of the majority of the visitors. Not that I ever had any visitors, but I'd observed others.

Mary had been incarcerated a while. The powers that be didn't like to call us "incarcerated," but a spade was a spade in my opinion, and if you couldn't waltz out the front door whenever you wanted to, I considered that "incarcerated." Mary spent a lot of time either doped into zombieville or locked away from everyone else. She was schizophrenic, but around here that was more the norm than not. Sadly, Mary was on the violent side of the spectrum—hence the doping and the locking away.

"Willow." She rubbed her head. "I don't think that's right."

"What isn't right?"

"Your name isn't Willow."

"It is."

"No!" The word was too loud. She hunched her shoulders, glanced around to make sure none of the orderlies were headed our way. None were.

Yet.

"It hasn't always been. It was something else. Before."

Very few people knew about my past, or lack of it. Mary McAllister certainly shouldn't. Unless she was part of it.

I'd been abandoned at birth. Found beneath a black willow tree on the banks of a babbling brook. Luckily for me it had been July, and there'd been a huge town picnic going on nearby. I'd been found almost immediately, or I'd have been dead.

I'd often wondered why the State of Wisconsin hadn't named me Brook instead of Willow, though I guess Brook Black is a bit of a tongue twister.

"Your hair was red." Mary leaned in close. "Your eyes were greenish-brown."

Mary might seem good today but she was still talking crazy instead of truth. Even if I'd dyed my hair from red to blond, which I hadn't, I didn't think I could change greenish-brown eyes to blue, unless I wore superexpensive contact lenses. As I didn't have enough money for new shoes, and putting anything near—never mind *in*—my eyes wigged me out, that hadn't happened either.

"You have me confused with someone else," I said. "That's okay. Happens to everyone."

Mary shook her head. But she didn't argue any more than that. The silence that descended went on so long, I nearly went back to my book.

"I know what you are."

I hadn't shared what I was with anyone, though I guess it wasn't a secret that I was here for the same reason Mary was.

"What am I?" I asked.

Might as well get the truth out in the open, although *murderer* was a bit harsh. The man hadn't actually died.

No thanks to me.

"A witch," Mary answered.

I laughed, but when her eyes narrowed I stopped. I'd been in here long enough, with people like her, to know better.

"Why would you say that?" Had I done something to her without realizing it? Or did she just think that I had?

"Because I'm one too."

"When you say *witch,* you mean . . . ?" I'd been thinking *bitch* but—

Mary cackled like the Wicked Witch of the West.

Maybe not.

That interpretation made more sense. If Mary thought she was a witch, it followed that she'd think I was as well. Which meant everyone in here was a card-carrying broomstick rider—at least according to Mary.

"You see things," she continued. "Then they happen."

Since becoming a resident of this facility I'd told no one of what I saw when I looked into the water. I'd stopped insisting that those incidents would occur. I wanted to get out of here while I was still young. So how did Mary know about my visions?

"I don't understand what you mean," I lied.

There wasn't much that could be done about what was wrong with me. No amount of medication made the visions stop. Talking about them with my shrink certainly hadn't. Pretending I didn't have them was my only option, and I was getting better at it.

"You know any spells?" Mary lifted a bottle of water to her lips and sipped. The sun sparkled in it like a beacon. Images danced.

I closed my eyes, turned my head. "No."

"We'll have to find some."

"Find spells? How? Where?" I should have asked, *Why?* My first mistake.

The sound of water splashing onto the floor made my eyes snap open. Second mistake.

The puddle on the ground at my feet reflected the ceiling tiles and the fluorescent lights for just an instant before I saw something that should not, could not, be reflected there.

A room with books, books, more books. I recognized

the library here at the facility even before I saw myself at the center—green scrubs, blue shirt, bare feet. I was alone. On the floor lay a volume. The title: *Book of Shadows*.

I seemed to be searching for something, or maybe someone. I appeared frantic—pale, scared, trembling. What had I done this time?

Then a face appeared in the water, blotting out both me and the library. A man slightly older than me. Long-ish dark hair, scruffy beard. I'd seen him many times before. He was important, but I didn't know why. He would keep me safe; he would save me. But I didn't know from what.

"Ladies." The mouth in the vision formed the word; those lips curved.

Strange. It was almost as if—

I lifted my gaze. He stood in front of us. Had I conjured him from my vision in the water?

I snorted. Conjured. Right. Mary's witch talk was invading my head.

"Something funny?" he asked.

I reached out, my fingers trembling as they had in the vision, and he took my hand with a gentle smile. A spark flared where we touched, and I tried to pull away, but he held on, though his smile faded to a frown. From the zap of electricity? Or my odd behavior?

This could not be him. He wasn't real. Even though he felt very much so.

I got to my feet, lifting my free hand toward his face. He was so tall I had to stretch. In my dreams of him I'd known he was big, strong. How else would he protect me from . . . whatever it was that he would?

He stilled, gaze on mine, but he didn't stop me from touching him. I pushed aside his tangled hair. The tiny golden hoop in his ear made my eyes sting.

"It really is you," I whispered.

Then I fainted.

Sebastian Frasier caught the girl before she hit the ground, swung her into his arms then stood there uncertain what to do with her.

The other woman, older, wearing a tan jumpsuit, which seemed to have come from the In Custody Collection, beckoned. Sebastian followed her to a room halfway down the hall.

The Northern Wisconsin Mental Health Facility had been built to follow the Kirkbride Plan of asylums in the mid-nineteenth century. Psychiatrist Thomas Kirkbride had had the idea that the building itself could aid in a cure. With long, rambling wings that allowed for sunlight and air, the structures were massive enough to provide both privacy and treatment. Built of stone, they were set on equally large grounds, often former farmland where the inmates could work as a form of therapy. They were damn hard to escape from, which was why this one had been designated by the state as the go-to facility for the criminally insane.

Inside the room were two beds. Made. Two dressers—one with stuff on top, one empty of everything but dust. Two closets—one also with stuff, the second just dust.

"That one's hers." The woman jabbed a skinny finger at the bed next to the nondusty dresser.

"Hers?"

The woman jabbed her finger again, and Sebastian laid his burden upon the mattress she'd indicated. He'd thought the girl an employee—nurse, orderly, maybe another doctor. She was dressed in scrub pants and a facility T-shirt. No ID tag, but he didn't have one either. At least not yet.

Nevertheless, her lack of one, and this being her

room, meant she was a patient not staff. She hadn't looked crazy. But he should know by now that a lot of them didn't. Her companion wasn't one of them. Sebastian knew a lifer when he saw one.

"I should probably . . ." He glanced around for a button, a phone, some way to call a nurse, but he didn't find one.

He stepped to the door, glanced into the hall. No nurse. Although he apparently wasn't very good at spotting them.

There was only one name on the door. *WILLOW BLACK*.

"Is this Willow?" He returned to her bedside.

"Yes."

"Has she been ill?"

Though Willow was tall, she was also very thin, her skin so pale he could see a fine trace of veins at her temple. Her hair was so light a blond it seemed silver, and her eyes before they'd fluttered closed had been such a vivid blue they'd seemed feverish.

He set his palm on her forehead, but he couldn't tell if she had a fever that way. The only way he'd ever been able to discern one with his sister had been to press his lips to her forehead.

In this case . . . bad idea.

"Would you get . . ." Sebastian paused. "What's your name?"

"Mary McAllister," the woman said, but her gaze remained on Willow and not on him.

"Would you get a nurse, Mary?"

"Nope."

"Why not?"

"First time she sees you and her eyes roll up, she goes down. You think I'm leaving you alone with her? I might be crazy, but I'm not crazy."

"I'm Dr. Frasier, the new administrator."

Mary eyed him up and down. "Sure you are."

At six feet five, two-fifty, Sebastian was huge, and his hands, feet, biceps reflected that. People often backpedaled the first time they saw him. He didn't blame Mary for being leery, though she didn't appear scared, just protective. Considering the fey frailty of Willow, he could understand that. Even if he worked here, that didn't mean he wasn't a creep.

"You're right," he said. "You stay with her; I'll get someone."

"If you're a doctor, why do you need to get anyone?"

"I specialized in psychiatry."

Mary gave him another once-over. Sebastian didn't look like a psychiatrist. Although, really, what did one look like? He'd never met any who looked quite like him.

He could have tried to fit in better. Wear a suit and tie rather than a leather jacket and motorcycle boots. But as he'd driven his late father's Harley from Missouri, wearing a suit and shiny shoes would have been awkward. He could have changed. Should have changed. But there'd been an accident near Platteville, then construction north of Wausau. He'd been lucky to get here on time.

He'd figured he could transform himself—as much as was possible considering his hair, his beard, and his dead sister's earring, which he would not take from his ear, ever—in his office. But he'd been distracted by Willow Black.

As a result he was still wearing a black leather jacket and black dusty boots. His overly long hair was matted from the helmet, and he hadn't shaved in several days. The guard at the front door hadn't wanted to let him inside until Sebastian had shown his license. Then the man had hesitated so long, frowning at the years-old photo of Sebastian sporting a nearly shaved head, a completely shaved face, and no earring that Sebastian had become concerned he'd never get inside.

"Head doctor's still a doctor," Mary said.

Sebastian *did* have medical training. Not that he'd used it much.

He sat on the bed, then set his fingers to the girl's wrist. Her pulse fluttered too fast. Which could mean anything or nothing at all.

Now what? He had no stethoscope, no blood pressure cuff, no thermometer. He was out of options.

"You have any idea what happened?" he asked.

"She saw something that upset her."

In the hall there'd been the two women and himself. Sebastian might seem big and tough and scary, but he'd never had anyone faint at the sight of him before.

Mary shook the half-empty bottle in her hand. "I dumped it on the floor."

"Accidents happen."

"Not an accident. I wanted her to stare into the water, to see."

"Microbes?"

Mary wouldn't be the first psychiatric patient he'd met who was a germophobe. She was probably nearer the hundredth.

Mary cast him a disgusted glance. "The future."

"You think Willow can see the future in the water?"

"I know she can."

"And does Willow believe this too?"

"She's never said so."

"Can't imagine why." Sebastian returned his gaze to Willow's beautiful, still face. What was it about her that called to him? His ridiculous need to save everyone, which had gotten worse after he'd been unable to save his sister?

"Why do you think Willow can see the future?" Sebastian asked.

"Wouldn't you like to know?"

As the explanation probably involved headache-inducing kooky talk, not really. Sebastian was saved from answering when Willow began to come around.

Her eyes opened. He was struck again by how very blue they were. Sebastian had never seen eyes the shade of a tropical ocean. He'd never seen an ocean—tropical or otherwise—although he'd always wanted to. It was on his to-do list.

Willow smiled as if she knew him, as if she'd known him a long time, and just as she had before, she reached out to touch his face. He should have gotten to his feet. He should not have let her touch him, but he was captivated by the expression in her eyes. Her palm cupped his cheek, and his heart stuttered.

"You're here."

Her voice made him shiver. Or maybe it was just her words, which also indicated that she thought she knew him. And that couldn't be true no matter how much he might want it to be.

"Miss Black, I'm not—"

Her fingers flexed, her nails scratched against his three-day beard. "You are. I'm touching you. You're real."

"You have difficulty understanding what's real and what isn't?"

Her smile deepened. "Never."

Sebastian lifted his eyebrows, and she laughed. This time his stomach twisted, and lower, in a place that had no business doing so anywhere near a patient, he leaped.

He stood so fast he bumped into Mary and had to grab her before she landed on her ass. "Sorry."

She gave him a look like his mother always used to

whenever he'd thought something he shouldn't. Mothers were like that. Then she took his place on the bed next to Willow.

"Run along, doc. She'll be fine now."

"Doc?" Willow repeated.

"Sebastian Frasier," he said. "I'm replacing Dr. Eversleigh."

"Shiny new paper pusher," Mary muttered.

"Among other things." In a small place like this, the administrator also treated patients, just not as many as the rest of the doctors. It was one of the reasons he'd accepted this position over the others he'd been offered. Sebastian liked being a practicing psychiatrist. He also liked being the boss.

His superior, Dr. Janet Tronsted, was in charge of state health services. When she'd appointed him the administrator of this facility she'd said, "You're in charge. Unless there's a problem, you won't be seeing me." Then she'd peered at him over the top of her vintage cat's-eye reading glasses. "You do *not* want to see me."

As this Janet reminded him of another Janet—Janet Reno: same haircut, same biceps, same build—he had to agree. Her reputation preceded her. She was hands-off as long as you did your job. If you didn't, her hands would be around your throat—figuratively, he hoped—and they'd definitely be all over your record, and you'd be lucky to get another job anywhere. Ever.

Someone called his name in the hall. "Should I send a nurse to check you out?"

"No." Willow sat up. She wasn't as pale. Her hands didn't shake. "I'm embarrassed more than anything. I—uh—didn't eat breakfast."

"Mary thought you might have had a vision."

"No," Willow repeated, scowling at Mary, who scowled right back.

Did that mean she hadn't had one now or that she never had?

Sebastian's name was called again—louder, closer. Not the time to press the issue. Really not his issue but her doctor's. He made a mental note to find out who that was and have a chat.

"It's nearly lunchtime," he said. "You should eat."

"I will."

As he had no more reason to stay beyond a strange desire to keep staring at her, Sebastian left. He headed back the way he'd come, just as the nurse who'd been calling for him barreled around a corner and bounced off his chest.

# Chapter 2

The man I'd been dreaming of my entire life, the one who would save me from . . . Lord alone knew; the one who was *the one* was a psychiatrist.

*My* psychiatrist most likely. He was replacing my former doctor, who'd told me the "new guy" would be my "new guy."

There was no way that the visions I'd had of him, of me—the lingering looks, the touches, the kisses, the . . . anything—would come to pass. What psychiatrist falls in love with his patient? Especially a patient like me?

"What was it about him that made you swoon?" Mary asked.

"Wasn't him," I lied.

She scooted closer on the bed. "What then?"

I didn't have the usual urge to get away, even though she had me trapped. There was something about Mary I trusted. As I hadn't met her before today—in reality or in dreams—I had no idea why. However, I'd had feelings like this before about people—both good feelings and bad—and I'd learned they were too accurate to ignore.

"Tell me about your vision."

I considered denying that I had visions, but I figured if I did, Mary would just keep tossing water around until I stopped.

"We need to keep it between us. Telling the shiny

new paper pusher that I have visions is a good way to get me locked someplace I can't have any."

Another lie. I could have them anywhere, but all I needed was for Mary to tell anyone—everyone—that I could see the future. From what I'd observed of Mary so far, she talked a lot. Usually to the corner, but still. She'd been lucid enough today.

"Okay," she agreed. "What did you see?"

"Our library."

"What's so scary about that?"

"Who said it was scary?"

"You fainted. Or do you always faint after a vision?"

"One had nothing to do with the other. I really didn't have breakfast."

"You never do," she said, making me wonder how long she'd been watching me before she approached. "Let's go to the library."

In my vision it had been night. There'd been a full moon shining through the skylight, and I'd been alone. Did that mean I was supposed to wait for the full moon and go alone or didn't it?

Couldn't hurt to check the place out in the light with a buddy. Why Mary was suddenly my friend I had no idea, any more than I did about a lot of things.

I let her help me up. In truth, I needed her to. When she continued to hold my hand as we walked down the hall I realized I needed that too. I couldn't remember the last time anyone had done so. Which might be all the explanation necessary for my new—my *only*—pal.

Mary appeared as starved for affection, as in need of a friend, as I was. If she thought I was a witch, if she thought she was too, so what? There were people in here who thought they were famous historical figures.

Why was it whenever folks went off the deep end they imagined themselves as Napoleon or Cleopatra?

Same goes for reincarnation. Farmhands from the sixteenth century were never reincarnated. But Anne Boleyn got recycled a lot.

The library wasn't far away, unusual in this facility, which had so many wings I don't think I'd yet seen them all. A lot of them had been closed off from lack of use. Northern Wisconsin might be vast, but the number of lunatics wasn't. Or maybe lunatics hid in the woods and didn't come out. I should have.

Not that it was bad here. It was just . . . here. And I didn't want to be.

What I would do once I was released was a mystery. I'd finished high school—wasn't easy, but I'd done it. I'd gotten a job at a nursing home. I was good at taking care of people. I had been considering applying for aid so I could go to nursing school, and then it had happened.

I'd seen the vision of my own death—the man who would do it and what he would do. The stabbing, the branding, the burning. I'd felt the knife go in, smelled my own flesh sizzling, seen the mark he'd imprinted on my skin with his ring—the head of a snarling wolf. Then the scent of gasoline, the snick of a match, the blaze as my body caught fire.

When the man from my vision appeared in real time I didn't wait for him to pull the blade that would end my life. I'd pulled my own and tried to end his.

I'd explained to my court-appointed lawyer that just because the guy had no ring or knife that night didn't mean he wouldn't come on another night and kill me as I'd envisioned.

He'd lit on that word—*envisioned*—used it to get me placed in this facility and not prison. It wasn't as if I hadn't been labeled crazy before. There was a reason I craved companionship, affection, a friend, some hint of family. None of the foster families I'd been assigned to had ever wanted to keep me.

Even as a baby I'd been a problem. You'd think someone would want to adopt a pretty little white girl like me. They had, until I woke up shrieking in the dark. Baths freaked me out. So did streams, lakes, rivers, and water in cups, glasses, bottles, and puddles. When I started talking and told them why, things really got strange.

"Now what?" Mary asked when we reached the library.

"You wanted to come here."

"What else did you see?"

"The *Book of Shadows,*" I blurted.

"All right."

She hurried off in the direction of the *B*'s.

The first time I'd told one of my foster moms that I'd dreamed her oldest would break his arm falling down the stairs, and then it had happened, she'd thought I pushed him. I ended up back at the group home. Counseling soon followed. It helped. I'd learned how to zip my lip.

Still, shit happened around me. Most of it bad. And when I tried to warn people that the bad was coming, I only got sent back even faster.

"It's not here." Mary's words were louder than they should have been. Her eyes darted this way and that. The guard—a solid older woman—glanced our way.

I smiled. "I'll help her find it."

The guard didn't appear convinced. I led Mary into the stacks.

She shoved her fingers into her hair and yanked. I tried to pull her hands down. She tried to put her elbow through my throat. I managed to deflect it.

"I saw the moon," I said.

Mary stilled. Her hands lowered.

"In my vision. It was the full moon." I pointed at the skylight. "Streaming in."

"Ah." Mary nodded. "The book probably won't be here until the moon is full. No point in searching."

"All right then," I said.

"Is there a problem?"

Peggy Dalberg, my caseworker, stood at the end of the row. As her office was right across the hall she'd probably heard Mary's shout. If not, someone had told her about it.

"No," Mary answered. "The book won't be here until the full moon."

Peggy didn't appear surprised. I'm sure she'd heard worse—and probably not just from Mary.

I wasn't certain how old Peggy was, though she spoke of grandchildren, and her hair was more silver than gold. Short. No-nonsense. Like Peggy.

If she'd ever had a waist, she didn't anymore. She wore soft colors, soft fabrics, loose and flowing tops and skirts paired with boots in the winter, Birkenstocks in the summer. I bet her grandchildren loved to sit in her lap. I would have. Her blue eyes were kind, and I liked them. I liked her.

"What book?" she asked.

*"Book of Shadows,"* Mary answered.

Peggy glanced at me, then back at Mary. "You're interested in Wicca?"

I wasn't sure what to say to that. Mary had talked about witches, not Wicca. They were similar, but not the same, though I wasn't sure of the difference. Still, I'd seen a *Book of Shadows* in my vision, so it would probably be a good idea to discover just what it was.

"We are. Yes. Definitely."

Peggy urged us to take seats along with her at a

nearby table. "Wicca is a pagan religion where the main tenet is to harm none."

"That's nice," Mary said, but her fingers twisted together with increasing agitation. I offered my hand, and she took it, calming visibly when our palms met.

Peggy lifted her gaze from our joined hands to my face. I shrugged. For some reason Mary and I had a connection. I couldn't explain it. But one of *my* main tenets had always been: If it works, keep doing it.

"I practice Wicca," Peggy said. "I could teach you more about it if you'd like."

"You're a witch?" I asked. She certainly didn't seem the type, but what did I know?

Peggy laughed, and Mary's fingers tightened around mine—once, very hard. I stifled a wince.

"Yes and no. Many followers of Wicca consider themselves witches. Though Wicca is a religion, and witchcraft is a skill set."

Peggy must have seen my confusion because she continued. "The Wiccan group I belong to meets in the woods and strives for peace and goodness. We try to become one with the earth, we are soothed by nature."

"Soothed how?"

"Healing herbs."

I lifted my eyebrows, and she shrugged. "They work."

I decided not to question too closely which "herbs" she was talking about.

"A day in the sun, a few hours beneath the moon, time spent on or near peaceful water pacifies the soul."

Water wasn't peaceful to me, and the time I'd spent in nature hadn't been all that soothing. Of course sleeping on cement and peeing behind a bush probably wasn't the kind of "nature" she was referring to.

"If Wicca is a religion, then what's witchcraft?" I asked.

"Spells and magic."

Mary squeezed my hand again, but she didn't speak. I had to. "You believe in magic?"

Peggy glanced over her shoulder toward the guard, but since Peggy had taken charge of us the other woman had lost interest and stepped into the hall. The door was open but she was too far away to hear anything that we said.

"Everyone should believe in magic. Otherwise what's the point?"

"Believing in magic is what landed a lot of us in here."

"What landed the two of you in here wasn't magic."

Technically, she was right.

"What's a *Book of Shadows*?"

"Every Wiccan group—sometimes called a coven— has its own *Book of Shadows* where they record their recipes for healing, the rituals they've performed. Some individuals keep a personal one as well."

"A witch's diary?"

"If you like."

"Why would there be one in the library?"

"I'm not following," Peggy said.

"Mary was searching for a *Book of Shadows*."

To be fair, she'd been searching because I'd told her to. But I'd seen one here in my vision. Something I couldn't tell Peggy, even if she did practice Wicca and believe in magic.

Mary was getting agitated again—chewing on her lip; her free hand twisted a lock of her hair. I should probably stop asking questions, but I couldn't help myself.

"Why would one of those be here?"

"It wouldn't. Or at least it shouldn't." Peggy gently took Mary's hand, the one that was twisting hair, and lowered it to the table. "Mary, why were you looking for a *Book of Shadows*?"

Mary glanced at me. Certainly Peggy knew that I had visions—or thought I did—but I was supposed to be getting "better." Admitting I'd seen the book in one of those visions was not going to help my case.

I shook my head—barely—but people like me and Mary got very good at reading the smallest of hints.

"I'm a witch," Mary blurted.

Oh boy.

"I know." Peggy patted Mary's hand. She didn't sound condescending at all, which, considering that she was one too, was impressive.

I waited for Mary to mention that I was a witch as well, but she didn't.

"I wanted to start my own *Book of Shadows*," Mary said. "But I thought I should read one first."

Mary might be crazy, but she was far from stupid.

"Good idea." Peggy released Mary's hand, which went right back to her hair and recommenced twisting. Peggy pretended not to notice. "I'll bring mine for you, all right?"

Mary's raised hand stopped twisting and lowered to the table. "Thank you."

Did the *Book of Shadows* I'd seen in the vision belong to Peggy? Was Peggy the individual I'd been searching for beneath the full moon that night?

That was the problem with a lot of my visions. I didn't know what they meant until the situations they illustrated actually happened. Even the ones I thought I understood often wound up being confusing when they became a reality. Those about Sebastian Frasier for instance.

Peggy glanced at her watch. "You have therapy, Mary."

"No. We have Wicca lessons."

"Come back afterward and we'll start then."

Mary's lips tightened.

"I promise," Peggy said. "But if you don't go, you know what'll happen."

Mary left without another word.

"What'll happen if she doesn't go?" I asked. It had never occurred to me not to go to therapy.

"Therapy is a requirement of her being here rather than in prison. If she doesn't go, she could lose that privilege."

"Do you think it's a good idea for you to teach her about Wicca when she thinks she's a witch?" I asked.

"I think I'm a witch."

I thought we were talking about two different kinds of witches, but Peggy didn't seem to get that. And why would she? In her mind witchcraft was a skill set not a delusion. Of course a woman who envisioned the future shouldn't throw the delusion stone around so freely.

"Wicca is about balance, communing with nature and finding peace. Mary could use all of that. Or any of it. Couldn't you?"

Probably wouldn't hurt, but I was still twitchy about Peggy's magic comment.

"You aren't going to teach us how to conjure a spirit or turn water into wine or anything, are you?"

"That's *Second Book of John* not *Book of Shadows*."

My mouth fell open, and Peggy laughed. "You think because I practice Wicca that I don't know the Bible? They aren't mutually exclusive."

"Aren't you more about the goddess than God?"

"Why does divinity have to be exclusive rather than inclusive?"

"Got me." Though I had a feeling statements like that had led to more witch*hunts* than witchery.

"The earth is a gift that we worship."

That one had idolatry issues, but whatever.

"If you aren't interested in learning, that's fine."

"No, I am interested. Very."

The more I knew before the full moon arrived the better.

"Mary thinks she's a witch," I said. "And I doubt she's talking the Wicca kind."

"Mary thinks everyone's a witch. It's one of the reasons she's here. Maybe if she learns what witchcraft is, what Wicca means, she might stop seeing broomsticks in every corner."

"Not if you teach her a spell that makes one fly," I muttered.

Peggy's gaze sharpened. "Do you believe that I could?"

"Do you?"

We held each other's gaze for several beats, then Peggy shook her head. "When I say spells, I mean rituals."

"That word just shouts serial killer."

"How did we go from a peaceful Wiccan chant beneath the moon to a serial killer?"

"It's a lot shorter trip than you seem to think."

"A ritual is merely a pattern for doing things."

"Said every serial killer ever."

Peggy's lips twitched. She found me amusing. So few did, it made me like her even more.

"Religion is based on rituals. The Rosary for instance, the seder. Rituals help people to feel included, safe, protected. A ritual is always the same. The way to keep it the same is to write it down, to practice it over and over, to share it with others of like mind. Wiccan spells, rituals, written in a *Book of Shadows*, is how we do that."

"Which would make each *Book of Shadows* similar to a book of the Bible."

"An interesting but fairly accurate analogy."

"You should probably keep that to yourself, unless you enjoy having your feet slow roasted over an open fire."

Something flickered across Peggy's face so fast I wasn't sure I'd seen anything at all. Probably just a bird's shadow as it flew across the skylight above.

Probably.

The nurse, who was also Sebastian's assistant, Zoe, had been looking for him because he had his first therapy session in less than a half hour.

Zoe was short, round, bespectacled, and far too young for the job. Not that Sebastian was ancient at thirty-two. He just felt like it.

He'd thought he would have more time to get acclimated. Of course if he hadn't been drawn to the two women in the hall he would have had it. Instead he'd had to hurry into his office, shed his boots and leather jacket, glance at his schedule, his messages. Before he was even able to find his patient files, let alone read them, Mary McAllister walked in.

"What's wrong?" He got up from his desk so fast his chair spun backward and hit the wall. "Is Willow all right?"

Mary's lips curved as if she knew a secret. He hated that expression. He'd seen it on the faces of many of his patients, and they were usually right. They knew a secret, and he had to pry it out. The secret was often bogus—as in lies, fantasy, delusion—but not to the patient.

"She's fine."

"Then what are you—?"

Mary took the chair in front of his desk, and he understood. She was his first therapy session.

He shut the door, tried to get his act together. Why was he so concerned about a young woman who wasn't his concern? Although . . . He glanced at the stack of files. Maybe she was. And wouldn't that just be fantastic?

Sebastian hitched a hip onto the front of his desk and rubbed a hand over his face. The scritch of his beard made him wish again that he'd shaved. Though maybe he'd just let it grow. The calendar might read August, but a chill already haunted every dawn.

He'd heard snow could arrive this far north as early as September. A layer of fur on his face might be welcome. He'd lived his entire life in Missouri—not the South, though it tried to be. The weather was definitely nicer than here. He could feel the difference already.

Sebastian dropped his hand. Mary was watching him.

"Where you from?" she asked.

"Missouri."

"Never been."

"I've never been this far north," he said, the words echoing his earlier thoughts about beards and snow.

"Is it warm there?" she asked. "Missouri?"

Sebastian nodded.

"You should probably keep the beard."

Sebastian blinked. Had she read his mind?

Mary smiled as if . . . she'd just read his mind.

"Coffee." He stood. "Would you like some?"

She shook her head, her gaze steady on his face. He felt as if she were leading this session and not him. Probably because she'd participated in a lot more sessions than he had.

Be it on one side of the desk or the other, Mary knew how things went. With a new doctor, there was small talk. Where are you from? What's it like? How's the weather? Then . . . slightly larger talk.

"What am I in for?" She laughed at his expression. "Been here." She waved back and forth between them. "Done this."

Again with the mind reading.

He went to the coffeepot on top of the file cabinet in the corner of his office. Dry as his mouth. Damn.

"Why don't you tell me what you and Dr. Eversleigh were discussing in your last session?"

"Same thing we always did."

"Which was?"

"Why I tried to kill my son."

Sebastian wished again that he'd had time to read her file. The tendency toward infanticide would have been good to know about beforehand.

"Did you come to any conclusions?"

"Not really," Mary said.

Sebastian returned to his chair, which put the desk between himself and Mary. He wasn't concerned. Even if she'd somehow managed to find a weapon in a place where they spent a lot of time and money making sure there weren't any, he outweighed her by over a hundred pounds. He'd played football in high school, boxed in college at Mizzou. Since he'd become Dr. Frasier, he'd commenced judo lessons. He hoped he could continue them here.

He'd wanted to learn a less violent method of self-defense. In theory his size should discourage aggressive behavior in patients. In practice, crazy people didn't care how big he was. He preferred using a pressure point application over a right cross.

"I haven't seen my son in a long time."

What was "long"? To some psychiatric patients, time was fluid, even imaginary.

"Or at least I don't think I have." Mary rubbed her head. "Sometimes things get fuzzy."

*Case in point,* Sebastian thought.

"Were things fuzzy when you tried to hurt . . . what's your son's name?"

"Owen. And no, well, yes." She smacked herself in the forehead with the palm of her hand.

"Mary," Sebastian said sternly. "Stop."

Instead, she did it again. Just once, then her hand fell to her lap and entwined with the other. "Things were staticky. I could see fine, so not fuzzy. But buzzy." She wiggled her fingers by her ears. "Loud."

"All right. I know it's hard to think when that happens."

Her gaze flicked to his, and she snorted. Sebastian couldn't blame her. It had never happened to him.

"It can be difficult to deal with small children when your mind isn't exactly . . ." He paused, searching for a word.

"Your own."

That might explain a few things.

"Whose mind—?" he began, and she continued right over him.

"Owen wasn't small. He was fifteen at the time."

"Teenagers." Those he had experience with.

After his parents had died in a boating accident—drinking and driving was equally dangerous on the water. Too bad no one had given the kid who had plowed into his dad's fishing boat that memo—Sebastian had taken care of his sister, Emma. He had been twenty; she had been fifteen. He hadn't done a good job. He'd failed her and she had died. He still wasn't over it. He wasn't sure he ever could be. Or should be.

"Teenagers can be very trying," he continued. When they weren't heartbreaking.

"Can't blame him for acting up. I was no good. People painted him with the same brush. Small town." She shrugged her bony shoulders. "Happens."

"Do you remember the inciting incident?"

"The what?"

"What set you off? What made that day *the* day? What did your son do that was the final straw?"

Observers might say there'd been nothing, but there was always something—even if that "something" was only in the mind of the beholder.

"The voice told me to."

*There you go.* The inciting incident as well as the explanation for her mind not being her own. Sebastian was two for two without even reading her file.

"Shouldn't have listened," Mary continued.

"Why not?"

She rolled her eyes. "It got me put here."

No remorse about trying to kill her son, only concern that what she'd done had affected her in some way. Sebastian had no doubt that when he perused Mary's file he'd see the word *psychopath* stamped in big red ink. She wasn't his first.

"In here I can't help anyone," she said.

"Help?" Psychopaths helped no one but themselves.

"They're out there." Mary stood and smacked her palms on top of his desk, leaning closer. "They're killing people."

"Who's they?"

"He whispers to them."

"Same voice that whispered to you?"

Mary nodded as her gaze went to the window at his back, darted right then left. Sebastian wanted to glance that way, but he shouldn't take his eyes off Mary.

"The more they kill the closer he gets."

"Who is he? Where is he?"

"Roland." Her gaze met his. "He's in hell now, but he won't be for long. He's coming."

Sebastian got a chill, and that was just foolish. Mary was talking nonsense. She needed her meds adjusted and fast.

Still her words, her fear, her utter conviction rattled him so much that when she sprinted for his window, he sat there almost too long, barely managing to catch her before she went headfirst into the bars that protected the glass.

# Chapter 3

"That's a shame," Peggy murmured as Mary was carted past the library kicking and screaming.

"She was fine when she left."

I contemplated Sebastian Frasier, who stood outside his office looking as if he'd kicked a puppy, or maybe been kicked by one. He'd taken off his leather jacket to reveal jeans and a white button-down. But the shirt was untucked and streaked with what I really hoped was dirt but might very well be blood. From this distance, it was hard to tell.

"With Mary, fine doesn't last very long," Peggy said.

"What do you think happened?"

"Hard to say. I'm going to have a word with Dr. Frasier. See if I can convince him not to medicate her into the stratosphere."

I could hear Mary screaming that "he" was coming. That she had to stop him. Stop them. Had she done anything like this before? I didn't know. Screaming fits were so common, I didn't pay much attention to them.

"You think that's a good idea?"

"Meditation might help more than meds."

Mary screamed gibberish then something metal crashed to the ground. A door slammed, and the volume of her shrieks became muted.

"Good luck with that," I said.

Peggy sighed. "Maybe once she winds down, we can—"

"We?"

"She trusts you."

"I just met her!"

"You seem to have a connection."

I'd thought the same. I'd also thought how crazy that sounded, yet here was my caseworker saying just that. I wasn't sure what to make of it.

"She was more like herself with you than I've ever seen her," Peggy continued.

"Did you know Mary before she came here?"

"No."

"Then how do you know what herself is?"

"I don't. You're right." Peggy bit her lip. "She's calmer today than ever before." Her gaze shifted toward the continued thumps and screams. "Or at least she was."

"Because you said you'd teach her about Wicca, and she thinks she's a witch. You were playing into her delusion."

Why did I feel like the psychiatric professional here?

"What delusion is that?" Peggy asked.

"That witches exist."

"I'm right here." Peggy faced me. "Look, denying the existence of witches, of Wicca, is not only a lie, it isn't helping. You think she hasn't been told that before?" She threw up her hands. "That's working out really well for her."

"You're a caseworker," I said. "Not her doctor."

"I'll talk to her doctor."

"You think he'll give the okay?"

"If he doesn't," Peggy said, starting in Sebastian Frasier's direction, "I'll turn him into a toad."

I followed, hanging back enough that I could hear what was said, but not be considered part of the conversation.

Peggy marched right up to him, hand outstretched. "Dr. Frasier. Call me Peggy."

His gaze went to Peggy's ID tag, which listed her full name and title. The guy hadn't been here long enough to have a staff meeting. Lucky him—his first duty as administrator had been to deal with Crazy Mary.

This close I could see that the stain on his shirt wasn't blood but dirt. I was more relieved about that than I had reason to be.

"I'm Sebastian." He shook Peggy's hand, then glanced at me.

I'd paused a few feet away and pretended to read whatever had been posted on the corkboard nearby. I wasn't fooling him, but he didn't tell me to run along either, so I stayed.

"You don't want to be called doctor?" Peggy asked.

The corner of his mouth lifted in time with one shoulder. "Seems silly when my degree is younger than my shirt."

Peggy nodded. "I wanted to talk to you about Mary."

"We should probably step into my office."

"I just wanted to get your permission to teach her the tenets of Wicca."

"Pardon me?"

"Wicca," Peggy repeated. "It's a peaceful religion—"

"I know what Wicca is. But—" He paused. "You?"

"Me," she said, unperturbed.

"She hears voices." He peered in the direction of the continued screaming about said voice, which was apparently named Roland. "Though how she hears anything above that racket, I'm not sure."

"I don't see what hearing voices has to do with Wicca."

He frowned. "You're kidding, right?"

"I don't hear voices," Peggy said. "No one in my coven does. We aren't crazy. Not even a little bit."

"I still don't—"

"Drugging her hasn't worked. Therapy hasn't worked. Telling her that she isn't a witch hasn't worked."

"She isn't a witch. There's no such thing."

"I'm a witch," Peggy said quietly.

I waited for the doctor to argue that point. He didn't.

"I apologize if I insulted you. I meant the flying, magical, nose-twitching, pot-stirring, *Macbeth*-type witch."

"I'll give you that," she said. "I'm just thinking that if I teach her the Wicca way, it might override the witchy way. Meditation, herbs, chants, the study of our history—all peaceful. What could it hurt to try?"

"That seems like an awful lot of time and energy for one patient."

"I'd like to try it for more than one." Peggy gestured to me, and I approached. "Willow wants to learn too."

"You do?"

I nodded.

"Why?"

"I don't have any pressing commitments."

He gazed down the hall toward Mary's room again. "Maybe you should keep your distance from Mary."

He was probably right, except I didn't want to. We needed each other.

"She's better when she's with me," I said.

Dr. Frasier frowned. "I don't think—"

He was going to say no, and suddenly I was desperate for him to say yes.

"I'll show you." I headed for Mary's room.

"She's out of control." Dr. Frasier hurried along at my side. "She tried to jump through my window."

"A lot of us do."

He cast me a quick glance. He wasn't sure if I was kidding. Neither was I.

Peggy caught up as we reached Mary's room. I opened the door and walked right in. Dr. Frasier began to protest, but it was too late. Mary, who'd been banging her head against the wall, saw me and sprinted in my direction.

The room was small. She reached me very fast. Her hands came up.

"Don't—" the doctor began.

Mary hugged me, and I hugged her back.

A short while later, Mary was asleep. Sebastian, Willow, and Peggy stepped into the hall.

"Well?" Peggy asked.

The change in Mary had been remarkable. The instant Willow appeared, she stopped shouting and banging her head. The minute they touched she calmed completely. When Peggy asked her the difference between Wicca and witchcraft she seemed to know. Or at least she talked a good game, and as she hadn't before now . . .

"I'll think about it," he said.

Peggy wanted to argue, but she didn't. Instead she glanced at her watch. "I have to go." With a wave at Willow she did.

Willow started to go too.

"Not so fast," Sebastian said. "I wanna talk to you."

"I should eat lunch."

"I'll have something brought to my office." He didn't know if he could but it sounded good.

He led Willow into the room. Someone had cleaned up the mess. He and Mary had knocked over a plant, hence the dirt on his shirt. He was just glad they hadn't broken his coffeepot. He was really glad she hadn't dived headfirst into the iron bars. His first day was shaping up real well.

Was he being sarcastic or not? He wasn't sure.

"Sit," he said, then went to the door on the opposite side of his office.

Zoe looked up from her computer, her eyes appearing goggly through thick lenses. He wondered if she'd talked to anyone about Lasik. He didn't imagine it was easy to get dates with glasses like that. Being short and pudgy probably didn't help either.

"Could you bring Miss Black and me a sandwich or something?"

As Zoe nodded and got to her feet, rather than scowling and calling him names, Sebastian figured he hadn't requested anything he shouldn't have.

"How well do you know Mary?" He returned to his desk.

"I've seen her around. They call her Crazy Mary."

"Pot, kettle," Sebastian murmured, and Willow laughed.

The sound was so light, so young, so out of place here that he could do nothing but stare at her, entranced. Which made the beautiful laughter stop.

Zoe came in then with a tray of sandwiches, chips, apples, and milk. Sebastian felt like he was back in kindergarten. He kind of liked it.

"Thank you, Zoe." He smiled at his assistant, and she stumbled, colored. She shoved the tray into his hands and fled, shutting the door firmly behind her.

"You need to be careful," Willow said.

"Careful?" he repeated, his gaze flicking over the tray, making sure all the utensils were plastic. They were. He made a mental note to put the kibosh on the sandwich wrap. A determined deviant could do some serious damage with that. Paper or tinfoil was less of a threat as a murder weapon.

"Any new man in town is going to be the subject of every young, single woman's fantasy."

"Huh?"

"You're hot. You're single. There isn't a lot of that in this neck of the woods."

"I don't think this discussion is appropriate."

"You're probably right. But be careful anyway."

"Zoe's too young for me," Sebastian felt compelled to point out.

"I don't think she agrees."

Sebastian was mystified at the conversation. But he usually was in conversations like this.

He offered an apple.

Willow's lips twitched. "You trying to tempt me, Doctor?"

"Tempt?" he repeated stupidly. Had his brains leaked out of his ears in the past half hour?

"Apple?" She plucked the fruit from his palm. "Serpent? Garden? Temptation? Ring any bells?"

She took a big bite, and temptation became a close, personal friend as he watched her chew, her lips impossibly pink, her teeth just-right white. He wanted a taste.

Sebastian's hand clenched against the sudden urge to smack himself in the head like Mary had. He glanced away, his gaze catching on the files atop the cabinet. Thank goodness he and Mary hadn't knocked those all over the ground too.

Needing a distraction, he moved to that stack and shuffled through them. Sure enough, one of those files was Willow's.

"You're my patient," he said.

"Yep." The crunch of the apple punctuated the word.

"So is Mary."

"Okay." More apple-crunching.

Sebastian turned. "You said you don't really know her, but—"

Willow held up her hand. "She likes me. Oddly, I kind of like her."

"She's dangerous."

"So am I." Willow took a last bite of her apple and tossed the core into his trash.

Sebastian glanced at the stack of files again, his fingers itching to rifle though hers, but that would be rude. At least while she was watching.

"You can read it if you want."

What was up with the mind reading? He didn't like it.

"It's nice of you to befriend Mary, however . . ."

He couldn't tell Willow what Mary was in for. Privacy rules abounded. But what if the voice—Roland— told Mary to kill Willow too?

Though Mary had said she shouldn't have listened when the voice told her to kill her son, that didn't mean she wouldn't rethink the decision if it told her to kill someone else. Those imaginary head voices were notoriously persuasive, as well as fickle. Today one might ask you to kill your child. Tomorrow the same one, or perhaps another, might decide any stranger would do.

Sebastian had worked in psychiatric facilities for years. A lot of the patients heard voices, a lot more of them were homicidal, but he'd never been consumed by the urge to share privileged information before like he was right now.

"I know why Mary's here," Willow said.

Sebastian had heard *that* trick before. He wasn't biting. If *she* knew, she could tell him. "Why?"

"Attempted murder." Willow picked up a sandwich, took off the wrapping and tossed it after the apple core.

"You don't seem worried."

Her ocean-blue gaze flicked to his, then back to the triangle of bread and what appeared to be ham and cheese. "Listen, you're going to read my file, so I may as well tell you that I'm in here for the same reason."

"You tried to kill your son?"

She'd just opened her mouth to take a bite. Instead, she closed her mouth without doing so. "Mary tried to kill her son?"

Shit. Sebastian had thought he was so smart he'd never fall for a leading question, then he'd dived right off that cliff. The idea of Willow having a son had surprised, and disturbed him, so much, he'd blurted his question before he could even think of holding it back. What business was it of his if she'd been married and had a child, or even if she hadn't been?

Well, it *was* his business, but only in relation to how that status affected why she was here and if she might ever get out.

"I can't—" he began. "I shouldn't have—"

She held up her hand again. "Don't sweat it, doc, I won't tell."

Her not telling anyone about his gaffe didn't make his gaffe any less wrong. But that was water under the bridge now.

Water. He straightened, the movement causing the edge of the desk to dig into his backside, but he ignored the uncomfortable sensation as another one took its place.

Mary had said that Willow saw visions in the water. Was that Mary's delusion or Willow's?

"I didn't try to kill my son," she said. "I don't have one. I have no family at all."

"Everyone has a family."

"No." She set the sandwich down untasted. "Everyone

has parents. But not everyone has a family. I learned the difference a long time ago."

Thunder rumbled—distant but threatening. The sky had gone a nasty, swirly greenish-blue. As Sebastian had just ridden a Harley for several hundred miles, he'd studied the weather along his route. There hadn't been a hint of rain for the next week. Not that he trusted meteorologists. They'd have better accuracy if they read tea leaves.

"I should go."

He tore his gaze from the storm, which seemed to be hovering, billowing, not moving, something that storms didn't do. Storms meant wind and wind caused movement. But this storm . . . not so much. He didn't like it.

Willow stood at the same time Sebastian did, and then they were so close he should have stepped back, would have, except the desk was there. She lifted her face. He wanted to lower his—maybe he even did, but he managed not to touch her. Nevertheless, if someone walked in, this would look very bad.

"You didn't drink your milk," he said inanely.

"I hate milk."

"I'll get you some water."

Her eyes widened. Lightning flashed, much closer than it should be. There was a crack, a snap, then a pop, and the lights, the computers—everything—went off. The loss of power caused a momentary silence that was so deep it hummed.

Then patients started shrieking, employees started shouting, Zoe opened the connecting door calling his name.

Sebastian reached for Willow, and his hands closed on nothing but air.

\* \* \*

I slipped out of the doctor's office while he was distracted, then slid into the commotion that filled the hall.

As weird as that storm coming out of nowhere was, weirder still had been that the backup generator hadn't gone on. In northern Wisconsin we had all kinds of storms—wind, rain, tornadoes, thunder, snow and ice. A backup generator was a necessity. One that worked, even more so.

But that wasn't my main concern—wasn't even *my* concern, I didn't work here. My biggest worry was first stilling the annoyance that bordered on anger over my lack of family, then slowing the overburdened pumping of my heart that had come from Dr. Frasier's offer of water. I'd never be able to convince him that I was getting better if I got mad when we discussed my past and I nearly stroked out at the mention of $H_2O$.

"Willow!" Mary stood in the doorway of her room. As she wasn't wearing a straitjacket, I figured it was all right for me to join her.

"You scared?" I asked.

She took my hand, nodded.

"They'll get the power back on soon."

She drew me into her room. "No."

"They won't?"

"I'm not scared of the dark."

Being midday it wasn't really dark, though the gloom outside looked suspiciously like twilight.

She went to the window, and as I was still holding her hand, I went too. Though it had bars like every other window in the place, they were far enough apart that we could see through.

"The sky was blue," she said, "then suddenly it wasn't."

"Storms can come up pretty fast."

"Not like this. Never like this."

"Okay," I said. I'd never seen one do it either, but as it *had* happened, then it *could* happen.

"Someone cast a spell," she whispered.

Aha.

"I don't think—"

"Is he coming?" Her voice remained low, as if afraid "he" might hear.

"Who?"

"Roland." Her fingers tightened around mine.

"Who is Roland?"

"Their leader."

"Who's they?"

*"Venatores Mali."*

"Latin?" Because of my nursing ambitions, I'd studied the language a little, knew the sound if not the meaning.

"Hunters of evil. Though we aren't. They hunt us. They brand us. We burn."

A chill rippled over me. I let go of her hand. The words *brand* and *burn* were far too familiar. "They hunt who?"

"Witches."

Considering the *us,* I should have known.

"Why?"

"They hate."

Hate plus witch historically equaled burn. I'd said the same to Peggy, though I had been referring to a bygone century. Who would be hunting witches now?

No one. I was listening to and believing Crazy Mary, two things I should not do.

"They want to purify us. But they are the ones who aren't pure."

"Purify how?"

While I shouldn't be listening, I couldn't stop, and when she answered me, I knew that I wouldn't.

"The brand."

My vision rose up—the scent of burning flesh, the sizzle, the smell. I swallowed, and I tasted it too. Who was crazy now?

"What brand?" I managed, voice hoarse, as if I'd been breathing in a lot of smoke.

"Their crest is the snarling wolf."

Lightning flashed, so close, so bright, I saw stars. I glanced out the window just as the rain hit, thunking against the glass like a hundred tiny birds.

A drop ran downward, joined with another and then another, and within them I saw a whole new world.

# Chapter 4

A woman stood in a clearing in the woods. The trees were mammoth—pine, some birch. Looked like Wisconsin, but I couldn't be sure.

The moon glinted off the two-edged blade in her hand. Shaped like a *Z*, it appeared to have carving on the handle, though I couldn't tell from this distance—both time and space—what it was.

I'd never seen her before. She was very tall—six feet at least. Her dark hair waved past her butt. Considering her height, that was a lot of hair.

The undergrowth rustled. Her lips curved. I didn't like that smile a bit. She had evil things on her mind, and she liked them.

A big, ugly dude with a shaved head strode out of the trees. Over his shoulder he hauled a woman, bound and gagged and struggling. Didn't seem like she wanted to be here any more than I did, and she had about as much choice in the matter as I did as well.

The tall woman pointed with her knife at the large flat stone that shone beneath the moon. It resembled a pagan altar, even before the man laid his burden on top.

Middle-aged, dark hair, brown eyes—I didn't know her either. She started to scramble off the stone, but with her ankles and wrists tied, then the big guy guarding one side and the big gal the other, the effort was mostly for show.

I figured there'd be chanting and other ritualistic oddities. Instead, the man picked up what appeared to be a meat cleaver, lifted it high over his head, then brought it down.

I tried to scream and couldn't. My throat worked, yet not a sound emerged. I'm sure we've all had dreams like that. We usually wake ourselves up with the strangled noises we make. I didn't. At least not soon enough. Not before I saw—

I came out of the vision gasping as if I'd been underwater almost too long. Mary held my hand. The rain still fell. I closed my eyes, turned away.

There'd been so damn much blood.

Mary led me to a chair, pushed me into it, went to her knees at my side. "Where was it?"

"Where was what?"

"The forest? The altar?"

My mouth dropped open. "You saw?"

Maybe she *was* a witch.

"As soon as I took your hand."

Or maybe I was.

My laugh sounded slightly hysterical. Not only was Mary starting to share my delusions, I was starting to share hers.

I didn't follow the tenets of Wicca, hadn't even learned them yet, and witchcraft was a skill set I didn't have. Spells? Rituals? I knew nothing about them. But maybe the man and the woman in my vision had.

"Were those witches?" I asked.

Though the idea of Mary seeing what I had should freak me out, instead I was kind of glad. I wasn't alone anymore.

"Witches harm none."

"I thought that was Wicca."

Mary waved her hand as if a fly buzzed around her head. "I think those were witch hunters."

*"Venatores Mali,"* I murmured. "Which would make the woman lying on the stone a witch."

"We have to figure out where they were. Who they were."

"Why?"

"To stop it!"

"We're incarcerated."

"What's the point of a vision if you can't do anything about it?"

I'd been asking myself that since I'd understood I was having them.

"No one will believe us." Even if they did, a stone altar in "some" forest wasn't going to get them very far.

"Try again." Mary pointed to the window. The storm had blown past, but there were still droplets on the glass.

I went back where I'd been, tried as hard to see something now as I'd tried to scream about what I'd seen before. I had the same amount of luck. The drops were just drops.

"I got nothin'."

"Try harder."

I'd never been able to have a vision by trying. Never been able to stop having one by trying either. Visions were funny that way. Or maybe *funny* wasn't the right word.

Annoying? Terrifying? Excruciating? Pick one.

Mary laced our fingers together and tugged. "Let's run water in the tub."

I pulled back. Even though I'd told Dr. Frasier that I was as dangerous as Mary, I still didn't feel like going into a small room with her and running enough water so that she could drown me.

"I need to rest," I said. "Visions are exhausting."

Another good word for them. I had a dozen. None of them were complimentary.

"You can sleep on my bed."

From the slightly manic sheen in her eyes, I knew how that would go. She'd either stare at me and keep me awake or pace the room with the same results.

"I'll go back to my own." She released me reluctantly, but she did it. I paused at her door. "Don't tell anyone what we saw."

"Not until we see something that'll help."

That wasn't what I'd meant, but it would do.

So far I'd never seen anything helpful.


"Freakiest storm I can remember."

The maintenance man, who'd introduced himself as Justice Finkel, was old enough for his observation to really mean something. He appeared to know how to fix a generator, or he was at least doing a good imitation.

Sebastian handed him a Philips screwdriver upon request. He was just glad the rain had stopped and the creepy green clouds had disappeared. From the utter silence of the machine and the decrepit appearance, they were going to be out here a while. He hoped the staff was able to quiet the patients. When he'd walked outside, the door closing behind him had cut off the sight and sound of bedlam. He'd searched for Willow amid the chaos—hadn't seen her or Mary. He wasn't sure if that was good or bad.

"Isn't the purpose of a generator to go on when the power goes off?" Sebastian asked.

"Yeah." Justice squinted into the motor, which gave off an odd but vaguely familiar smell.

"What's its excuse?" Sebastian pointed to the machine with a hammer that he was trying his best not to use on the still-silent generator.

"It's not talkin', but I'm thinking lightning strike." Justice sat back. "This thing is toast."

Sebastian sniffed again and got a whiff of . . . not burned bread but ozone, with a hint of gasoline. They were lucky the whole place hadn't gone up in flames. Probably would have if the building weren't made of stone.

Sebastian gave in to temptation and smacked the flat of the hammer on the corroded shell of the junk generator. Justice didn't seem disturbed by his lack of control. Justice didn't seem disturbed by much—a good trait for an employee of a mental health facility. Sebastian wished he could say the same about himself.

He set the hammer back in the man's huge toolbox. "Now what?"

"I'll get another."

"When?"

"An hour. Two if the first store's out and I have to go to a different one."

"Isn't there a Walmart around the corner?" After riding a motorcycle from Missouri to Wisconsin, he swore there'd been one around most of the corners.

Justice rubbed his dirty palms on his damp jeans. "There is. But the corner's probably twenty miles away."

This far north the next town—or the next corner— was not as close as it was anywhere else except maybe Alaska. His own apartment was in a complex that had been specifically built for employees of this facility. If the job worked out and Sebastian stayed here for more than a year, he'd like a house. Except he'd been told a house of his own would most likely involve building one since houses in the area were scarce and empty ones available for purchase even more so.

"Maybe you should buy two generators," Sebastian said.

"What for?"

"What if the next one gets hit in the next storm?"

Sebastian didn't care for the lack of power. Although this place was old enough to have locks that needed keys, rather than electrical doors and fences, he still felt twitchy. All he needed was an escaped patient on his first day of work. On any day of work for that matter.

"Lightning don't strike twice in the same place, son. You know that."

It was a saying, sure, but did that make it true? Justice seemed to think so and Justice knew more than Sebastian did. At least about lightning storms and generators.

The old man headed for his truck, and Sebastian for his office. Inside the patients were quieter than they'd been when he'd left—Sebastian checked his phone—a half hour ago.

He beckoned to Zoe. "Any problems?"

She shrugged. "Anything out of the ordinary gets them riled up."

"They seem fine to me."

"Those who don't unrile on their own are given pharmaceutical help."

Sebastian would prefer less drugs not more. However, a riot in the dark didn't work for him either.

"My patient?" he asked.

"Which one?"

"The one I was talking to when this happened." The one who had seemed to disappear into thin air.

Zoe cast him an unreadable glance—mostly because the sky was still overcast and the lights were still out. He could barely see her let alone read her glance.

"Last I saw Willow she was coming out of Mary's room and headed for her own." Her lips thinned. "You should be careful."

"Of?"

"Willow. Mary too."

"So I hear. Has either of them tried to kill anyone lately?"

"What's lately?"

"In here?"

"Hard to say. Mary gets agitated. She's gone after a few orderlies, a nurse. But as she has no weapons beyond tooth and nail, was she trying to kill them or wasn't she?"

"Did she say?"

"When she gets like that she says a lot, not much of it coherent."

"And Willow?"

Zoe gave him a look again, one he still couldn't read. "She's always coherent. She just doesn't say much."

"Has she attacked anyone?"

"Not yet."

"Don't be such an optimist."

Someone called for her, and Zoe lifted a hand, stepped in that direction, paused and glanced back. "I've been here a long time, Dr. Frasier."

As she appeared too young to have been anywhere but grade school for a long time, Sebastian smiled noncommittally and said nothing.

"Patients like Mary and Willow, the ones with serious delusions and homicidal tendencies, don't get better. They just get dead."

Sebastian's smile faded.

"If they manage to get dead before they make someone else that way . . . it's probably for the best." She trotted in the direction of whoever was calling her name.

Sebastian stared after her, uncertain if her attitude was anything he should worry about. It was the most honest opinion he'd ever heard, and how could that be bad? Zoe hadn't said *she* was going to take matters into her own hands. *That* would be a problem. Still, he should take a gander at her personnel file, just for kicks and giggles.

Sebastian went to his office, leaving his door open so he could hear any undue commotion. He'd sat at his desk and reached for his keyboard before he remembered there was no electricity and he would be unable to access any personnel files until there was. He made a note about that, then reached for the physical files. Thank heaven for old-school Dr. Eversleigh, who still liked to treat patients while perusing a hard copy of their information. Sebastian turned on the flashlight feature of his phone and got to work.

*Mary McAllister—born March 12, 1962.*

She looked older than she was. Lifers usually did.

He didn't see much in Mary's file that he hadn't suspected. Schizophrenia diagnosed in late twenties. The usual medications, which she often stopped taking when she felt "better." Then she wasn't better anymore.

Alcoholism. Recreational drugs to the point that they were no longer very recreational. Harder drugs—narcotics, heroin, coke.

There was mention of her trying to ride a broom off the roof, which resulted in a compound fracture. Sebastian wondered if she'd started to believe she was a witch before or after that incident.

"Probably before." The falling and the breaking should really have convinced her otherwise, but it hadn't. Maybe Peggy was right and actually learning about Wicca could help. At this point, probably couldn't hurt.

He read on. The file was pretty thick.

Theft to support her habit. Dealing for the same. Nothing out of the ordinary or surprising until he got to the reason she was in here.

The voice of Roland—he paged back through the file. None of the voices had ever been named before. Didn't mean she hadn't decided to name one of them then. Didn't really matter if this voice was new or old. What mattered was that it had told her to kill her fifteen-year-old son, and she'd listened.

Owen McAllister was now twenty-eight. A marine, in the K-9 Corps. Multiple tours in Afghanistan, which might explain why his mother had tried to kill him and not managed it. Certainly he'd been fifteen at the time, but anyone who spent that long in the Marines had probably started out pretty tough in the first place. Considering the kid's entire life . . . he'd had to be.

According to the file, the last time Owen had visited, Mary hadn't remembered him. That had been over a year ago. He hadn't been back since. Sebastian hoped he was all right, though there was no notation in the file of anything different.

He should probably call the man. Sebastian made another note.

He drew out the next file, opened it, grew quickly bored. The patient was a few days from release. Not much for Sebastian to do but have a final meeting and sign the papers. He set the file aside and gave in to his desire to search for the one he really wanted.

*Willow Black—birth date unknown.*

How could that be? Sebastian read on and found out.

Abandoned at birth. Foster home after foster home after group home, to the street and back again. Failure to bond. Confusion. Delusion. Lies. Alcohol. Drugs. Runaway. Around Willow, bad things seemed to happen. That she sometimes knew about them before they did only made her seem guiltier of causing them in the first place. Then came the night she'd used a knife.

According to Willow, the man she'd stabbed had planned to do horrible things to her with a knife of his own. That there'd been no weapon on him had been brought up several times at the trial, along with the lack of a ring sporting the face of a snarling wolf, which Willow insisted he meant to brand her with before he burned her body. None of this helped her defense. It only made her sound insane.

He spun his chair toward the window, staring at the heavy gray sky. Raindrops still pattered from the tree leaves, the wind flinging them against the glass in clumps.

He found it interesting that as a child she'd had an irrational fear of water, had said on several occasions that she saw the future in it. Then, Mary had said the same.

According to Dr. Eversleigh, Willow had been doing well since coming to this facility. In their discussions of water and visions, she'd admitted that what she'd believed could not be true. For Mary to know about those visions contradicted this. If Willow had just met the woman as she claimed, why would she tell Mary these things, especially if she no longer believed them? Of course, Willow wouldn't be the first patient to tell her doctor what he wanted to hear.

Sebastian let out a short huff of amusement. Why was he trying to find sense in the nonsensical? Because even though his patients were often delusional, those delusions made sense within the world of the delusion. And this . . . it just didn't.

"Dr. Frasier?"

He glanced up to find Peggy Dalberg in the doorway. "Everything all right?" he asked.

"Yes."

"The electricity should be back up in an hour or so," he continued.

"You psychic?"

Considering the file he'd just been reading, he gaped. "Excuse me?"

"It's pretty hard to predict when the electricity will go back on otherwise."

"Oh. Right." He scrubbed a hand through his hair. His mind was still full of Willow. He wondered how he was going to make that stop. "Justice went to buy a new generator. The other one got hit by lightning."

"That's weird." She glanced behind her with a frown.

"Apparently." Though the way she was acting, she thought it was a lot weirder than he did. "Peggy? You okay?"

She turned back. "Why wouldn't I be?"

"Question with a question usually means you don't want to answer."

She smiled at him as if he were an adorable, yet precocious child, but she didn't answer his question, only asked yet another of her own. "Do I have your permission to teach Mary and Willow about Wicca?"

"What's the rush?"

She shifted her shoulders. "I kind of told Mary that I would. If you say no, she's probably gonna need to be sedated."

"Seriously?"

"Yeah."

"You know better." Or at least she should.

"I do. And I'm sorry. Seemed like a good idea at the time." She spread her hands. "It still does. I think the peace of it all would help her. At the least, learning that witches can't fly couldn't hurt. I just shouldn't have promised before I asked you."

"Your jumping the gun is relatively minor in the scheme of things."

"Thanks."

"Go ahead and teach them. But—"

"I know. If one of them suddenly starts to fly or turns into a chicken, my ass is grass."

He'd been going to say if either one of them became more agitated, she'd have to stop but—

"Whatever works."

# Chapter 5

"This is a spell of transportation." Peggy pulled items out of a paper sack and set them on the floor in preparation for our first lesson.

We were gathered in my room almost a week later. The upheaval caused by the storm had caused a lot of problems. Peggy had been swamped, which had pushed our lesson back a day and then another and so on.

"Where are we going?" Mary asked.

The mental health facility was at last back to normal, or as normal as a place like this got. The electricity had been restored about five minutes after the new generator had been installed, which always seemed to be the way of things like that.

Dr. Frasier was still getting acclimated. I hadn't been called into his office again. But I was scheduled for a therapy session in the morning. By now he'd read my file. We'd have plenty to discuss.

I was also certain the whiff of sexual tension that I'd caught the last time I was with him would be gone. I wasn't sure how I felt about that. On the one hand, I didn't want to be the cliché patient who had the hots for her therapist any more than I wanted him to be the creepy therapist with the hots for his patient. On the other hand, we were meant to be together. I'd known this since the first time I'd seen him in a vision fifteen years ago. Yes, I'd been twelve, but I was a very old twelve, and the visions had been G-rated. At first.

"We aren't going anywhere." Peggy removed a red candle and set it between us on the floor. "Transportation is another word for joy."

"Why would we conjure joy?" Mary asked.

Peggy cast her a quick glance at the word *conjure,* but she didn't correct her.

"Why wouldn't we?" A bell jangled as Peggy removed it from the bag as well.

"That's not magic," Mary scoffed.

"Sure it is. Joy is some of the best magic I know." Peggy withdrew a stuffed toy dog, which looked like a boxer, and set it next to the other items.

"What's that for?" Mary pointed at the dog.

"It represents an item that makes me happy. My dog. He's very joyful."

"Unless you're going to teach us how to turn a toy into a real live boy, or bring the actual dog here from somewhere else, I'm not interested," Mary said.

There were times Mary was more lucid than anyone gave her credit for.

Peggy glanced at me. "How about you?"

"Joy sounds good to me."

Mary rolled her eyes. "This is bullshit."

Peggy ignored her. She'd been around Mary longer than I had. She probably knew best.

Our caseworker lit the candle, picked up the bell, rang it once, and said, "I open myself to joy."

She handed the bell to me, with an encouraging nod. "Now you."

I rang the bell, repeated her words, and handed it to Mary, who hesitated, fingers tightening on the bell as if she meant to fling it against the wall. I gave a tiny headshake and she jingled it, then parroted Peggy's words. We repeated the chant and the actions three times each.

Peggy clapped and said, "I open myself to joy and

I am happy." She set the bell next to the candle, blew it out and beamed at us.

"Lame," Mary said.

Peggy's smile faltered. "Don't you feel happier?"

"I feel tricked." Mary glanced at me. "How about you?"

"I feel okay."

Peggy bit her lip. "We should probably try it again with items that bring joy to the two of you."

"Screw this," Mary said. "We need a spell that's going to help us."

"Joy helps," Peggy said. "More than anything."

"Not against knives."

Peggy stiffened. "What knives?"

I took Mary's hand, which had started to lift toward her hair, I'm sure with the intention of yanking some out. "There aren't any knives."

"Then why—"

"Mary had a dream."

Lie. I'd had the dream.

"It upset her."

Truth. My dream had upset us both.

"Aren't there spells of protection?" I asked.

Probably wouldn't help but it couldn't hurt.

"Sure." Peggy was eager. "We can do one next time."

"We need it now," Mary muttered, her gaze on my window.

I saw nothing out there, but even if there were something it wouldn't be getting in here. I still didn't like her expression.

"You're safe," Peggy said. "I did a spell of protection around this place the first day I started working here."

Mary's gaze flicked back. "You did?"

"Of course."

I was beginning to worry about Peggy. Did she think her spell actually worked?

"Why'd you chant in English?" Mary asked.

Peggy appeared confused. "What other language would I chant in?"

"Latin."

"We chant in the language we speak. And no one speaks Latin anymore."

"Did they ever?" I wondered.

Peggy shrugged.

"Show us a spell that's worth something," Mary ordered.

"Worth?" Peggy echoed. "Like money, fame, fortune?"

"Do you know any?"

"I can't cast a spell for personal gain."

"Why not?" Mary demanded.

"Spells created for selfish reasons are considered black magic. A true Wiccan does not dabble in the dark side."

"Who does?"

"I won't speak of them." Peggy's gaze touched on the shadowy corners as if someone might materialize there.

"If you speak of them will they come?"

Peggy just shook her head.

"Roland?" Mary said. "Roland!"

"Shh." I tightened my fingers around hers. Shouting usually brought someone along to see what the shouting was about. That never ended well. At least for Mary.

"Why would you want to bring the voice that told you to hurt your son into existence?" Peggy asked.

The voice that had told Mary to hurt her son and the voice of Roland were the same one. As Roland was a murderous voice, I should have added that up before now.

"He's more than a voice," Mary whispered. "Or he will be soon. He's almost here."

"We should probably move on," I said. Talking about voices . . . Rarely a good idea. And Peggy should know it.

"Using a spell for selfish or trivial reasons can cause the Foster Effect," Peggy continued. "That's dangerous. Spells can multiply out of control."

"And then what?" I couldn't help but ask.

"Natural disasters."

I blinked, remembering the storm that had come out of nowhere, the lightning that had hit closer than ever before. Had someone been performing black magic?

I couldn't believe I was thinking that, almost believing it. Except my caseworker was thinking and almost believing it too.

Peggy glanced at her watch. "I have to go."

She withdrew a final item from her bag of tricks—a *Book of Shadows*—and handed it to me. One glimpse of the cover and I understood it was the *Book of Shadows* that I'd seen in my vision.

I dropped the thing, and it hit the floor with a muffled thunk. Mary snatched it up as Peggy returned the candle, bell, and toy dog to the now empty bag.

"Be careful with that," Peggy said. "It's my only copy."

Which made me wonder why she was giving it to us. Though from the way Mary was handling the book— as if it were gold—she wasn't going to be ripping it to shreds or dropping it in the bathtub, which were the only two ways she might have to destroy it in here as fire and sharp implements were frowned upon.

"I'll keep it safe." Mary held it against her chest with both arms.

"Next lesson I'll teach you a protection spell." Peggy headed for the door.

"If spells cast for selfish reasons cause problems, then wouldn't a spell to protect ourselves do the same?" I asked.

Peggy paused. "A protection spell protects anyone and anything in the charmed circle. Which makes it about others as well as oneself. You see?"

Not really but I nodded anyway and Peggy departed.

"Thought she'd never leave." Mary opened the book.

"You're the one who wanted to learn the spells." I leaned in so I could see what she was looking at.

"I didn't think they'd be namby-pamby find-the-joy shit."

I found her brutal honesty both refreshing and far too funny.

"What did you think they'd be, considering Wicca harms none?"

"I figured she was lying. She wouldn't have been able to get permission to teach us if she told the truth."

"What truth?"

"Ha!" Mary pointed at the book.

I leaned in even closer to read what was there. "That's the same spell we just did."

"Not exactly." Mary tapped a chewed-on fingernail beneath the final line on the page.

"Works best beneath the full moon," I read. "So?"

"No wonder it didn't work! It's daylight."

"It says 'best,' not 'only when.'"

"She just didn't want us transporting under her watch. Can you imagine the trouble she'd get in?"

"I can't imagine what you're talking about."

She punched me in the arm. "Focus."

I rubbed what would no doubt be a bruise. Sometimes

I forgot that Mary was called "Crazy Mary" for a reason. She seemed so lucid. Until she didn't.

"Peggy showed us how to do the spell," Mary said. "But she gave us the book, which tells us when to do it so that magic actually happens."

Mary's eyes appeared a little wild, so I decided not to argue. Especially since I was still rubbing the "ouch" from the last time I had.

"The full moon is tomorrow night," she continued.

"I thought it was full last night."

"The moon appears full a bunch of nights, but there's only one when it actually is."

Was that true or wasn't it? Did it matter? Not really. All of this was bogus, except in Mary's head.

"I'll come here after everyone's asleep tomorrow night," Mary said, "and we'll do the spell right this time."

I hesitated, but what better way to prove to Mary that magic wasn't real and the spells wouldn't work than to actually do one and have it not work?

"Okay."

Mary got to her feet, picked up the *Book of Shadows,* kissed the top of my head like I thought a mother might, and went away.

Sebastian had been dancing as fast as he could to get up to speed on both his administrative and psychiatric duties. He'd scrolled through the personnel files, found nothing particularly disturbing beyond a lack of experience in some channels and less education than he'd prefer in others. Considering their location and the nominal local population totals, the employment pool was limited. Dr. Eversleigh had done the best that he could.

He'd taken a close look at Zoe's file. She was as young as she appeared, but a lot smarter than most. She'd graduated from high school early, plowed through her BSN—Bachelor of Science in Nursing degree—in three years, and accepted this job at the age of twenty. Her grades were stellar, her employment record the same. That she was only twenty-two now made her the youngest employee at the facility. According to her last review, they were lucky to have her and should do whatever possible to keep her.

Sebastian had to wonder why a smart young girl like Zoe would continue to live in the middle of nowhere and work in a place that—from the outside at least—resembled a Gothic castle. Of course someone might ask him the same thing.

He'd taken his patient files home the first night. As Zoe had hinted, Mary and Willow were the patients he should be most concerned about. Almost everyone else in his pile had yet to try and kill anyone, or if they had, they hadn't gotten caught.

Sebastian had considered assigning Willow to another psychiatrist, but what possible reason could he give for that before they'd even had their first scheduled session together?

He was new here. He was the boss, brought in from the outside and given oversight of several doctors who could easily have had the job, considering their records and tenure. Sebastian didn't want anyone thinking he was incapable of handling the tough cases. He certainly didn't want anyone to discover the truth.

He daydreamed about kissing Willow Black, and in the night he dreamed of doing a whole lot more.

He'd seen her several times over the past few days, always with Mary. Neither one of them seemed to have any friends but each other. He found that both endearing and very sad.

Mary was better when she was with Willow. Everyone

said so, even Willow. However, a young woman should have dozens of friends her own age. But, in here, that wasn't going to happen.

"Doctor?"

Sebastian lifted his gaze from the file he'd practically memorized to find the subject of that file standing just outside his open door. She was wearing practically the same thing she had the first time he'd seen her: tennis shoes with Velcro straps—no shoelaces in here—scrubs, and a T-shirt advertising this facility. The only difference was her scrubs were green and the shirt was blue, one shade lighter than her eyes.

"Come in." Sebastian stood too fast, sending his chair clattering backward. "Shut the door, please. Have a seat."

She shut the door. Her gaze flicked to the obligatory couch.

"Unless you'd rather—"

"No!" She sat in the chair so fast it clattered too.

Her cheeks had pinkened, causing her eyes to shine nearly as blue as her shirt, making Sebastian wonder what she'd thought when she glanced at the couch. He knew what he'd thought whenever he glanced at it lately.

Sebastian took his own chair. "What were you and Dr. Eversleigh discussing the last time you met?"

Best to keep this professional from the beginning. In that vein he didn't voice his usual "call me Sebastian if you like" spiel. He needed all the distance he could get. If she called him Dr. Frasier, it might help. Certainly couldn't hurt.

Willow's gaze went to the file on his desk. "I'm sure you've read all about our last session, and any others too."

"I'd like to hear it in your own words. Unless you'd rather discuss something new. That's fine too."

"You shaved your beard."

The statement might seem random, but it wasn't. Willow was trying to form a bond with Sebastian, which was what he, as her therapist, should be trying to do with her. According to the file, Willow had been receiving therapy longer than Sebastian had been dispensing it. Like Mary, she knew the drill better than he did.

"I did," he agreed.

"It suited you."

"It didn't make me scary?"

"I don't think shaving off your beard is going to change that."

"You're scared of me?" he blurted, surprised. She didn't seem to be.

"No." She laughed. "You'd never hurt me."

She said that as if she'd known him longer than the few days she had. Before he could question her about that, she questioned him.

"How much longer?"

He glanced at the clock. "We just started."

"I meant how much longer do I have to be in this place?"

"That depends."

She tilted her head. "On?"

"Are you still having visions?"

Her brow furrowed. "You say that as if you believe I had them."

"You believe you had them."

"I did."

"Had them or believed that you did?"

She shrugged, glanced away. "By believing I had them does that mean I actually had them?"

"If a man speaks in the forest and no one hears him is he still wrong?" His sister's favorite joke, though whenever she'd said it to Sebastian she hadn't been laughing.

Willow's gaze flicked back to his. "What?"

"Joke. Sorry. Variation of 'if a tree falls in the forest and no one hears it does it still make noise?' "

"Yes?"

"I'm inclined to agree in the case of the tree."

"But not in the case of a vision?"

"Or in the case of men being genetically wrong."

She didn't laugh. She didn't even smile. Sebastian gave up trying to amuse her. He'd never been very good at it.

"What do you think about the visions?" he asked. He could tell her that they were delusions, but for her to get better she had to believe it too.

"There's no such thing," she said.

Her voice, her face made him inclined to believe her. Which was foolish. He knew as little about her expressions as she did about his. He'd met people in the past who were so convinced of their own delusions they'd made others believe in them too.

Jim Jones anyone?

Sebastian curled his hand around the glass he'd placed out of sight behind a stack of files on his desk. He set it right in front of Willow. The sunshine sparkled off the water inside.

"And what about this?" he asked.

Her gaze fixed on his and not the water. In her eyes he could have sworn he saw hurt, betrayal, perhaps fear, but her words revealed none of those things. "What about it?"

"I'm not going to be able to release you if you still think you see the future every time you look into the water."

"How do I prove to you that I don't?"

"It would help if you actually looked into it."

Instead she closed her eyes, took a breath, let it out. Her lips compressed; her fingers clenched.

"Willow?"

Her eyes snapped open. She focused on the glittering water. For an instant he thought everything would be all right.

And then, suddenly, it wasn't.

# Chapter 6

At first I thought I was only seeing Dr. Frasier's reflection in the water. Even when I saw myself there too, I didn't get it. But when a man came out of the trees and pulled a knife at the sight of me, I started to catch a clue. What was it with men, knives, and me?

The guy wore black from head to toe. I would have thought it was in order to blend into the night, except his clothes were strange—as if he'd stepped out of a past where men still wore hats and clunky shoes.

"Another of you!" he exclaimed. "You're like rabbits."

He had an accent, a brogue, I thought, though how I knew that I had no idea. When he lifted the knife, the full moon glinted off his ring.

Snarling wolf. I'd seen one before.

"One of you be dead and soon there'll be another."

The blade arced downward. Sebastian stepped between us.

Panic flared. I tried to push him out of the way, but he wouldn't go. The blade struck him in the side. He grunted, but he didn't fall. Instead he did some fancy roundabout twirl and kicked the dark man in the chest.

"Ooof." The attacker's breath rushed out.

You'd think having the air knocked out of you would cause anyone to stop, or at least slow down. Not this guy. He came forward again, wildly swinging.

Sebastian punched out with the heel of his hands—right, left, right. He couldn't get close enough to land a strike with the knife flailing about, but he did get the man to back up.

They were almost to the trees when Sebastian staggered, nearly going to his knees. I'd only taken a single step forward, hands outstretched, before he hauled himself upright again. The lurching movement revealed that his shirt, once light brown, now glistened maroon with blood.

Our attacker smirked. "Give me the witch and live."

Sebastian flipped him off. The fellow didn't seem to know what he meant. Who didn't know that?

The question became irrelevant when he began to circle, knife out. From the way Sebastian swayed, we didn't have much time.

I cast around for a weapon—even a big stone would be better than nothing—and I saw the wolf.

The surprise made me blink, and the forest was gone, along with the dark man, a bloody Sebastian, and the black wolf with the green eyes. Why had she seemed so familiar?

Dizziness washed over me as it always did after a vision. Luckily I was sitting, and I didn't fall down. Hoping against hope that the vision had happened so fast I could pretend it hadn't, my gaze flicked to Dr. Frasier's.

He knew.

"Guess I'm not getting out any time soon," I said.

He didn't answer, which was answer enough.

I grabbed the glass of water and drank it with my eyes closed. When I set it back on the desk, the tap sounded so final.

I was going to be in here for the rest of my life.

\* \* \*

I slept the day away, not only because visions wiped me out, but because I was too damn depressed not to.

Dr. Frasier had tried to be kind, to give me hope, but what hope was there? As long as I saw things in the water, I couldn't go home. As I didn't have a home, that was probably for the best.

I might have continued sleeping indefinitely if Mary hadn't woken me just after midnight.

"It's time." She held up a paper sack, which looked just like the one Peggy'd had yesterday. Not that paper sacks were all that distinct. Then she drew out the red candle and the bell, set them on the floor.

"Where'd you get that?" I sat up.

"Where do you think?" She tossed the stuffed dog over her shoulder like it was spilled salt and pulled matches out of her jumpsuit.

I snatched them out of her hand. One thing we didn't need was Crazy Mary playing with matches. The building was made of stone, but I wasn't.

Peggy might have given Mary the items for the spell, but there was no way she'd given her matches. Which meant Mary had probably stolen all of it. Surprisingly, I didn't have a problem with that. As long as the matches stayed in my hand.

"Moon's up." She sat on the floor next to the candle and the bell. "Time's a-wasting."

She produced Peggy's *Book of Shadows,* handed it to me, and I sat too. I opened to the spell of transportation. "Did you bring an item that gives you joy?"

"No."

"Should I use one of mine?" I glanced around, at a loss. Not a single item in this room gave me joy. What did?

"Joy, schmoy. I want out of here."

"Mary—" I began.

"You promised you'd try."

I had. And the reason was to prove to Mary that not only was I not a witch, but neither was she, and neither was Peggy—or at least not the kind of witch Mary was hoping for. One who could actually transport someone using a transportation spell.

I lit the candle, rang the bell, and said the words. Mary did too. We repeated the spell and actions three times each. Nothing happened.

"See?" I leaned over and blew out the candle. "This stuff isn't real, Mary."

Instead of agreeing, disagreeing, or punching me in the nose, Mary snatched the book out of my hands, then the candle and the bell off the floor, and ran out of the room. I sat there blinking for a minute before I followed.

The hallway was shadowed, deserted—creepy, in a mental-asylum sort of way. Somewhere in the distance someone cried out, closer still, someone moaned. Probably dreams, nothing more. Then again, who knew?

I heard the bell jangling as Mary hurried along. Sooner or later someone besides me—guard, orderly, nurse, doctor—was going to hear it, and then Mary would be in solitary again. Or maybe I would. I was the one holding the stolen matches. I tossed them back in my room and hustled after that bell.

All the way down the corridor to my right, then left and right again. The bell stopped jangling. I squinted into the gloom as Mary slipped into the library. A quick glance behind me revealed we were still alone. Considering the racket, that was magic right there.

By the time I went in too, Mary had set the candle and the bell on a table and was paging through the *Book of Shadows*. She was muttering and twitching, her eyes so wide the whites shone, and I considered calling an attendant. I'd meant to help, but it appeared I'd done more harm than good. Story of my life.

"Mary." I approached slowly, keeping my hands where she could see them and my voice soft. "We should probably go."

"It's tonight, remember? It's here!"

Unease rippled over me, and I cast a glance at the shadowed stacks. "What is?"

She ran to the center of the room, where the bright full moon shone through the skylight like a beacon from a spaceship. Memory flickered.

I glanced at my clothes—green scrubs, blue shirt, bare feet. Exactly what I'd been wearing in my vision. Except I'd been alone. Searching for someone. Frightened. Agitated.

"We should probably go," I repeated.

"Yes! We should go." Mary held out her hand.

I took it. Or I thought I did.

One instant my palm was touching Mary's, the next my hand was empty. The book Mary had been holding—Peggy's *Book of Shadows*—fell to the floor with a crack that made my breath catch. The sound far too loud in the silent, lonely room; outside the wind began to whistle.

"Mary?"

My only answer was an increase in the speed of the wind.

I walked around, found nothing but books. The more time that passed, the more frantically I searched. The rain that pattered against the skylight sounded like sleet. Oddly the moon still shone down.

My sense of déjà vu increased with every second that passed with no sight of Mary. Eventually I had to admit what I already knew.

Mary was gone.

* * *

Sebastian's phone rang in the middle of the night. Wasn't the first time. However, it was the first time a patient had escaped.

Dopey with sleep, he bobbled the phone. "Who?"

"Mary McAllister."

"How?"

"No one knows." The caller, a guard who went by the nickname Deux because he was the second Tom that was employed at the facility, sounded pretty freaked out.

Sebastian wasn't. Yet. The facility was secure. Certainly it was huge, but she had to be somewhere. If he was lucky they'd find her before he even got there, which meant he wouldn't have to call Dr. Tronsted at all.

"Surveillance footage?" They had cameras outside and on the doors. Only a few inside, on the entry, main hallway, and cafeteria. Those things were expensive.

"No sign of her."

"Then she's still inside the building. She's hiding."

"Better than anyone's ever hidden before."

"Keep searching. Have you called the police?"

"Should I?"

Sebastian rubbed his forehead. Did they have protocol for an escape? He was pretty sure they did, but maybe he was the only one who'd read it. He'd have to remedy that. Perhaps update that protocol, considering. But not now.

"What's the closest police force?"

"Nearest town is twenty miles in one direction. Twenty-five in the other. As the crow flies . . . maybe fifteen."

"When was Mary last seen?"

"Lights out."

Which had been two hours ago. "On foot she couldn't have reached any of them yet."

He'd have to call them all, just in case, and the state patrol while he was at it.

"Names of the towns?"

Deux rattled them off.

"I'll call them before I head in," Sebastian said.

Fifteen minutes later he pointed his motorcycle toward the facility. A storm swirled on the horizon. He wasn't going to be able to ride the Harley much longer. Soon enough, any storm would mean snow. He'd have to start shopping for a reliable winter car. The thought made him melancholy.

The Harley had been one of his dad's favorite things. Sebastian had fond memories of riding on the back, arms around his father's waist, as they explored together—just the guys. Whenever Sebastian rode it, he felt closer to his father. Which was stupid. His dad was dead, along with everyone in Sebastian's family. He still wanted to ride the motorcycle all the time.

Though the wind seemed to be picking up, and mist hit him in the face, the clouds did not move. Just like the last storm. Though the phenomenon seemed odd to him, apparently it was the way storms behaved around here. Even stranger, as he got closer, he could see that the weather system was twirling right above the Northern Wisconsin Mental Health Facility.

He'd definitely never seen anything like that before.

The sky appeared clear in every other direction. If Mary had truly escaped, and Sebastian still didn't think she had, she wouldn't be getting rained on. Though maybe if she were, she'd run toward the facility instead of farther away.

None of the police officers Sebastian had spoken with

had seen her, or had any reports of the same. Which made Sebastian all the more certain she was messing with them.

He strode into the facility. "Find her yet?"

The guard on the door buzzed him through. "No, sir."

Sebastian tightened his lips to keep the curse from slipping out. He had maybe half an hour before he had to inform his boss. He didn't have time to curse.

Deux waited on the other side. He shook his head without Sebastian even asking.

Sebastian figured the kid had played football—around here, who didn't?—perhaps a running back since he was low to the ground and wide, with thighs that pushed against the seams of his uniform and biceps that did the same. While he didn't seem like he was the brightest crayon in the box, Deux knew his job and he did it well enough that staff and patient alike looked up to him. He had small, dark eyes set in a large, flat face and dirt-colored hair cropped so close to his head, his milky pale scalp shone through.

"You wanna see the security tapes?" Deux asked.

"In a minute." Sebastian headed for Willow's room.

All the patient doors were open, left that way to show that the room had been searched and the occupant tallied. As he passed each one, he glanced inside. Some of the patients were awake, others had gone back to sleep, or perhaps stayed asleep the entire time, depending on their meds.

Willow's lights were off. He stopped his headlong rush just outside her door. She was asleep or pretending really well. She probably didn't know any more than he did, but he still had to ask. Maybe he could do so from right here. He could try.

"Willow?"

She stirred, turning away from the door, from him, and toward the wall. Sebastian's hope of keeping his distance fled. He crossed the room.

"Willow," he said more loudly.

She pulled the pillow over her head.

Now what?

He glanced toward the hall. Should he call a nurse just to wake her up? What kind of doctor was he if he couldn't do that much for himself?

Sebastian shook Willow's shoulder. Beneath his palm she seemed so frail—her bones fine, her skin soft but so warm. He should have removed his hand. Instead he rubbed his thumb along the curve of her neck.

Outside, thunder boomed. Inside, he could have sworn lightning crackled.

She removed the pillow from her face and turned toward him. For an instant the two of them stared at each other. He had no idea what to say.

He should probably lead with *sorry,* or *forgive me,* perhaps *don't scream,* or *please don't sue me.*

She lifted her hand to where his still rested against her. He started to draw away; she caught his fingers and held on. The thunder that had been rumbling above stopped.

"What's wrong?" she asked.

Beyond his being in her room, in the night, and being unable to keep himself from stroking her skin? Not much.

"Found her yet?" Sebastian glanced over his shoulder, but whoever had asked the question was not asking him.

"Not a trace," someone answered.

Sebastian straightened, stepping back, and taking his hand with him. "We seem to have misplaced Mary. Have you seen her?"

Willow sat up and the covers fell down. She wore her usual T-shirt and scrubs, thank goodness. What if she'd slept in the nude?

"No," she said.

*No* was right. What was he thinking?

Sebastian took another step back, his gaze lifting to hers. She didn't appear afraid, disgusted, horrified. He wished he could say the same about himself.

"Where could she be?" she asked.

Mary. She was saying she hadn't seen Mary. Which was what he'd asked. Sebastian resisted the urge to smack himself in the forehead.

"Has she mentioned, or perhaps shown you, a special place she likes to be alone?"

"In here?" Willow's voice was incredulous. "The only place we're alone is in our rooms, if we don't have a roommate. Even the bathrooms and showers are communal."

"There's nowhere?"

"In a place like this, Dr. Frasier, I don't think there's supposed to be."

"Sir?"

Deux stood in the doorway. He stared at Willow as if he'd never seen her before. In the half-light, tousled and sleepy eyed, she appeared more ingénue than incarcerated.

Sebastian stepped between them. "What is it?"

"They found her."

Sebastian hadn't realized how tense he'd been until the words caused his shoulders to relax and his lungs to at last draw a complete ration of air. Hallelujah! He *hadn't* lost a patient on his watch. He'd just misplaced her.

"Show me." He started for the door.

Deux didn't move. "Sir?"

"Where's she hiding?"

The guard glanced at Willow, then back at Sebastian. "We didn't find her here. The police chief just called from Glacier Point."

"That's twenty miles away," Willow said.

"How could she have gotten there in two hours?" Sebastian asked.

"Maybe if she was a track star." Deux twitched one hulking shoulder. "But she isn't."

Willow shook her head like a child frantically trying to convince a parent that she hadn't raided the cookie jar, despite the chocolate chip residue all over her face. An odd reaction, one that caused Sebastian to consider her more carefully. She froze, blinking like a rabbit caught in the beam of a headlight.

"Someone had to have given her a lift," the guard said.

"Why?" Sebastian kept his gaze on Willow.

"Because she definitely didn't walk there."

Willow choked. Sebastian tilted his head. Had that been a laugh? A sob? Both? She really was behaving strangely. Then again, wasn't that why she was here?

"I meant"—he turned back to Tom II—"we have signs posted that warn against picking up hitchhikers."

"From what I've observed, people don't like to read."

Sebastian had observed the same thing. Either they were lazy, stupid, or both. No matter. If they were driving, they could see. And anyone with eyes should know better than to pick up someone who looked as loony as Mary.

"Let's go get her."

"Well—uh—" Deux shifted his wide shoulders. "There might be a bit of a problem with that."

"What did she do?" Willow asked.

"Tried to strangle a guy."

"Big bald guy?"

Deux blinked. "How'd you know that?"

"I—uh—" Willow glanced at Sebastian and shrugged. "Lucky guess."

I sat in my room, wide awake, as the lights went out one by one in the hall and the noise level became less and less, finally fading to nothing just as the storm had.

Not only had Mary disappeared from the library, but she'd reappeared in Glacier Point. No one in their right mind would have given her a ride. Even if they had, there was still the little matter of Mary being on the road at all.

How had she done it? She'd say the spell had worked. I'd like to argue, but how could I? Mary had been here and then she hadn't been. The only explanation I had for that was *shazam,* which wasn't an explanation at all.

I stared into the dark until dawn threatened and the facility began to wake up. I took a shower, put on fresh scrubs—gray—a new T-shirt—orange. As I headed for the cafeteria and coffee, Dr. Frasier, Deux, and Mary returned. Mary was in handcuffs. She wasn't happy about it.

She shrieked and kicked and tried to get away. "He was a hunter! She showed me! He'll kill a witch if we don't stop him. I couldn't find the bitch-whore. But I will. Let me go!"

I winced at both the volume and the language. Taking into account the lack of a reaction from her companions, they'd heard it all the way back from Glacier Point.

"If you don't knock it off," the guard said, "you'll be in solitary longer."

"Solitary?"

All three of them glanced in my direction with varying degrees of surprise.

"Willow!" Mary tried to run to me. The guard yanked her back. She stomped on his foot. He grunted, but he didn't let go. Dr. Frasier sighed and rubbed his eyes.

I came closer and hugged her, ignoring both the guard's "bad idea" and Dr. Frasier's "I don't think—"

"Shh," I whispered in her ear.

Her answer was a smile and a pat on my cheek. The handcuffs rattled, the metal cool against my skin.

"Does she really have to be in solitary?" I asked.

"Until she tells us how she got out of here, yeah." Deux led her away, leaving Dr. Frasier and me alone.

Or as alone as we got in the hallway of a psychiatric facility, which wasn't very alone at all. Nurses, guards, attendants, cafeteria workers all scurried past.

"I'm kind of surprised they let you take her," I said. "Considering the assault."

"The guy she attacked disappeared."

I'm sure he meant the guy had driven off and not that he'd morphed into nothingness, but who knew? As it wasn't something I could ask, I didn't.

"No one to press charges," Dr. Frasier continued.

"Convenient."

"For Mary."

For the guy too if he'd had something to hide. If he were the man I'd seen in my vision—the man Mary had seen too—he did. Or he soon would. He certainly didn't want his name in a complaint, or the hassle of too many questions and a trial.

"I was able to bring her here since this is basically—"

"A prison."

Dr. Frasier shrugged, but he didn't argue and I liked him all the more for it. What was, was, and with the locks on the doors, the bars on the windows, it certainly wasn't an all-inclusive resort.

"I asked her how she escaped."

"What did she say?"

"What she said just now is what she said all the way back. Not a word about how she got out, just jibber-jabber about the guy and what he'd do if she didn't stop him. You know anything about that?"

I shook my head, hoped he couldn't see or smell the lie, but I thought he kind of did.

"What did you say to her that made her stop ranting?" he asked.

"Shh."

"That's it?"

"She likes me."

"You want to tell me how you knew she'd attacked a big, bald guy before anyone else did?"

I'd been thinking about this all night. The answer was simple. "She told me."

"Told you," he repeated. "When?"

"Mary has a lot of delusions. Voices that tell her things."

"And one of them is a big, bald guy?"

I shrugged.

"She *hears* voices," he said. "She doesn't see the owners of them. Or at least she never did before."

"First time for everything."

"Why did the first time a patient escaped have to be on my watch?"

I figured that was rhetorical.

"You think she'll tell you how she got out?" he asked.

I blinked. "Me?"

"She appears to adore you. You could ask."

"You want me to snitch?"

"You want her in solitary forever?"

What I wanted was to talk to Mary, find out what had

happened. Solitary meant I shouldn't be able to get near her at all, but I was being given a free pass.

Well, not exactly "free." Dr. Frasier wanted me to extract a confidence from someone who trusted me, then blab it to him.

That didn't mean I had to.

# Chapter 7

"All right." Willow smiled at Sebastian so sweetly he forgot what he'd asked her.

He'd had very little sleep, a lot of stress, and no coffee. He was lucky he remembered his own name.

"When can I talk to her?"

Mary. Right. Willow had agreed to speak with Mary about how she'd escaped a secure mental health facility.

"Later," he said. "She's being sedated."

He probably should have waited on that—he needed answers sooner rather than later—but she'd been off-the-charts cuckoo all the way home. He doubted even Willow would have been able to get sense out of her at this point.

The problem was he needed to call Dr. Tronsted. But he'd prefer to do so with an explanation as to how Mary had gotten out. Calling his superior about an escape with no explanation for it other than *not a clue* wouldn't look good. Certainly the information that Mary was back in custody and no one was hurt, including her, would help, but an answer for every question thrown his way would help even more.

"I'll make sure you're allowed in to see her as soon as she's awake and more herself," he continued. "Probably this afternoon or maybe this evening."

"She was herself when you brought her in here."

Sadly, she was right.

"Mary had a big night. She needs some rest."

Willow laid a hand on his arm. "You look like you could use some too."

Sebastian stilled, fighting the urge to set his palm atop hers. What was it about Willow that called to him? Certainly he was lonely. Had been for a long, long time. Raising a kid sister while going to college meant his social life had been nil. Later, he just didn't care. He'd devoted his life to his work and his patients. Only recently had he started to want more. But he certainly shouldn't be yearning for it with Willow. He needed to stop or he'd be on a fast track to not only losing this job but his license.

He stepped back, and her hand slid away, hovered in the air for a minute before she curled her fingers inward as if holding on to the sensation of that touch.

God, he was tired.

"Let's get some coffee."

Had he said that? Must have, because she headed for the cafeteria. He shouldn't have followed, but he did.

The early-riser patients had filled Styrofoam cups of coffee, tea, and juice, and sat either in small groups or alone. A few glanced Sebastian's way; one of his patients waved.

He stood behind Willow while she filled her cup, then moved to the side and dumped in milk and sugar. She smelled like institutional soap and shampoo, which shouldn't be appealing but was. Everything about her appealed to him.

Except the reason she was here. He had to remember that.

Compared to Sebastian, Willow seemed so tiny, so frail. In reality, she was tall for a woman—at least five seven in bare feet—though she was too thin. He was tempted to dump more milk and sugar into her coffee himself. He managed not to by pouring coffee of his own.

"Let's take these outside," he said. She could use some sun, and he could use some air.

"Outside?" she repeated, as if he'd spoken in Dutch.

"There's a garden. I've been meaning to sit there." He always meant to sit in gardens, never did get around to it. Not only did he not have the time, he had no one to sit there with. He shouldn't sit in one with her. He knew it, but he did it anyway.

He led Willow to the door that opened onto the walled inner courtyard at the center of the facility. He had to use a key to get inside—entry was a privilege accorded a certain few.

A picnic table sat in the center of the open area. Above loomed the sky. Around them, wildflowers, a few bees, even some birds.

In the old days, patients had been required to work on the acres that surrounded the facility. Farming, gardening, lawn care had been part of their therapy. Sebastian thought they might have been onto something with that plan. Not only did sunshine work wonders healthwise, but being busy rather than bored didn't hurt either.

Of course now that many of their patients were criminally insane, allowing them outside to plant posies was no longer an option. To be certain they wouldn't escape, they'd have to wear chains on their ankles like a chain gang and that was inhumane. But locking them up behind stone walls and tossing away the key was a-okay. However, he didn't make the rules, he just followed them.

Kind of.

"Have you been out here before?" Sebastian took a seat across from her at the table.

"No."

"Never?" If Willow wasn't one of the "certain few," who was? Certainly not Mary.

"Dr. Eversleigh was old school."

"Meaning?"

"We didn't have sessions outside."

And he'd been thinking "outside" was old school. All a matter of perspective, but what wasn't?

"Is this a session?" He took a sip of coffee.

"Do you want it to be?"

"You sound like me."

She sipped her own coffee and smiled.

Since Sebastian wanted to taste that smile, he looked away, and the stone walls captured his attention. He disentangled himself from the picnic table—not an easy task for a man as big as he was—then walked over to one, lifted his arm, curled his fingers over the top. He could probably pull himself up. It wouldn't be easy, but he could do it. Could Mary?

First she would have had to get into the garden. Had someone let her out here and now didn't want to mention it, considering? Or perhaps a key had been lost, misplaced, even stolen—also not something that the loser might want to admit at this point.

Sebastian reached farther and encountered what he thought was a pebble, but when he drew it back down discovered it was a piece of broken glass. He stood there frowning at it so long Willow came over to see it too.

"Better than barbed wire," she said.

"She didn't get out this way." Sebastian put the glass back on top of the wall. If she had there would have been a blood trail, both on the ground and on Mary.

"Did you think she had?"

"I don't know what to think."

"You need to stop thinking for a bit."

"I'm not sure I can."

"Try." She started down the path that meandered through the grass and the wildflowers. Unable to stop himself, he followed.

They didn't talk, and that was all right. It was soothing for a man who spent most of his day listening to others, to not have to for a change. Willow remained just ahead of him; the trail was narrow. Though he could have crunched through the unmowed grass to walk at her side, he didn't. He liked the sight of her against the tall grass and flowers. If he just stared at her, at the path, it was as if the walls were gone.

Willow pointed to a monarch butterfly perched on a fluffy white flower that resembled a snowball. Sebastian caught a glimpse of a statue overturned and half hidden beneath a swath of bright orange wildflowers. He stepped off the path, pulled it free, held the angel up for her to see. Willow brushed her fingers over the jagged edge of one broken wing.

"I'll see if Justice can fix it," Sebastian said.

"No." She took the statue out of his hand, taking great care that their skin did not touch.

He was both glad and sad. Glad because whenever they did touch there was a snap of electricity—both static and sexual. The first couldn't be helped; the second had to end and the only way to make it do so was not to touch at all. But also sad, because he'd never had a reaction like that to any woman in his life, and he'd started to wonder if he ever would.

Certainly there hadn't been many women—lately there hadn't been any. As a psychiatrist he knew that he'd been subconsciously punishing himself. He didn't deserve love, a home and family when his sister would never have any of those things. But just because he knew what he was doing—and if he'd been his own patient he'd tell himself to forgive, if not forget, and move on—that didn't mean he could do it any more than most of the people he advised could.

"Not everything should be fixed." Willow knelt and set the angel in front of the flowers, then glanced up at him. "Not everything can be."

His eyebrows lifted. How many times had she spoken exactly what he was thinking? More than could be a coincidence, except the other options were mind reading and witchcraft.

He shook his head at the foolishness of his thoughts. "Doesn't hurt to try."

She straightened and moved down the path again. "Sometimes it does."

He felt compelled to follow. He'd thought her fey. Was she weaving a spell?

He was a lot more tired than he'd thought.

His mother had been of Irish descent, and she'd told stories of fairies and elves—the little people—that her gran had told to her. As a kid both he and his sister had begged for those stories.

His father had been Scottish—Frasier—as well as German and Norwegian. None of the three was a fanciful race and David Frasier, John Deere equipment salesman, had been the same.

Despite Sebastian's choice of occupation, his personality was more like his mother's. Not that he believed in fairies and such, but he had liked hearing about them. He missed his mother daily, but he missed her most at night when he had the strongest memories of her sitting close and telling tales. Perhaps if he'd taken the time to tell his sister those same tales she wouldn't have—

A startled yelp had him hurrying forward just as Willow came barreling back. She bounced off his chest.

He grabbed her forearms before she could land on her ass. That dual spark—physical and mental—zapped him again. But one glance at her ashen face, and he pushed her behind him.

"No," she said. "It's nothing."

She caught at his clothes, but he wouldn't be stopped. He charged into the tall grass.

He'd slay whatever dragons she had.

Because Dr. Frasier was so tall, I could see him still, despite the wild overgrowth. His shoulders drooped on a sigh when he saw what I had, then he looked back. The disappointment in his eyes hurt, just as I'd known it would. He wanted to fix me.

But I wasn't broken. I'd been born like this.

"Come here, Willow."

I shook my head.

"It'll be all right. I promise."

It wouldn't be. That much I knew. But I went anyway, even though I wanted to flee in the other direction. What choice did I have? Not only had we needed a key to get in here, but I was pretty sure we'd need a key to get out, and I didn't have one.

My doctor stood in front of the stone birdbath. The storm of a few days past had filled it to the brim with water. The instant I'd seen the shimmery expanse of gray-blue I'd run.

He held out his hand, and like a fool I took it. It was so damn hard not to. In my mind I knew him. In my heart I loved him.

He smiled. I melted. Did he feel it too? This connection between us? At times he seemed to, and at other times he did not.

His eyes were so kind, so familiar. I focused on them as he drew me closer.

The sun was warm; the breeze was soft. He began to lower his head. I'd seen this before.

My eyes drifted closed. My mouth lifted. I waited for the first touch of his lips, and the world shimmied with that sense of déjà vu.

He smelled the same, like limes beneath the sun, or perhaps on ice. His hand in mine was so familiar I could rub my thumb along his index finger and feel the callus that had always been there every other time I'd envisioned his touch. The cadence of his breath was the cadence of my own. I knew exactly what he'd taste like when our lips touched.

Then his mouth brushed my temple. His free hand patted my shoulder. "Shh," he whispered. "Shh."

My eyes snapped open. That might work with Mary, but it wasn't going to work with me. "I'm not a dog."

He stiffened as if he'd been poked. "Of course not."

He seemed like he wanted to pat me again. I narrowed my gaze, and he stepped back.

Had everything I believed I knew about us—the kisses, the touches, the whispers, the love—been a lie? I didn't think so. Nothing else I'd ever seen was. As this—him, me, us—was the only thing I'd ever prophesied that was good, it had to come true. It just had to. Otherwise what was the point of going on?

"Willow?"

I refused to meet his gaze. I'd see pity in his eyes and that I couldn't bear. What kind of patient falls in love with her doctor?

The pathetic kind. I was already pathetic enough.

"Did you want to look into the water?" he asked.

"Hell, no."

There was a reason I'd run from that still blue expanse. All I'd seen in it lately were death and destruction.

"The more you face what scares you the less frightening it will be."

I was in no mood to be psychoanalyzed. Would I ever be?

I fled in the direction of the picnic table and my no doubt cold cup of coffee. Why had I thought he would kiss me here in the sun? Our kiss would take place beneath the moon.

I stepped free of the tall grass. Dr. Frasier's assistant, Zoe, stared at our two cups, which still sat on the picnic table. She flicked me a glance. "Where is he? What have you done?"

She seemed both frightened and furious; for an instant I wondered. Had I lost time? Had I done something I shouldn't?

No blood on my hands, my clothes. Why would there be? Certainly there had been once, there would be again. It would even be his. But it wouldn't be because of me.

Zoe stalked toward me, fists clenched. My own fingers curled. I knew better than to punch a nurse, but if she swung first the rules changed.

"Zoe?"

She stopped short a few feet away. Her fingers unfurled. The set of her jaw relaxed, though the flush of anger remained.

Dr. Frasier set his hand on my shoulder, and my own fingers loosened. I wanted to reach up and twine ours together, but I knew better.

"What's wrong?" he asked.

I kept quiet. I wasn't exactly sure.

Zoe's gaze fixed on his hand, which he kept on my shoulder, the heat of his skin warming the sudden odd chill. "Are you all right, Doctor?"

"Why wouldn't I be all right?" He urged me forward with light pressure. I didn't move.

There was something about Zoe right now that disturbed me. Not only didn't I want to get any closer to her, but I really, really didn't want her any closer to him. Maybe I *should* have looked into the water. There was a reason it had been there, and maybe this was it.

"Deux said the two of you came out here, but you didn't come back. I got worried so I decided to check." She shot me a glance; her fury seemed magnified by the thick lenses of her glasses. "Then you weren't here."

"We were here," he said. "We were admiring the birdbath."

"What's in your hair?"

I glanced over my shoulder. Dr. Frasier had leaves in his hair.

"Huh," I said, and he cast me a quizzical glance.

I reached up and pulled one out. Long and thin, I knew a willow leaf when I saw one.

"Huh," he agreed.

We both peered back the way we'd been.

There wasn't a willow tree in the bunch.

Logically I knew that the leaves had blown over the wall and stuck in Dr. Frasier's hair. It was a coincidence that the leaves were those of a black willow. Though I was starting to wonder how many coincidences there really were in life. Especially in my life.

"Black widow," Zoe muttered as she picked up the coffee cups and emptied the dregs into the grass.

"Willow," I said.

She snorted. I was going to have to keep my eye on her. She didn't like me. I was pretty sure I knew why.

I glanced at Dr. Frasier and he smiled. I didn't smile back and his faltered.

We were meant for each other. I knew that too. But Zoe could make life difficult for me, and from the expression on her face she planned to.

"I'll walk you to your room," he said.

"I'll do it." That was Zoe.

"I know where it is." I went to the door. Then I had to wait for one of them to unlock it.

Luckily Dr. Frasier was closer, and he got there first. I had a feeling Zoe would have stepped on my foot, elbowed me in the ribs, or perhaps opened the door into my face. Childish behavior, but it had happened before.

Not with her. Not yet. But it would. I didn't even need to look into the water to know that.

"When Mary wakes up I'll come and get you." He held the door for me as if we were on a date. Or at least I thought it was like that. The number of dates I'd had matched the times I'd been kissed.

*Zero.*

"I can get her," Zoe said.

Dr. Frasier didn't even glance her way when he answered. "Your shift will be over by then."

"So will yours."

He ignored her. "You've been up all night, Willow. Get some sleep."

"You too."

I reached for the door as he retreated, and our hands brushed. Our eyes met. Time seemed to stand still.

I'd sleep so much better when I slept with him.

Memories of things that hadn't happened yet tumbled through my mind. My face flooded with heat, and I fled.

Before I went back to my room, I detoured to the library. I wanted to see if Mary's *Venatores Mali* actually existed. Not that she couldn't have Googled them same as I planned to, but it wouldn't hurt to know what was truth and what was not. And if she'd totally invented them, I should probably know that too.

According to Wikipedia, which wasn't always accurate but didn't make a habit of inventing witch-hunting societies from the seventeenth century, the *Venatores Mali* were secretly commissioned by King James. The one with his name on a Bible. He'd also written a book on witchcraft.

You'd think the two were mutually exclusive. But not when your name began with *King* and ended in a Roman numeral. James had two of the latter, being King James VI of Scotland and I of England. That many numerals would give anyone a God complex. He also had a hard-on for witches that would not quit. Hence the *Venatores Mali*.

James had kept the society a secret, not wanting to appear more backward to the English than they thought a Scottish king already was. Having lost a buttload of people in the merrily burning pyres at Smithfield thanks to Bloody Queen Mary, the English had had it up to their eyeballs with religious fervor. The relative peace and prosperity of the Virgin Queen Elizabeth's reign had made them less tolerant of anymore.

The leader of the *Venatores Mali* was Roland McHugh. He'd executed more witches than anyone in history. Before he burned them, he branded them, believing the mark would cleanse their souls, banish their demons, and purify them of satanic whispers.

Though no mention was made of what the brand looked like or what he had used to do it, I figured there were enough coincidences between Mary, Wikipedia, and my vision to think I'd found the right guy. That Mary thought Roland was coming back, even though he'd died in the Plague of 1636, was disturbing. That she thought he'd been speaking to her was even more so.

I went to my room, but it was a long, long time before I fell asleep.

I woke in the dark, and I wasn't alone. I didn't move,

kept my breathing even, got ready to fight back if I needed to.

Then the scent of sun and limes reached me an instant before Dr. Frasier murmured, "Willow?"

I wanted to reach out, take his hand, draw him next to me on my bed, curl into him, go back to sleep. Instead, I sat up, tossed off the covers, stood. Lying in bed with him anywhere near only caused me to yearn.

"Mary's awake," he said. "And she's asking for you."

I bet she was.

I stepped into the bright fluorescent lights of the hall and blinked until my eyes didn't ache. Together we walked toward solitary.

"Did you sleep?" I asked.

"I had work."

"You should go home."

"I have to find out how Mary escaped. What if she does it again? What if someone else does?"

I didn't think that was going to happen, but as I couldn't tell him why, I kept quiet.

We walked down several long hallways. Solitary was located in the farthest wing still in use. Beyond it there were many more, but they were dark, cold, and dusty. Their entrances were blocked by padlocked gates so none of us could scoot down there and do things that we shouldn't.

Dr. Frasier stopped at a locked door, with a single small window. He glanced in. "I told her you would visit. It seemed to calm her."

I waited for him to open the door, but he didn't.

"I should probably go in with you," he mused.

"She isn't going to tell me anything if you're there."

"What if she tries to hurt you?"

"I can take care of myself."

His gaze was drawn to the window again. I got uneasy and glanced in too. Mary sat on the bed, hands folded, waiting.

"Why does she have a bandage on her forehead?"

"There was some head banging. She stopped when I promised she could see you."

"Then let her see me before she starts up again."

"What if she decides to head-bang you?"

"I've been in places rougher than this, with people scarier than Mary."

His forehead creased.

"I'll be fine." I'd envisioned the faces of several people who wanted to hurt me. None of them had been hers.

He unlocked the door and I went inside.

"Willow!" Mary rushed forward, hugged me a little too hard. When she let me go, she scowled at the window. "Is he out there?"

The glass was one-way. "Could be. But he can't hear us if we're quiet."

He'd expect me to tell him what she said, but he wouldn't believe the truth, would write it off as crazy talk. I'd have to figure out something.

"What happened?" I asked, as we sat on her bed, side by side.

"We did the spell, and I was transported."

I wanted to argue, but we *had* done the spell. She *had* disappeared from here and reappeared there. There'd been a time lag between the first and the second, but it had happened. I might have tried to convince myself that I'd imagined her blinking out of the library, except she'd been gone. I wasn't the only one who couldn't find her.

"I saw the big, ugly, bald guy. He had the ring. He was a *Venatores Mali,* a hunter."

"What was he doing?"

"Eating a bratwurst."

I blinked.

"Maybe a hot dog."

"Did he say something to you? Recognize you?"

Mary's forehead creased. "Why would he? He didn't see me in a vision. Did he?"

"No idea," I said absently. "Why did you try and strangle him?"

"He's going to kill that woman on the altar with a meat cleaver. The witch. From the looks of it, she wasn't his first."

I'd thought so too. Still—

"You tried to kill him because he might someday kill someone we don't even know?"

"Has one of your visions ever not come true?"

She had me there.

"I don't think you're supposed to go around killing the people I see in them."

"I do."

"Mary—"

"Willow," she interrupted. "If I wasn't supposed to see, then why did I? If I wasn't supposed to try and stop him, then why was I transported to the place where he was?"

I had no answer for that either.

She took my hands. "I didn't see the tall, long-haired woman. But I bet the next time we do the spell, I will."

"Next time," I echoed, and yanked my hands away. All I needed was for Mary to go poof while Dr. Frasier was watching.

Or maybe I did. If someone other than me saw Mary disappear, or vice versa—I wasn't exactly sure which one of us was causing this phenomenon, it might even be both of us—then I'd know for certain . . . what? That I wasn't crazy?

Technically, I *was* crazy, but not about this. Still, I'd like someone who wasn't certifiable to see the same thing I had.

"We have to wait for the full moon," Mary said.

Another month. It seemed so far away.

# Chapter 8

Sebastian watched the two women through the small window. He couldn't hear what they were saying, but they both seemed to be saying a lot.

The most interesting thing was how normal Mary appeared. She was still dressed in the tan jumpsuit accorded to the least stable patients; loaferlike slippers graced her feet. Her hair was matted and snarled. The white bandage on her forehead nearly matched the ice-pale shade of her skin.

But when she talked to Willow, her hands didn't wring, pull at her hair, or smack her own head; her eyes didn't dart, and her voice didn't lift toward a shriek. The two carried on a conversation like ordinary adults. Sebastian only hoped that when Willow came out she had more to report than gibberish.

Willow patted Mary on the shoulder and kissed her head. Mary beamed at her as if Willow had given her the world. Why, then, when he'd done the same to Willow, had she glared at him as if he'd farted in church? Probably for the same reason that Zoe had glared at him all day.

With a woman's sixth sense, they knew he wanted more from Willow than he should. He wasn't sure what to do about that. He barely knew her, yet he felt as if he did. He felt as if he'd known Willow all his life. And that was nearly as crazy as . . .

Willow tapped on the door, and he glanced inside,

afraid he'd missed something dire while daydreaming. But everything was fine—or as fine as it got in solitary. Mary still sat on her bed, hands folded. Willow waited for him to let her out, which he did.

"What did she say?"

"Not much."

"You were talking quite a bit."

"Not much that made sense," she clarified.

"Maybe you should tell me everything. It might make more sense to me."

"Doubtful."

"Try me."

"She transported from here to there."

"Like *Star Trek*?" he asked.

"*Star Trek*'s not real."

"Neither is transporting from here to there."

"I didn't say it was true." Willow studied the toe of her shoe. "I said that's what she told me."

"Is this an idea she got from the Wicca lessons?" he asked.

Willow coughed. "You think Peggy Dalberg knows a spell that can make someone disappear from one place and appear in another?"

When put like that he had no choice but to say, "No." Still . . . "I should probably put a stop to the lessons."

"You're the administrator," Willow said. "But if you want my opinion . . . ?"

He nodded.

"The lessons are about finding joy, focusing your mind, discovering yourself. Mary's a lot calmer because of them."

"I think she's calmer because of you."

"Not me. Us. Friendship heals. The lessons are something to look forward to. Learning improves the mind."

Mary spent a lot of her time reading the *Book of Shadows*. Since she was calm and quiet when she did so, no one, including me, cared. We both went to our sessions with Dr. Frasier, as well as group sessions with counselors, art class, journaling. Anything to pass the time. Other patients had weekly visitors. Mary and I had each other.

Peggy joined us at our lunch table. We were alone. Since Mary had been released from solitary several patients had tried to get her to tell them the secret of how she'd gotten out of the facility. I wondered if they'd been enlisted to snitch by Dr. Frasier as well.

Mary took my advice and clammed up. One inmate pressed the issue. Mary stomped on her toe pretty hard before I could stop her. As they both wore designer crazy-house slippers, Mary didn't hurt the woman but she got the message. After that everyone left us alone. They were familiar with Mary.

"Dr. Frasier said you believe you transported yourself out of here," Peggy said.

Mary glanced at me and ate her pudding.

I shrugged. "Mary believes a lot of things."

Peggy leaned closer and lowered her voice. "What concerns me is that I taught you a spell of transportation."

"For joy."

"As Mary pointed out, the word *transportation* means more than one thing. With a slight tweak in the spell anything can happen."

"Are you asking us if it actually worked?" I put an edge of laughter in my voice, a tinge of disbelief in my expression.

"No." She sat back. "Of course not. That's cr—" She pressed her lips together.

"Today's the protection spell," Mary said.

Peggy twitched. "I'm not sure—"

"You promised!"

I gave a small headshake at the volume of her voice.
Mary returned to her pudding. It was almost gone. We
needed to wrap this up.

"You did promise," I said. "And what can protection
hurt?"

What *would* hurt was not having it.

"Dr. Frasier might—"

"What?" I interrupted. "Think you taught Mary a
spell that made her disappear from here and appear over
there?" I tilted my head. "Did you tell him that?"

"Of course not. That's not possible."

"Exactly. I spoke to him about how much this has
helped Mary."

"He did mention that."

"He said we could continue, didn't he?"

Peggy nodded, still appearing uncertain.

"You want to tell him why we aren't?"

I waited while Peggy did the math. If she stopped
teaching us, Dr. Frasier would want to know why. Any
explanation wasn't going to look good. Some of them
might sound a bit insane. If Mary lost her shit, which
was a definite possibility if Peggy stopped the Wicca
lessons, things were going to look even worse. Despite
Mary's comment, Peggy *was* sharper than the average
tool. She added things up pretty quickly.

"All right. A spell of protection is always a good idea.
They're usually done in the water. River, lake, bathtub."

"No, thank you," I muttered.

Uncertainty flickered over Peggy's face. "Maybe a
bowl of water that we set our fingertips in. Would that
work?"

"You're the witch," I said. I should be able to avoid a

glimpse into a bowl if I tried hard enough. Being in a river, lake, or tub . . . that wasn't going to happen.

"I brought what we'd need, just in case." She stood. "Stay here."

"Should I get a pot of water?" Mary asked.

"I'll get it." Peggy hurried off.

Mary made a disgusted sound. "She thinks I'm gonna drown someone in a pot of water? How would I do that?"

"Probably easier than you think."

"It is," she said.

I decided not to ask.

By the time Peggy returned, juggling the pot of water and a cloth bag, only Mary and I remained in the cafeteria. Peggy pulled six white minicarnations from the sack and handed them to Mary. "Pull off the flower tops and float them in the water."

Mary seemed thrilled to have something to do.

Next Peggy removed a small brown bottle and poured a tablespoon of citrus-scented oil into the water, then a second. "Florida oil."

She put the cap back on and withdrew a nylon bag that crinkled with whatever she'd stuffed inside. "Sea salt, lavender, peppermint, five-finger grass, chamomile." She set the sack in the water as well.

"Are we making tea?" I asked.

"Cool water, not hot. And we aren't going to drink it."

She pulled three candles out of the bag, setting each one on the table as she identified them. "White for purity. Purple for healing. Black for protection."

She lit them then drew a circle around the pot with chalk. "The spell calls for immersion in the water. We'll dip in our fingertips."

She did so then waited for us. Mary plunged hers in so fast, the water nearly sloshed out of the pot and doused the candles. I kept my gaze on Peggy and immersed mine more slowly.

"Breathe in through your nose, out through your mouth. Center yourself. This spell calls on the elements— earth, air, fire, and water. They will shield us from harm. Close your eyes and think of each one."

I was perfectly happy to. If my eyes were closed, there was no chance I'd see anything I didn't want to in the water.

"The earth beneath us—brown dirt, green grass, flowers, trees. Plants need air. Fire purifies. Water is life." Peggy's voice was low and soothing, almost a chant. "The air all around us—soft, a breeze—it smells of the earth, gives life to the fire, and swirls the water. Fire is fueled by air, doused by the earth and by water. The elements intertwine. They are separate, but connected. Like us. Together they are more powerful than they are apart. Like us. Do you have a sense of peace, of safety?"

"Mmm." I felt trancelike. Calm. Protected.

My mistake.

"Water." Peggy moved her hands and water sloshed as only water can. The tremors tickled my knuckles. "Hear. Feel. See it," she intoned, and I did.

First I saw a gray-blue expanse of water, stretching out to an unknown horizon. Rippling, flowing, and then . . .

I saw a playground. Children running, laughing. Parents sitting on benches watching. From the height and density of the trees surrounding the place it was Wisconsin or somewhere farther north, Minnesota, Michigan, Canada. The choices were limited.

Everyone wore coats and hats, gloves. Snow dotted

the green-brown grass. Might be April, might be October. Hard to say when all of the trees were pine.

The wolf that came out of the forest was a beauty. Big and black, with exquisite jewel-green eyes. No one saw it at first.

No one but me, and I wasn't really there.

The great beast—a female, I thought, no obvious male parts in sight and on a wolf they would be—stalked to an unattended baby carriage. No slinking. No hiding. That, in itself, was weird. What was really weird was that this was the same wolf I'd seen before—in the vision of me, Sebastian, and the knife-wielding man with the brogue. It had to be. Certainly there were other black wolves. But one with eyes that green? I doubted it.

No time to think about what that meant. The wolf reached the carriage and stuck her snout inside. Was there a baby in there? If so, what was she going to do? Take it? Bite it? Eat it? Why?

I didn't know much about wolves, but I'd never heard of one doing any of the three to an infant. Dingoes, yes. Coyotes occasionally. Wolves seemed smarter than that. Hurt a baby, pay the price—bullets, traps, poison, sometimes a wolf head on a spike. Depended on the era.

I glanced into the carriage. I'd only seen a few pictures, but the baby inside was me.

A shriek made us jump. The wolf snarled; the baby gave one "Eep" and went quiet. She—me—stared at the wolf and smiled, then reached for it. Her—my—palm stroked the creature's snout an instant before the animal wheeled and ran.

A woman snatched up the baby. I didn't recognize her. How could I when she'd been one of my foster parents in the days before I remembered anything?

The sky that had been as blue as my eyes darkened

and thunder rumbled as deep as the wolf's snarl. Rain began to fall in a torrent, and the vision shimmied, dissolved. But I wasn't back in the cafeteria, and that was as new as the jump into the past. The park was gone; a small bathroom took its place. Same woman, same me. I lay naked in the bathtub, shrieking the way I should have shrieked about the wolf.

Candles lit the room—one white, one purple, one black. The water smelled of citrus. The oil clung, making my skin shiny, slippery, shimmery. Six white roses floated in the water, bobbing beneath, then springing on top as I kicked and flailed and cried. My tiny heel smacked against a bag transparent enough to reveal herbs.

"Earth, air, fire, and water, shield Willow from harm. Cloak this child's existence from all who seek her out."

The candles flickered in a breeze that wasn't then went out. I opened my eyes just as the candles on the table in the cafeteria did the same.

Mary's gaze rested on my face. Had I said or done something to indicate I wasn't "here"? If I had, I certainly didn't want to talk about it now, in front of Peggy.

The caseworker set about cleaning up, dipping a cloth into the liquid and erasing the chalk circle from the table as if nothing strange had happened. Obviously neither one of them had been party to my vision or they wouldn't be so calm. The only explanation I had for that was that we hadn't been touching each other, only the water.

I'd never envisioned the past before. Why had I done so now?

"How long does a spell of protection last?" I asked.

Peggy skimmed the flowers and herb bag from the water and tossed them into the trash. "Until it's removed."

"How do you remove it?"

She glanced up with all three candles in her hands. "Why would you want to?"

"I didn't say I did. I just said how do you?"

"I don't know."

"Can you find out?"

"Protection is good. Why would anyone not want to be protected?"

She was right. However, I couldn't help but think that the woman in my vision had protected me right out of anyone in my family ever finding me. Did she know something about them? And how did I find out what?

"Is there a way to get a list of my foster parents?"

Peggy's forehead creased. "Don't you remember them?"

"Not before I was three."

"What does it matter now?"

"I have questions."

"About what?"

*The wolf and the witch*, I thought.

"Me," I said.

"I'll have to talk to Dr. Frasier."

"What does he have to do with it?"

"He's your doctor."

"My keeper."

"Six of one, half a dozen of the other," Peggy said.

"I'll ask him." I had therapy today anyway.

"Suit yourself." Peggy tried to retrieve the *Book of Shadows* from Mary and got smacked on the hand for her trouble.

"Still readin' it." Mary cradled the book against her chest. "When's the next lesson?"

"I'm going to visit my new granddaughter for two weeks. When I get back, we'll do whatever spell you choose. Until then, no performing spells without me. That's like driving without a driver's license."

Considering what had happened the last time we'd done so, I nodded.

"Mary?"

"No new spells." Her fingers tightened on the book.

Peggy didn't seem to notice that Mary hadn't agreed not to do old spells. With Mary, that was an omission that shouted louder than words.

Sebastian should have felt settled into his new job by now, but he didn't. It might have something to do with the unsolved mystery of Mary McAllister's escape.

Weeks later and he was no closer to discovering what had happened than he'd been the night it *had* happened.

He'd had Justice go over the place stone by stone. The old man hadn't left a single one unturned. Just to make sure, Sebastian had hired a contractor and an exterminator. One had made sure none of the walls were unsound, as in secret passageways to the outside that were secret even from them. The other had made certain there weren't any holes. If a mouse had a hard time getting in, Mary should have had a harder time getting out.

He'd questioned every staff member—twice. No one had seen anything, done anything, lost anything—including their keys or their IDs. He'd not only asked but required said keys and IDs to be produced.

He'd had every counselor and psychiatrist question their patients. Not one of them had come back with anything concrete. Although there seemed to be more aliens in town than Sebastian had known about. But none of them had opened the doors either.

His conversation with Dr. Tronsted had gone as well as could be expected, considering. She'd been impressed with all he'd done to discover the truth, not so impressed that he hadn't. She'd ended the phone call with one sentence and no good-bye.

"Make sure it doesn't happen again." *Click*.

As he had no idea how it happened in the first place, he wasn't going to be able to follow her order.

"Hey."

Willow stood just inside his office. Today her scrubs were charcoal gray, her T-shirt bright red. The colors were too harsh for her fair coloring, but she was still the prettiest girl in school.

Sebastian rubbed his eyes. He really needed to assign her to another doctor. But so far he hadn't been able to make himself do it. She might know something, or she might discover something from Mary, and he was the one best equipped to stay on that case. Or so he explained to himself whenever *himself* wanted to argue about impropriety.

He hadn't touched her. Lately.

"You okay?" She shut the door and sat in the chair across from his desk.

"Yes. Sorry." He glanced at his notes from their last session and frowned. After writing *"nothing new with Mary"* he'd doodled all over the page.

They'd talked about nothing in particular. Television, movies, books. They had similar taste in all three—TV dramas, movie comedies, fantasy novels. They might have talked for days about *Game of Thrones*. Who couldn't?

He should probably press her on the visions again, but their conversations were so pleasant he didn't want to. That had to stop. They weren't dating, despite topical evidence to the contrary.

"Have you had any—" he began at the same time she said, "I'd like to ask—"

They stopped speaking.

"Go on," he urged. Maybe she'd discuss her visions without him having to press.

"You know I was in foster care all my life."

Sebastian nodded.

"Do you have a list of the families I stayed with?"

He sat up, leaned forward. "You don't remember them?" That would be something to talk about besides the "getting to know you" discussions they probably shouldn't be having.

"Not all of them. Before the Dandridges, for instance. I went to live with them when I was three."

"It would be pretty amazing if you remembered much before then."

"Which is why I was wondering if there were any pictures they might have taken, or memories they might have that I don't. It's disturbing not to have a past."

"You have a past," he protested.

"Do I if I don't remember it?"

"Back to the tree-in-the-woods question, and I think the answer is the same."

"If a falling tree makes noise even when no one hears it, then I have a past even if I don't remember it?"

"What do you think?" he asked.

"I think I'd like to talk to the people who fostered me. Is that possible?"

"I'll make some calls."

# Chapter 9

Navigating the foster system was nearly as frustrating as talking to Crazy Mary. Sebastian had planned to enlist the help of Peggy, but he'd forgotten she was on vacation.

Therefore it took him the better part of the afternoon to get an actual person on the phone. Once he did, that person transferred him to another, and then another. Each subsequent transfer resulted in more messages and phone tag.

Willow came by every day. "Any luck?"

"Not yet."

Her disappointment made him call again and again. Over a week passed. When the phone was picked up he waited for the beep instead of listening to the words. It wasn't until Renee Jones said, "Hello?" the third time, with a good dose of snip in her voice that he realized he'd reached the real deal.

"Hello. Sorry. This is Dr. Sebastian Frasier, from the Northern Wisconsin Mental Health Facility."

"I got your message, Doctor. I've been swamped. Just pulled the file on Willow Black." Pages rustled. "I'm sorry to hear she's in your facility, though I can't say I'm surprised."

"Why's that?"

"You've read her file. Visions, voices, that kind of nonsense usually leads right to your doorstep, and that's if they're lucky. The unlucky wind up in prison or dead. Is she any better?"

Willow seemed pretty sane to him. Except for those nonsensical visions.

"Asking about her past is a good sign," he hedged. He wasn't sure if it was or not, but at least she wasn't telling him the future.

"I'll fax you the list of her foster families and the contact numbers we have for them. Everyone is still active in the system and willing to answer questions, except for the one family, of course. Such a tragedy."

"What tragedy?"

"The murders were all over the news a few months ago."

"I just arrived from Missouri recently. What happened?"

"The Gilletts were stabbed to death in their home. An odd case. Nothing was taken and the wife's body was set on fire but not the husband's."

"Any suspects?"

"None."

"When did Willow live with them?"

"Second family. She was eight months old. They kept her two months."

"Why did they send her back?"

"Same reason most everyone else did. Screamed whenever she came near water like a kid possessed. We didn't know then that she thought she was having visions."

Willow had been a baby. How could she have "thought" anything? Wouldn't she have had to actually see something in the water at that age to be afraid of it? But just because she believed she had, didn't make it so. Visions weren't real. They were the mark of the nut.

"Thanks for your help. I'll wait for your fax." Sebastian hung up.

He didn't like that one of Willow's foster families had been stabbed. He was sure they hadn't been wild about it either.

That Willow's weapon of choice had been a knife was disturbing but irrelevant. She'd been in here when the Gilletts were killed. Still, Sebastian was concerned enough by the information that he Googled the murders. Pretty much everything Renee had said was reported— stabbed, wife burned, no suspects. There was one tidbit she hadn't mentioned and it bothered him. The Gilletts had been tortured. As nothing had been taken, said torture was either to get information or just for the fun of it.

He dialed Renee again, didn't bother with hello. "Has anyone else called about Willow?"

"Hold on." He could hear her moving things. "Yes. But we didn't tell them anything. Privacy."

"Who was it?"

"They didn't say."

"When was it?"

She stated a date.

"A few days before the murder."

"What does that mean?" Renee asked.

"I'm not sure." He thanked her and hung up a second time.

Had the same someone who'd called the foster care system for information on Willow tortured her former foster parents for the same? How had that person found out that Willow had been with them? Hard to say. Whoever had told them had probably figured it didn't matter since they hadn't seen her for over twenty-five years. They'd been wrong.

Had the Gilletts known Willow's whereabouts? If so,

the culprits should have turned up on this doorstep. According to the visitor log, none had.

Sebastian sent an e-mail to the head of security that Willow was not allowed visitors until further notice. Then he called the detective in charge of the Gilletts's case—Jim Hardy—and told him what he knew.

"I can't see how a foster child the Gilletts took care of for a couple of months over twenty-five years ago has much bearing on the case," the detective said.

"Even when a stranger was asking about her a few days before the victims died?"

"Even then. Without a name, it's going to be hard to figure out who to question."

"Phone records?"

"I'll try, but with a phone call coming into a government office it ain't gonna be easy. And if this person was planning murder . . . they probably didn't use their home phone, or even their personal cell."

Hardy had a point.

"The FBI is in on the case now," Hardy continued. "I'll let them know. They might have other ideas, better luck. They definitely have better resources."

"Why is the FBI involved?"

"This case is similar to a bunch of others around the country."

That made Sebastian think that the Gilletts's killing had been random—or as random as a serial killer got—but at least not related to Willow, as he'd feared, despite the bizarre coincidence in somebody asking about her around the same time.

"You'd think that stabbing a person and burning the body is a serial methodology that would show up in the national news."

Something about saying those words aloud made Sebastian's brain tickle.

Stabbing. Burning. He pulled Willow's file open once more.

"Snarling wolf," he said.

"Say again?"

"Were the victims branded with the image of a snarling wolf?"

"How do you know that?"

"I can't tell you." Sebastian shut the file. "Privileged information."

"That detail was not released. Only the killer or someone the killer spoke to would know."

Unless it was someone who'd seen the killer in a vision, something Sebastian couldn't tell Hardy any more than he could tell him anything else.

"Doctor, the killer is still out there. If you know who it is you have a duty to stop the next murder. Imminent harm negates privilege."

It did. But had the man Willow stabbed been the killer? While Sebastian couldn't tell the detective what Willow had said in any of her sessions, he could direct the man to information he already possessed.

"There should be a police report on Willow Black. Court case too."

One of the reasons Willow was in here was that she'd thought the man she stabbed was going to stab, then brand and burn her. That he had no stabbing, branding, or burning tools hadn't looked good. It might look a little different now.

"I'll check that out," Hardy said. "Expect a call from Special Agent Nic Franklin, FBI."

"Great," Sebastian muttered.

I was in the common room watching an episode of *Seinfeld* for the eighty-fifth time. Surprisingly, it was still funny. Some shows were like that.

The door opened, and Dr. Frasier beckoned. As Mary was reading the *Book of Shadows* with such concentration she wouldn't miss me, I followed him into the hall. He handed me a piece of paper that appeared to be a printout of a newspaper article, complete with a photograph.

"That's her," I blurted.

"Who?"

The woman in my vision, but we weren't going there.

"She was one of my foster moms."

"You recognize her?"

I nodded.

"But not him." He tapped the photo.

I didn't recognize him because he hadn't been in the vision, but whatever. According to the text beneath the photo their names were Sadie and Malcolm Gillett.

"He seems familiar too," I lied.

The headline read: LOCAL COUPLE MURDERED.

They had both been stabbed. Only Sadie had been burned. Had she also been branded?

Considering what I'd seen of Sadie—the protection spell, which just shouted witch—and what I'd heard from Mary, combined with what I'd read online about the *Venatores Mali*, witch hunters who wore a snarling wolf ring and branded their victims with it, after killing them but before burning them, I kind of thought she had.

Had Sadie's spell of protection been meant to keep away the *Venatores Mali*? It hadn't worked. For her or for me.

Dr. Frasier waited for me to explain something I had no explanation for.

"I didn't remember their names," I said. "I didn't know this had happened."

"I'm not accusing you of anything, Willow. You were here when they died."

"You thought I might have killed them?"

"No." He shoved a hand through his hair and his earring glittered.

The memory of tickling that ear, tasting that earring, distracted me for a minute. When would those flashes of the future stop? When they became actual memories of the past? Doubtful, but at least they might not make me so dizzy.

I leaned against the wall so I wouldn't sway, tried to make my slouch appear cool and not weak. From the sharp glance the doctor threw my way, I didn't manage. But at least he didn't mention it. He had more important things to talk about.

"They were murdered the same way you said you would be by the man you tried to kill."

Which probably meant I'd been right about the branding. Yay, me.

"Can you explain that?"

I could but I wasn't going to. Instead I shrugged and spread my hands.

"According to social services, someone called asking for you. Social services didn't tell them anything, obviously. However, the attack on the Gilletts occurred soon after."

"You think the Gilletts told their killer where I was?"

"I have no idea, but I don't like it."

Me either. I had no family. No friends. Who would bother? Specifically who would bother to torture and kill someone who hadn't seen me for decades?

The *Venatores Mali* were witch hunters, and Mary thought I was a witch. Mary thought she was too. I could see where Mary's belief might be common knowledge, considering. But no one had been looking for Mary.

That they were looking for me was disturbing on a whole lot of levels. Because that meant someone not only knew about my visions but believed they made me magical and not crazy. Until a few weeks ago, I'd have said they were insane too. But now . . .

I considered sharing what I knew with Dr. Frasier, except I'd have to tell him I'd seen the witch hunters in a vision. I didn't wanna.

"I've rescinded your visitor privileges," Dr. Frasier continued. "Not because of anything you've done, but because I don't like that someone was asking questions about you around the time your foster parents were murdered."

"I don't get visitors. Ever."

"Exactly," he said. "And now's not the time to start."

I didn't return to the common area. *Seinfeld* no longer held any appeal. Instead I headed for my room.

I hadn't remembered the Gilletts until my vision, but now that I had, they felt like family. Not that I knew what family felt like. Mine was most likely all dead. Unless they were searching for me and being blocked by the protection spell. The only person who'd ever found me had tried to kill me. Or would have if I hadn't tried to kill him first.

Now that I thought about it, that dude knew where I was. He could easily have told anyone who asked. Why the torture of the Gilletts? Why the anonymous calling of social services?

The door to my room opened and Mary came in. "You okay?"

I nodded. I didn't want to explain, wasn't sure I could, or should. It probably wasn't a good idea to tell Mary any of this, considering she'd been jabbering about the burning, the branding, and the *Venatores Mali* for a while now. She appeared saner by the minute, and what did that make me?

She held the *Book of Shadows* in one hand and a coffee cup in the other. She joined me at the desk, where I sat, hitching a hip onto the edge. "You're upset. Here."

She set the mug in front of me. I glanced into it and—

"Goddammit, Mary . . ."

There wasn't coffee in the cup but water. It rippled, reflecting the white surface of the cup for an instant before it reflected something else. I reached for Mary, and she took my hand as I fell.

A house in the woods. Two stories. Big place.

A pickup parked on the side of the dwelling. A non-descript four-door car sat in front—navy blue, forest green, black? It was hard to tell in the deep woods darkness.

One window lit up. The shadow of a woman appeared. I couldn't see her face but she seemed familiar. How could that be? I'd never been here.

Next thing I knew I was inside. Bottom of the steps, peering up. I sensed more than one person in the house. I sensed a lot of people, some more there than others. I had no idea what that meant.

I climbed the stairs, headed for the only room where light spilled into the hall. I stopped in the doorway and watched a woman stab a pillow and a mattress to death. What had they ever done to her?

The woman spun. She was the same woman who'd been in my other vision in the forest, when the big ugly guy had killed someone. She walked past me, and pounded down the stairs toward the open door.

"Who the hell are you?"

A man stood in the entryway to the kitchen on the first floor. Never saw him before either. Short, with a solid build, maybe fifty, give or take—silvery-blond hair, pale complexion, and light blue eyes.

The big woman with the knife was already out the door. An instant later gravel spewed as she took one of the vehicles and made tracks.

"Bitch-whore!"

I blinked and the house, the trees, the man, the mattress and pillow that were never going to be used again were all gone and Mary was back.

I closed my eyes and drank the water in the cup, then set it down. "You need to stop doing that."

"How else are we going to find out anything?"

"What did we find out? Do you know that guy? The house? Recognize anything?" She opened her mouth, and I lifted my hand. "Besides the bitch-whore?"

"Yeah. Her knife."

There had been something strange about it.

"The blade," I said. "Like a *z* and double-edged."

She'd had it in the clearing, as well, but I'd been too distracted to notice much more than the meat cleaver and the murder. I was funny that way.

"Did you see the hilt?"

I thought back. The hilt had been carved into the likeness of a snarling wolf. "What does that mean?"

We already knew the long-haired woman was a *Venatores Mali*, that they were a witch-hunting society, and they used the snarling wolf as their symbol. But usually on a ring.

"I saw a knife like that in this book." Mary started to page through.

"With the wolf?"

"No." She turned the book so I could see. "The blade."

The page she'd opened to had drawings of four magical items. A pentagram, a chalice, a wand, and—

"'Athame,'" I read. "'Used by a fire witch to cut herbs and draw the sacred circle.' But this one isn't curved."

"No," Mary agreed. "But that doesn't mean it couldn't be."

Mary riffled through more pages, then indicated a five-pointed star drawn on one. "Four elements." She tapped each point and read what was written within the triangle. "Fire, air, water, earth." Then the final one, which pointed up. "Spirit."

She turned the book to face her so she could read what was written beneath it. "The pentagram with the point ascendant indicates the spirit is more important than earthly concerns."

"What if the point is down?"

She shrugged. "Maybe that's for the other guys."

"What's a fire witch?"

"There's a type of witch for every element, and they each have their magical instrument. Wand for an air witch. Pentacle for an earth witch. Your instrument would be a chalice, because you're a water witch."

"Sure I am."

Mary's eyes narrowed at my disbelief. She handed the book to me. "Read."

" 'Sometimes called a sea witch, a water witch aligns with all types of water. Water reflects. A water witch can see things others cannot. She is adept at divination. She can foretell the future.' "

"See?" Mary said.

From her tone, I half expected her to stick out her tongue.

"I don't—"

Mary snatched the book from my hands. "Elemental witches are born. They have real magic. Like you."

"I'm not magic."

"You transported me. Of course you are."

"You think that was me?"

"I know it was you." She set her hand on mine.

"Tomorrow night's the full moon again. We'll do the spell. Then you'll believe."

"That's probably not the best idea in the world."

"I need to stop those bastards from killing people," Mary said. "Die, witch hunters!" She pumped her fist into the air for emphasis.

"If I do the spell tomorrow night and nothing happens, can we stop?"

She lowered her fist. "People are dying, Willow. Witches are dying. How can you stop?"

She was right. I might want to stop, but I couldn't. Not if I could help. And if the only help I had was sending Mary out there like an insane version of *The Avengers* . . .

So be it.

# Chapter 10

"Do you think we should meet again at midnight?" Mary whispered at supper the next day.

My gaze lifted to the guard on duty. Tom, the original, slightly less gung-ho than Deux but not by much, had his gaze on us—or maybe just on Mary. Since she'd disappeared the last time, there seemed to be eyes on her 24/7.

"Have you noticed you're a guard favorite these days?"

Mary turned her head and stuck out her tongue. She began to lift her middle finger too, but I grabbed her hand, held it between my own. "That won't help."

"Helps me."

"Let's watch TV. They'll get bored watching us watch the screen. Eventually."

If they didn't I wasn't sure what I'd do. Or what Mary would do. I could easily see her banging a guard's head against a wall to make him stop staring at her. I'd like to avoid that.

After supper we returned to the common room, took some chairs near the back. I wasn't certain if we had to have the moon shining on us, or if the moon just had to be shining. Or if this would even work. I guess we'd find out.

"We need the bell and the candle." Mary stood.

"No." I pulled her back down. "We might be able to

ring a bell, but we certainly aren't going to be allowed to light a candle."

"But—"

"We didn't use them in the library, remember?"

Her eyes widened. "When we used them, nothing happened." Mary patted my hand, beaming at me as if I were a prize pupil. Why that made me feel like one, I wasn't sure.

An obnoxious reality show blared on the television. From what I could gather they'd locked a bunch of people in a house. They seemed sane when they went in, except that no one in their right mind should agree to such a thing. Which kind of explained what was going on in the show now.

"Ready?" Mary asked halfway through the televised fiasco.

The room was full of patients staring zombielike at the screen. The guard's attention had wandered. He stood outside the room, talking to the night nurse. They were flirting. It was kind of cute—even more so because they weren't watching us.

"You remember the spell?" I asked.

She rolled her eyes. I wasn't sure if that meant she remembered it or she didn't. In the end, it didn't matter.

She held out her hand. I held out mine. The instant I touched her, Mary vanished.

Sebastian got the call just as he reached his apartment. He pointed the Harley back the way he'd come.

Mary was gone. No one had seen how. At least the staff had already called the local police. His review of emergency procedures must have helped. By the time he got back, a county cruiser sat in front, its flashing lights pulsing against the night.

Sebastian reached the door just as the sheriff came out. He introduced himself, shook hands.

"We'll find her, Doctor. She can't have gotten very far."

Sebastian resisted the urge to snort and hurried inside.

Tonight's second-shift guard—the first Tom—waited. "They were watching TV."

"Who's they?"

Tom spread his hands. "The patients."

"All of them?"

"Most. Mary and Willow for sure. I've been keeping a special eye on Mary, like you said."

"Not special enough," Sebastian muttered, and Tom winced.

"I was at the door. No one went in or out."

Sebastian rubbed his forehead. "Where's Willow?"

"Here."

Her voice trilled along his skin like a feather. He dropped his hand. Had she been standing there in the shadows all along? Must have been, it wasn't like she'd warped in the way Mary had warped out.

"Where is she?" he asked.

"I have no idea."

She sounded like she was telling the truth, but what did he know? Not much. Not enough to keep his job if he continued losing patients.

Make that patient. Same woman, different day. Would that matter? Probably not.

"You were sitting right next to her." Tom loomed over Willow, making her seem smaller, frailer, paler than ever before. He grabbed her arm, shook her a bit. "You had to have seen something."

Sebastian didn't even realize he'd moved until Tom's

back hit the wall and his head bounced off it with a sickening thunk. That's what happened when a bigger man put his hand around a smaller man's throat and shoved.

"Don't touch her," he said, in a voice that didn't sound like his own.

"I'm all right." Willow tugged on Sebastian's arm.

He released the guard. "Never touch her again."

Tom nodded, rubbing his throat.

"Or any of the others," Sebastian thought to add, though from Tom's expression he wasn't buying it. "Go."

Tom went.

Sebastian took a deep breath—in, out, in again—waiting for the pounding in his ears to recede along with the orange haze behind his eyes. He didn't have much luck until Willow took his hand. Everything calmed. He wanted to hold her hand forever, but he couldn't. He shouldn't have held it this long.

"Come along." Not waiting to see if she followed, Sebastian released her and headed to the courtyard door, unlocked it and stepped through, closing it behind them both. "What happened?"

She lifted her face to the moon—full and silver, it shone on her for just an instant before shadows danced between that moon and the earth. He lifted his face too.

Odd. There hadn't been a cloud in the sky and now the sky was full of them.

"We were watching TV," Willow said.

Sebastian lowered his gaze to hers. "And then?"

She stared at her feet. "Someone screamed that she was gone. That she'd been there and then she'd disappeared."

"What does that mean?"

"I don't know."

"Look at me."

She continued to stare at the grass. He stepped

closer—too close. Inappropriately close. Thunder rolled on the horizon.

"Please," he murmured.

When she did, he fell into her eyes as if he'd fallen into the ocean from a rocky cliff. The world shimmied like déjà vu, which was crazy. He'd never stood with her in the night, beneath the moon, with a storm blowing in, electricity humming along his skin, making the hair on his arms buzz. He'd never stood like this with anyone.

They were as close as they could get without touching. Every breath she took, her breasts rose closer to his chest. He couldn't seem to move, to speak, to think. He could do nothing but listen to the cadence of her breath, inhale the scent of her skin, tingle at the memory of a touch that had never happened.

The wind picked up and whipped her hair across his face. She shuddered, and the movement caused her breasts to brush against him at last. He was going to kiss her. He shouldn't. He couldn't. Nevertheless—

"Tree," she said, and shoved him in the chest.

He was big; she was not. He only took a single step back, surprised more than anything else. Then she launched herself into his arms; his feet tangled. Together they fell.

An instant before a giant limb from the largest tree in the courtyard cracked and slammed into the ground exactly where they'd been.

I'd had a lot of visions in my life. Most of them I remembered, some of them I didn't until right before they happened.

Like tonight.

I knew this wasn't our first kiss. Wrong place. Wrong time. However, the instant my breasts had brushed his chest and the entire world stilled, I'd seen again what I'd seen once before.

The tree was going to break. It was going to break us unless we moved.

We fell hard. My chin hit his chest. I bit my tongue. Blood filled my mouth. He grunted when my knee connected where it shouldn't. Then we both lay there kind of stunned.

The earth shook—the tree or the thunder? Perhaps both. Then the courtyard filled with lights and sound and people. Someone dragged me off Dr. Frasier, pinned my arms behind my back.

"What did you do?" Nurse Zoe yanked my arms up so high I saw stars, or maybe it was just the sizzle of lightning far too close.

"Stop." The doctor's voice was hoarse. He held up a hand. One of the guards hauled him to his feet. He limped over and physically extricated me from Zoe's clutches. "You're bleeding."

He wiped my chin. From the wash of red on his palm, I was bleeding a lot.

"I'll fill out the incident report," Zoe said.

"What incident?" Dr. Frasier asked.

"She attacked you. You had to defend yourself."

I didn't have to be psychic to understand the look she gave me. I was in for a rough time whenever she was around. Nothing new there. She hadn't been able to do much more than pinch and shove with Mary around. But Mary was gone.

"Willow did nothing but push me out of the way of that tree limb."

Everyone stared at the limb that was more of a log. It had put a dent in the ground. It definitely would have put a dent in one or both of us.

Zoe didn't appear convinced. Neither did anyone else.

I suppose the idea of me pushing Dr. Frasier was a bit far-fetched. But terror fuels adrenaline. It had certainly fueled me.

"Let's clean you up." Dr. Frasier took my arm and led me inside.

I was a mess. Blood had dripped all over my shirt. My face was probably worse. He led me to his office, sat me on the couch, went into the nearby restroom and came back with a cloth. Then he knelt at my side and gently washed the blood from my face and neck.

I probably should have stopped him, but I'd started shaking. What if I hadn't remembered the future/past in time?

He took my trembling hands between his own. "You're like ice. Lie down."

I shook my head.

"Doctor's orders. You're going into shock." He glanced over his shoulder at the continued pandemonium in the hall. "Really, Willow, I don't have the time."

"Time?" I echoed.

Worry haunted his face. "This is a secure psychiatric facility. Or at least it was before I took over. To lose the same patient twice isn't going to be good for me. As much as I'd like to sit here with you, I need to find Mary. Now."

"It's not your fault."

He urged me to lie down and covered me with a blanket. Then he smoothed my hair. "Who else's fault would it be?"

I couldn't tell him it was mine, but I could help him find her. "May I have a glass of water, please?"

"Of course." He fetched it, handing it over without glancing at me at all.

Which only showed how distracted he was. I'm sure

the fact that I *never* drank water by choice was very prominent in my file.

At first I saw nothing in the tiny bathroom-sized cup. I sipped and when the water hit my lacerated tongue it burned. A fleck of dried blood floated across the surface. It spread out, dissolved, became one with the water, and I saw a small town—different from the last one but similar enough to be in the same general area. A coffee shop—a woman and a man sat in the booth by the window. He was slim and blond; he had a goatee. She was the same long-haired woman I'd seen twice before.

Someone shot out of the darkness, ran up to the window, started hammering fists against the glass.

"Bitch-whore!" she screamed.

"Mary," I said.

"What?" Dr. Frasier asked.

I dropped the cup. It soaked first the blanket and then me. "The restaurant is called Missy's Café."

"What restaurant? Where?"

"Google it." I pointed to his computer. "Quick. I'm not sure how much time you have."

"Before what?" he asked, but he was already sitting at his desk and bringing up the search engine.

"Before Mary tries to kill her."

He flicked a glance at me, then back at the screen. "Who?"

"That bitch-whore she keeps talking about? She found her."

Sebastian located the restaurant through the wonder of Google in Carlton's Cave Township.

"That's forty miles from here," he said. "There's no way she could be there yet. Even if she got a ride."

"You need to hurry," was all Willow said.

"She told you she was going there?" He typed in the Carlton's Cave PD, found the number, dialed.

"Whatever works."

Sebastian frowned at her answer, but he didn't have time to ask "what the hell?" because the phone was picked up on the other end.

"Carlton's Cave Police Department."

"This is Dr. Sebastian Frasier from the Northern Wisconsin Mental Health Facility. One of our patients may be in your area. Perhaps headed to a restaurant called Missy's Café?"

"That's not a crime," the dispatcher said.

"Not yet." Sebastian couldn't believe he'd just said that. "If you could have an officer patrol there tonight, be on the lookout for an older woman, long gray hair, tan jumpsuit, slippers not shoes. Can't miss her."

Especially if she put her hands around someone else's throat and started to squeeze.

"And if we find her?"

"Detain, please. I'm on my way." He hung up as Willow swung her feet to the floor. "You should stay there until you feel less shaky. Would you like more water?"

Sebastian heard what he'd just said and frowned. Because of what she thought she saw in it, Willow only drank water to get rid of it. She never asked for it. Why had she tonight?

To find Mary. And she had. Or at least she thought she had. Who was he to throw stones? He was heading to Carlton's Cave because of her "vision." But he had to do something.

What if Mary was actually there? He'd deal with that after he found her. He'd deal with calling Dr. Tronsted then too. Breaking with procedure again but why stop now?

"I'll come with you." Willow stood, swayed.

"Not."

"She'll behave better if I'm there."

"Willow, I cannot take you out of here."

Well, he could—in cuffs maybe—but he wasn't going to. He wasn't taking anyone. Willow because he didn't want to lose two patients in one night. And anyone else because he didn't want an audience if he got to Carlton's Cave and found nothing but locals.

He set his hand on her shoulder. "Just rest, okay?"

She tangled their fingers together. She wasn't as icy as she'd been a few moments ago, thank God.

"You need to be careful," she said.

"If I have to I can sedate Mary."

"I wasn't talking about Mary."

A shadow flickered in the doorway. Zoe stared at their still-joined hands with an odd expression. Sebastian yanked his away.

"I had a call about Mary," he said. "I'm going to check it out. Willow can lie down in here until she feels better."

"I'm fine."

She seemed pale. The remaining streaks of blood on her chin and lips only made it worse.

"You want some ice cream?"

Her eyes widened. "Really? Ice cream? I'm not five."

"Sugar and fat would help."

"Help what?" Zoe asked.

"Yeah, help what?" Willow echoed.

"Shock?"

"Are you asking if I'm in shock or if it helps shock?"

"Yes."

She laughed. Zoe didn't.

"Why would she be in shock?"

Willow cast the nurse a narrow glance. "I'm not."

Sebastian was uneasy about leaving. "You're sure you're—"

"Go." Willow made a shooing motion. "Find Mary."

He shooed.

An hour later—forty miles on county highways took longer to travel over than miles on just about anything else—he rolled into Carlton's Cave in the facility's minivan.

Small-town police departments were usually located on a side street. Less cost for the real estate than the main drag and room to expand if necessary, which it usually was. As he drove toward the first cross avenue, a sign halfway down on his right drew his attention.

MISSY'S CAFÉ.

He slowed as he approached. Framed in the window sat a woman with long dark hair and a blond man. They were in earnest conversation, leaning toward each other, gesticulating.

Then a figure shot forward, pounding the glass with fists and shouting. He couldn't hear what. As the figure was undoubtedly Mary, he could imagine.

He threw the vehicle into park, leaping out just as a CCPD cruiser pulled up and the officer behind the wheel did the same. He reached Mary an instant before Sebastian did, shoving her against the window and cuffing her.

Mary continued to shriek about the bitch-whore. Sebastian tuned her out.

He expected the "bitch-whore" and her companion to come outside and see what was going on. He'd ask if either one of them knew Mary, though considering Mary, that wasn't a prerequisite for her flipping out. When no one joined them, Sebastian glanced inside.

The woman and the man were gone.

"Would you return to your vehicle, sir?" The police officer's question brought Sebastian back to the issue at hand.

"I'm Dr. Frasier. I called earlier about Mary." He indicated the struggling woman in cuffs.

"Great." The man stepped back, and Mary tried to run off. He pushed her against the wall again. "I don't think she wants to go with you."

Sebastian bit back the *no kidding* that rose to his lips. "Can you put her in the van?"

"I can try." The guy looked doubtful. Mary was giving him a lot of trouble.

"Hold on." Sebastian went to the vehicle, which would have been in traffic, if there was traffic. The only car that passed in either direction was a bright yellow Jaguar with tinted windows, which caught his attention not only because of its glaring uselessness in northern Wisconsin but because of the ostentatious color. Although, if the thing went bumper deep in a snowbank, which was a given sometime soon, it wouldn't be hard to spot.

Sebastian retrieved the sedation he'd brought along and returned to the officer and his charge.

Mary tried to bite both of them when he used it, but it worked fast. The fellow was able to lead her to the van, strap her in, remove the cuffs. Sebastian thanked him and drove away.

Mary had calmed, but she was still conscious. Sebastian wasn't sure how long either one would last.

"How'd you get out, Mary?"

"Same's last time."

"And how was that?"

"Transportation."

*Star Trek* again. He wasn't surprised.

"He will burn them all."

As Mary had been screaming about a "bitch-whore" Sebastian was curious. "Who's he?"

"Brand, then burn. It's what he does."

Considering what he'd learned about the murder of the Gilletts, that was disturbing. How could she know? According to Hardy, the branding part of the program had been withheld from the media.

Might Mary have been involved in the couple's deaths? No. She'd been in the facility at the time, and she hadn't yet "transported" out. But maybe someone inside had committed the murders or told Mary who had. Or maybe Willow had shared her vision with Mary as well.

"Who brands and burns, Mary?"

"Roland."

Roland was the name of the voice that told Mary to do bad things. As Roland had been talking to Mary for over a decade, Sebastian had to consider that Mary's answers tonight were more Mary-variety gibberish.

Unless Roland was real.

# Chapter 11

"I know what you're up to."

I'd been watching Dr. Frasier make his way down the hall toward the exit. He stopped and spoke with one of the other doctors, then a guard.

I met Zoe's gaze. "Wish I did."

"You think if you fuck him he'll let you out?"

"Excuse me?"

"I won't excuse you." She grabbed my upper arm and hauled me out of the office. "He deserves better. He deserves—"

"What's going on here?"

Peggy was back. I was ecstatic, and not because of Zoe. It might land me in solitary, but I knew how to handle her.

"Mary's gone again." Zoe continued to hold on to me.

Peggy's gaze flicked to mine, then down to Zoe's too-tight grip. "What does that have to do with Willow?"

"I don't know. But I'm sure it's something."

"I'll take over from here, Zoe."

Zoe's fingers tightened. I refused to wince. It was what she wanted. Since Peggy was waiting, Zoe released me, but she'd be back. I'd be ready.

Peggy kept her eyes on the nurse as she joined the others. "Is she behaving badly, Willow?"

"No." I knew better than to point fingers. If Zoe were reprimanded, I'd bear the brunt of her fury. The only way to deal with bullies was to be a bigger bully. Been there, done that. Was pretty good at it.

"Hmm."

Peggy didn't believe me. Imagine that?

"How did Mary get out?"

"Wow, déjà vu," I said.

"Don't be a smartass. Was it the spell?"

"Really?"

"Willow, did you do the transportation spell?"

"No." I lifted my arm. "Hand to God." We hadn't gotten that far.

"I wonder if I should call her son?"

"The one she tried to kill?"

"He's the only one she has."

"What's he going to do?"

"True." Peggy let out a breath. "He's in Afghanistan anyway."

"By choice?"

"Marine."

*Good.* I'd been a little worried about Mary's son. But if he was a marine, he might just be able to take her.

"How was your visit with your granddaughter?" I asked.

"Great."

"Bet you're thrilled to be back."

"I was until I walked into this." She waved at the gaggle of patients and staff still milling around in the hall. "You truly have no idea how Mary got out?"

"You think if I knew I wouldn't have gotten out too?"

"I thought you were happy here."

"No one's happy here." Although now that Dr. Frasier had arrived, I was less *unhappy*.

"You wanna tell me why Zoe has a bug up her butt about you?"

"No."

Peggy took my hands. "I saw the way he looked at you."

"He who?"

"Dr. Frasier. You want to tell me anything?"

"Nothing to tell." That had actually happened in reality and not in a vision.

"Willow, I'm on your side. I'm your advocate. If he's done anything—even said anything—he shouldn't have—"

"No. Of course not!"

"You understand what's inappropriate?"

"Better than most."

"For a doctor, a nurse, a guard to take advantage of a patient is criminal."

"There has been no advantage taken."

There never would be. There couldn't be.

Perhaps I'd seen what I had about Dr. Frasier and me so I could stop it from happening. He was a good man. A fantastic doctor. And if he hung around me, he was going to wind up in a lot of trouble.

Who didn't?

The return trip to the mental health facility was uneventful. After dropping the name Roland, Mary had dropped off to sleep.

Sebastian dialed his boss. As it was the middle of the night, he got her voice mail, which was what he'd been hoping for, and left a message. She had an emergency number, but he didn't consider the situation an emergency anymore.

Delusion? Rationalization? Cowardice? Yes. And he was okay with that.

He notified the facility of his arrival time and Tom I

met them at the intake bay, then rolled Mary off in a wheelchair to solitary.

Sebastian returned to his office and did some research. The name Roland got him diddly. Too broad.

He typed "snarling wolf" into the search engine. Same thing. He got gazillions of hits, but they were all pictures of snarling wolves.

"Snarling wolf ring" didn't work too well either. He found a lot of jewelry on Etsy.

"Snarling wolf symbol" brought up several groups who'd used one; the most infamous were the Nazis. Certainly that group was still around—more's the pity—however, if they were behind these murders the FBI would have been all over that already. It wasn't like the Nazis kept a low profile. Ever.

There were several motorcycle clubs. Having watched *Sons of Anarchy*, Sebastian figured the FBI knew about them too.

He hit the jackpot when he combined Roland and snarling wolf symbol. Someone had recently updated the Wikipedia information. He had to wonder who.

*"Venatores Mali,"* he read. "Hunters of evil."

And for these bozos evil meant witches. As the patient who'd led him to this information thought she was one, Sebastian was both intrigued and a little freaked out.

On the one hand, Roland was a real person as he'd suspected—namely Roland McHugh, leader of the bozos. On the other hand, just because Mary's voice was named Roland, didn't mean it actually *was* Roland—this Roland. Sebastian was pretty sure it wasn't. The guy had been dead for centuries.

Mary had probably read about Roland at some point. Started applying his name to every bad man who spoke to her—be they real or imagined. She was obsessed with witches, paranoid too. Why wouldn't she think the voice in her head belonged to a dead witch hunter?

Although she'd started out listening to the advice of this voice, when she should have been smacking herself and telling it to shut up. Unless the latter was behind her brain banging. In his experience, those head voices were pretty persuasive.

"Dr. Frasier?"

Peggy Dalberg stood in his doorway. Sebastian was damn glad to see her.

"You're back! Great. Come in." He indicated the visitor's chair and she took it, though she seemed uncomfortable.

"You found Mary."

Not a question, so he didn't answer. Sebastian had questions of his own.

"Have you ever heard of Roland McHugh?"

Her forehead creased, and she shook her head.

"He was the leader of a witch-hunting society in seventeenth-century Scotland."

"Little random," she said.

"Not really. You're a witch. Mary thinks she's a witch." Apparently someone thought Willow was one too.

"No one's hunting us." When he remained silent, she sat up straight. "Are they?"

Quickly he told her what he knew. She appeared suitably concerned.

"Have you ever heard of the *Venatores Mali*?" he asked.

Peggy shook her head again.

"Isn't that something you should know?"

"No one's hunted witches for centuries."

"That we know of."

"You think the *Venatores Mali* are back?" she asked.

"If not, someone's doing a damn good imitation."

"Why?"

"I've never gotten very good explanations for crazy."

"You think someone's after Mary?"

"No one's been asking questions about Mary."

"Willow then. Because of the visions?"

Yesterday he would have pointed out that Willow didn't actually have visions. Today, he just shrugged.

"What should we do?"

"The FBI is involved." He should probably call them, though most of what he knew was Mary-variety gibberish. "I'm not sure what we can do beyond our jobs. If Mary and Willow are here, they should be safe."

"Except Mary's getting out somehow, which means there's a way in."

"Unless she's actually transporting."

"Don't start," Peggy said.

"We'll have to keep a closer eye on both of them."

"About that," Peggy began, then went silent.

"What about it?"

"People have noticed."

"Kind of hard not to."

"Sir?"

"When Mary's gone, people notice."

"I meant people have noticed you and Willow."

"Me and Willow?" he echoed.

"Doctor," she said in the same tone of voice his mother had always said *Sebastian* whenever he'd disappointed her. "You need to assign her to another psychiatrist."

Sebastian didn't argue. She was right.

Mary remained in solitary for several days, but as her explanation for escape continued to be that she transported, and she obviously believed it, she was released.

If I'd thought we were being watched before, it was nothing compared to what happened after she disappeared the second time. I couldn't turn around without bumping into staff.

I wouldn't have minded bumping into Dr. Frasier. But he not only assigned me to another psychiatrist—an elderly woman who'd probably known Freud and liked him—but he avoided me with a deftness I might have appreciated if it hadn't hurt so badly.

My new psychiatrist liked to ask me about sex. As I hadn't had any, ever—at least in reality—they were short conversations. I wasn't surprised when she didn't believe me.

Most girls of my background used sex for currency—food, shelter, drugs. There'd been times I'd been close to using it myself. But I'd found other ways—stealing, cheating, lying, hiding were all better than sex with a stranger, in my opinion.

If I hadn't had those visions of Sebastian, the knowledge of what sex with love would be like, I wouldn't have understood what I was selling so short. But I did have those visions; I did know. And they'd given me strength in so many ways.

Unable to psychoanalyze what had never happened, my psychiatrist moved from questions about sex to inquiries about my parents. Those conversations were even shorter.

Dr. Frasier's boss, the head of all the facilities in the state, made a surprise visit. Both she and several of her assistants trolled the halls, poking into empty rooms and storage closets, pushing up ceiling tile and peering down bathroom drains—as if Mary could turn to smoke and get out that way—but they didn't find a physical path of escape any more than anyone else had.

Dr. Tronsted spent a lot of time talking to Justice. I

suppose he knew the place better than anyone, but the few times I'd seen them together they'd stopped talking as soon as they'd seen me, and made a beeline away from each other as if they were guilty of something other than chatter. Maybe they had a thing goin' on. Or maybe she had convinced Justice to spy. He seemed to be everywhere I looked lately.

Tronsted interviewed me twice. I suppose a lot of people in this facility changed their stories as often as the wind changed direction, but not me. I told her the same thing both times that I'd told Dr. Frasier whenever he'd asked. Mary thought she'd transported outside the walls, and I hadn't seen anything to contradict that.

She interviewed Mary too. Their meeting was short— no crashes, no shouting—then the doctor left, and as far as I knew she hadn't been back. Although the facility was huge. I might be wrong.

As Peggy continued our Wicca lessons, Mary must have convinced the big boss all was well. Or Dr. Frasier had convinced her that the more Wicca Mary learned the saner she became, which seemed to be the truth. Most likely, no one had mentioned Wicca at all.

One afternoon, over three weeks after Mary had disappeared the last time, we were in the cafeteria where our lessons habitually took place between lunch and dinner, when Mary brought up blood magic. I thought Peggy might have a stroke.

"Where did you hear that?" she demanded.

Mary lifted Peggy's *Book of Shadows,* which, since it never left Mary's possession anymore might need to be renamed. "Where do you think?"

"Blood magic is the most powerful kind of magic there is," Peggy explained. "Using blood in a spell makes that spell not only personal but permanent. It shouldn't be used unless there's no other choice."

"If it's that powerful, why not?" Mary asked.

"Blood magic is the bridge between white magic and black. That connection can draw a witch from the light to the dark. It's dangerous."

"A bridge works both ways," I said. "Wouldn't it draw the dark to the light too?"

"It rarely does. Once power like that is used, it seduces. In white magic, the blood is given. In black it is taken. You see the difference?"

"Sacrifice versus—" I tried to think of the opposite of sacrifice and couldn't.

"Theft," Peggy supplied. "Torture, slavery, bondage."

"Got it," Mary said. "Taking bad. Giving good."

"The results of a blood spell cannot be undone," Peggy continued, ignoring her.

"Why not?" I asked.

"Those spells use the elements in some way. What is burned cannot be unburned. What sinks into the earth, can't be drawn out. What is tossed into the wind is irretrievable. Blood becomes one with the water."

As if it were happening again, right before my eyes, I saw the fleck of dried blood from my bitten tongue dispersing into the cup of water, disappearing, becoming one with it, right before I had my last vision. That hadn't been a spell, but it had been something. I'd seen what I wanted to, what I needed to, rather than random flashes that made no sense.

"Let's try one." Mary opened the book.

"No." Peggy closed the book. "Did you hear what I just said?"

"I'll *give* you my blood. All good."

Peggy lifted her gaze to Deux—our guard for the day—who lounged just inside the doorway, gaze fixed on us as if we were pork chops dancing in front of a wolf. I kept expecting him to lick his lips.

"You might *want* to give me your blood," Peggy said just above a whisper. "But if I start taking it, that'll not only be the end of our lessons, but the end of my job. You think no one's going to notice me cutting your arm?"

"I'll cut my own arm," Mary said.

"Not," Peggy and I blurted at the same time.

Mary scowled and hugged the book to her chest, but she quit arguing.

"I wanted to do a spell of healing today," Peggy said.

Deux made a derisive sound and turned away. But he didn't *go* away. Lately, none of them did.

"Where is it?" Mary began to shuffle through the pages.

"I haven't tried it yet. If it works, we write it down."

Mary snapped the book closed. "Okay."

Peggy withdrew three blue candles and a knife from her bag. She picked up one of the candles and began to carve a word into the wax.

"Whoa!" Deux plucked the sharp instrument from her hand. "Are you high?"

"Not at the moment," Peggy said, and held out her hand. "Give it back."

"Nope." He tucked the knife into his pocket and strolled back where he'd been.

"Now what?" The gaze Mary turned on the guard worried me.

"Now I do this." Peggy used her fingernail to write Mary's name in all three candles.

"I'm not hurt," Mary protested.

Peggy just lit the candles, held out her hands and waited until we took them before she began the chant. "Healing light, shining bright, let this sickness flee in fright."

"Not sick either," Mary muttered.

Peggy kept chanting. "With harm to none, including me, as I will so mote it be. Now together."

We repeated the chant three times.

"Close your eyes and imagine Mary well."

"Not. Sick."

Mary's patience was waning. Couldn't say I blamed her. A lot of Wicca involved meditation. Mary wasn't the type.

"What about sleeping?" Mary asked.

Peggy opened one eye. "Now?"

"Is there a spell to help me sleep?"

Both Peggy's eyes opened. "You have trouble sleeping?"

Mary nodded. I kept silent. This was news to me.

Peggy released our hands and started to dig through her handbag. She came up with a mesh bag that smelled herby. She pressed it into Mary's hand. "You can have this one. I'll have my friend make another."

Mary tightened her fingers around the bag and the smell intensified. "What's in it?"

"Cardamom pods, salt, cloves, peppermint, rosemary, and the peel of one lemon. Crushed, mixed."

"That's it?" Mary held the thing away by two fingers. "I don't want to nod off all the time."

"You have to do the incantation while you, or whoever you wish to help, has the bag on their person—held or tucked in a pocket perhaps."

Mary dropped the bag to the table. "What is it?"

"Sleep be with me. Ease my mind. Calm my body. Wings of darkness bring the sight of night and ease my dreams."

"Doesn't rhyme," Mary said.

"Doesn't have to."

"It works?"

Peggy winked. "Like a charm."

"Then why wasn't it in the book?"

"Not my spell. Someone in my coven gave it to me."

Whenever grandmotherly Peggy brought up her coven my ears rang.

"If it worked for you, shouldn't you write it in the book?"

"Would you like to write it there for me?"

Peggy's voice was a little first-grade teacher, and Mary's gaze narrowed. But she wrote down the spell.

"All right." Peggy gathered her things. "We'll try something new next week, okay?"

"Okay," I said.

Mary was still writing.

Peggy left.

Mary's gaze went to Deux and she smiled.

I suddenly understood what the sleeping spell was for.

Several nights later I was trying to decide if I was going to help Mary escape again. On the one hand, she was trying to kill people. On the other, so were they.

Mary must have sensed my waffling, because she came to my room. She brought along her shadow. Tonight it was Zoe.

The nurse had been keeping her distance from me. I figured she'd been warned. Didn't prevent her from throwing daggerlike glares in my direction.

"If looks could kill." Mary threw a killer look of her own at the nurse, then slammed the door in her face.

Zoe opened it right back up. "This stays open."

"Where are we going to go?" Mary threw out her arm, indicating the windows with bars.

"Open," Zoe said, and Mary gave her the finger.

"Wow." Zoe put her hand over her chest. "That hurt."

"I'd really like to learn how to turn her into a slug."

I'd seen Zoe talking earnestly to Dr. Frasier, setting her hand on his arm, basking in his smile. "Wouldn't mind it myself."

Zoe rolled her eyes and leaned against the wall in the hall.

"I hope she's working a few nights from now," Mary whispered.

"Why?"

"It would be so much fun to disappear on her watch."

"About that—" I began.

"Remember what Peggy said when she explained blood magic?"

"It's a bad idea."

"That's not what I heard."

I wasn't surprised. Mary usually heard what she wanted to, and sometimes what wasn't even said.

She held out her hand and I took it. Her palm was slick.

"Eighty percent of blood is water," she whispered.

I didn't even have time to curse.

An old house—dusty, grimy, garbage in the corners—all the windows busted. But most disturbing was the upside-down pentagram on the wall above a table full of dead things.

I smelled blood. Theirs or Mary's? Did it matter?

Voices outside, coming in. Can't be seen. Need to hide. Hurry to the stairs, rush to the top. Wait. Listen. Can't hear. Creep closer. I see myself, but not myself—red hair, greenish-brown eyes. I/she is speaking to someone in the room with the dead. The voices, the words jumble together. Confusing. Head hurts. Skin on fire. Need to, need to—

A shriek fills the air. Down the stairs, into the room, lift the knife—

Why is there a knife? Why does that knife appear familiar?

"What are you two doing?"

I yanked my hand out of Mary's. Zoe blocked the light from the hall. She flipped the switch in my room, and the glare made me blink and stutter. "I . . . uh . . . W-w-we—" At least I had the presence of mind to curl my fingers over the blood.

"Praying," Mary snapped. "Get out."

"You wouldn't know a prayer if one bit you on the ass," Zoe returned.

"I'm going to bite you." Mary started to stand.

"Shhh." I drew her back down.

Together we closed our eyes. Then we stayed that way until Zoe got bored and left. I opened one eye. Her shadow spread long across the hall. Good enough.

"What was that?" I whispered.

"My house." Mary rubbed her forehead, leaving a bloody fingerprint. I licked my thumb and rubbed it off. "I think . . . my son was there."

There'd been other people, other voices, but I'd only seen the redhead with my face.

"You don't know?" I asked.

"It's been so long."

I let it go. My main concern was—

"The woman?"

Mary sat up straighter. "Exactly like you, except with different hair and eyes."

"We need to work on your understanding of *exactly*." But she was right. Whoever that had been she'd looked "exactly" like me.

Might I have a sister somewhere? My stomach jittered. Excitement? Anticipation? Trepidation? Yes.

"She was my son's friend, when they were kids. I

haven't seen her since I went away. She grew up. So did he. That's why I was confused when I saw you."

"Where did you live?"

"Three Harbors. I have to go there."

She started to stand again. Again, I pulled her back down.

"Willow, you saw what was going to happen. Someone had a knife."

"Mary," I said. "I think that someone was you."

# Chapter 12

"Owen's in danger," Mary said.

"Peggy told me that Owen's a marine. He'll be fine."

"I have to help him."

"With a knife?"

"It was your vision, Willow."

"I think it might have been yours."

It had been strange. I usually saw the future, but I saw it through my own eyes. While this might have been the future, I'd been seeing things through Mary's eyes.

"He needs me. I failed him before. I can't fail him now."

Mary sensed my reluctance and began to get agitated. Never a good thing with Mary.

"You have to send me to him. Why else would you have the vision?"

"Because you brought it on with a bloody hand?" I reached for that hand, and she slapped mine away.

"Promise me that when the full moon comes you'll do the spell."

"Let me see what you did."

She held her arm out in the other direction.

"Don't be juvenile."

"I'll let you see it if you promise to do the spell."

"Mary—"

"He's getting louder. He's closer. He's coming."

"Roland?"

She nodded.

"You know he's dead, right? Has been for centuries?"

"Sweetie, evil never dies."

She sounded so lucid I got a chill. "All right. I promise."

She shoved her hand at me so fast I stiffened, afraid she meant to punch out my lights. There was a slice across the meat of her palm. "What did you do?"

She removed a knife from her back pocket with the hand I wasn't holding. The same knife she'd had in the vision. I realized why I recognized it. It was the knife Peggy had brought to our lesson. The one Deux had taken away.

"How'd you get that?"

"Sleeping spell works like a charm." Mary's lips twitched.

"Ha-ha." I beckoned with my fingers. "Give it to me."

"No." She shoved it back in her pocket. "I had it in the vision. I need it."

"If someone sees you with it you're gonna be locked away for a lot longer than you ever have been before."

She snorted her opinion of that. "You had the vision of me with Owen and this knife. Which means it'll happen."

She was right. My visions came true. But there was a first time for everything. Nevertheless, I let her keep the knife. I doubted I'd be able to get it away from her without more bloodshed anyway, and we should probably avoid that.

"You shouldn't have cut yourself. What were you thinking?"

"I had to know what was coming, and Peggy said blood magic was the most powerful kind."

She had. She'd also said it couldn't be undone. I wondered what that meant for the vision we'd had.

"He's getting harder to ignore," Mary continued. "He wants me to kill you. But I won't. Don't worry."

Hmm. Did I believe her? Oddly, yes.

"Why me?"

"Something about your parents."

"I don't have parents."

"Everyone has parents."

"I don't know who mine are."

"Roland does."

"Who are they?"

Mary's forehead crinkled. "That's what makes no sense."

None of this made sense, but I tightened my lips so I wouldn't say so.

"He speaks about witches and a wolf."

A wolf. Strange, but what wasn't lately?

"What does a wolf have to do with my parents?"

She shrugged. "There's a lot of crazy talk with him."

*With him?*

"He really wants you and your sisters dead."

"Sisters? Plural?"

"Definitely. The redhead must be one of the two."

If I hadn't seen her too, I might point out that Mary had delusions. Then again, a lot of her previous loony talk was proving not so loony.

The idea that I might have sisters was a concept so foreign I wasn't sure what to think about it. Though having someone—two someones apparently—would be better than having no one at all. Better than better. If it were true.

"What about the other one?" I asked.

"I haven't seen her."

Neither had I, which was odd. You'd think if I had sisters, I'd have "seen" them before now. All those times I'd been alone—sad, frightened, needy—knowing I wasn't alone would have lessened all of it. But I'd never had any control over what I saw—until lately.

"We could try again." Mary turned her palm up. The fluorescent lights made the fresh blood glisten.

The world wavered, and I glanced away. "No."

"But—"

"It's nearly lights out. You need to clean up before someone besides me sees that."

She didn't seem happy, but she nodded.

"How are you gonna clean your hand without Zoe noticing?" I asked.

She cast a narrow glare in Zoe's direction. "I could knock her senseless."

"As much fun as that might be, solitary would follow."

Which would mean no transportation spell. I'd say that would be my way out of doing it, but I was worried about Mary's son too, as well as the woman who looked exactly like me, but different—one of my sisters.

"Can't have that."

"What about the sleeping spell?"

"I used what I had on Deux. Kind of hard to make more from in here." Mary stood. "I'll take a shower. So far no one's watched me do that." She stuck her bloody hand in her pocket. "And knowing Nurse Ratched, she'll stay with you." Mary cast a concerned glance toward the hall where Zoe still hovered. "Maybe you should come along."

It was sweet that Mary wanted to protect me. But if there was one thing I didn't want to do it was watch Mary McAllister take a shower. Stuff like that was almost impossible to unsee.

"I'm going to bed."

"Good. You should get your rest before the full moon." She kissed the top of my head and left.

As Mary walked past Zoe, she gave her the finger

with her nonbloody hand. I had to try really hard not to laugh.

Zoe took a step after her, then glanced at me with a frown. I shut off my lights and crawled into bed, turning toward the wall and presenting her with my back. Then I wished I hadn't. I could swear she was creeping closer with evil intent. I turned toward the door just as Zoe hurried after Mary.

I let out a long sigh and closed my eyes. I was so tired I drifted off almost immediately. I wouldn't have woken until morning if someone hadn't put that plastic bag over my face.

My eyes snapped open. Everything was hazy, first because of the dark, the plastic, then because of lack of oxygen. I reached up to scratch a hole and my wrists were grabbed, held over my head.

Black dots danced merrily. I could have sworn I heard a rumble like thunder. Lightning flared. Electricity buzzed against my fingertips. Something went *zzzt!*

A start, a gasp, and I was released. I was almost too weak to yank the plastic off my face, but I managed. Ozone lingered in the air. The tips of my fingernails were blackened. When I touched them, they disintegrated into ash and fell away. The blood on my palm had dried, but that was the least of my worries right now.

I managed to sit up. I was feeling better by the minute. There was something I needed to do and now. What was it?

"Mary," I whispered. If someone had tried to kill me, they were probably going to do the same to her. At the least, I should warn her.

I stood, swayed, gritted my teeth, and stumbled out my open door.

\* \* \*

Sebastian worked late trying to catch up on paperwork. It was the one thing about his job he never got on top of. Probably because he hated it so much.

He enjoyed people—both helping his patients and managing his staff. But the constant, repetitive reports were so mind-numbing he'd started doing them one night a week rather than a bit every day as he should.

He'd bought a Ford Explorer the first time there'd been frost on the grass in the morning. But it had warmed up again—they called it Indian summer—and he'd been able to continue riding his bike to work. He doubted the reprieve would last much longer. According to the locals, the weather was uncommonly warm for late October.

He finished what he'd planned to for the evening—not enough, never was—and powered down his computer, then stepped out of his office. He glanced in the direction of Willow's room—shouldn't but he couldn't seem to help himself, and looking wasn't a crime, at least not yet—and she stumbled into the hall, nearly going to her knees before she righted herself.

He was at her side before she'd taken another step. "What's wrong?"

She blinked at him as if she'd just woken from a deep sleep. Her room was dark—maybe she had—the hallway was brilliant. He would have written off her staggering and blinking to waking from a bad dream and stepping into fluorescent lights, if her lips hadn't been tinged blue.

He set his palm along her chin and tilted her face. She focused on him and smiled. "I missed you."

"I—" he began, and saw movement in the hall. A quick glance revealed a patient shuffling to her room and not Zoe lurking as she seemed to do a lot lately, along with Justice, Deux, and Tom I. Everyone was on edge, concerned about their jobs. He was.

He could have sworn he smelled the remnants of fire and glanced into Willow's room to make sure she hadn't run out because of just that. But he saw nothing there beyond her sheets on the floor. She'd probably had a vivid nightmare and kicked them off, which would have made her cold, though not cold enough for blue lips. He wanted to warm them, but the *way* he wanted to warm them was definitely illegal.

He took her arm. "You should lie down."

"No, I need to—"

Her head snapped up. Next thing Sebastian knew she'd tugged free and raced toward the communal facilities. Concerned she was going to be ill, he followed. But once there he hesitated. A shower ran; he heard more voices than hers.

"Willow?" he called. "You need help?"

Silence was his answer. A prickle of unease skated over him. He considered searching for a nurse—where was Zoe when you needed her? When he didn't need her, there she was.

"I'm coming in," he said.

Steam billowed from the single shower stall that had both the curtain drawn and the water running. None of the toilets appeared to be in use—all the doors were unlocked, no feet on the floor that he could see.

"Willow?" he tried again as he reached the shower in question. "Answer me please or I'll have to—"

The shower curtain opened with a screech of the rings across the rod, revealing Willow, hair damp and curling, clothes wet in splotches, all alone inside. She was still too pale and her lips looked like she'd eaten a blueberry Popsicle a few hours ago.

"Are you all right?" he asked.

She nodded.

"What's going on here?"

Zoe stood at the entrance to the showers, hands on her hips, scowl bouncing from Sebastian to Willow and back again.

He had no idea what to say because he had no idea what had happened. He couldn't figure out why Willow would step into a shower fully clothed like that. Though if she hadn't, she'd be naked and he'd be in huge trouble.

She'd also been talking, and not to herself, unless she'd been using a different voice to answer. Which was another set of trouble altogether.

"Where's Mary?" Zoe shoved past Sebastian, peering into every shower stall on the way to the one Willow occupied, where the water continued to run.

"Mary?" he echoed.

"She was taking a shower." Zoe jabbed a finger at the floor. "In this stall."

"Where were you?" Sebastian asked.

"Right here until I went to check on a commotion in the next hall." Zoe spread her hands. "Mary barely had time to dry off and get dressed before I came back. There's no way she had time to escape."

Yet she probably had. Mary was getting far too good at this.

"Did you see her?" Sebastian asked Willow.

She shook her head and turned off the water.

"Bullshit." Zoe grabbed Willow's wrist and yanked her out of the shower.

Willow slid on the wet tile, nearly falling, but Zoe dragged her back up.

"What did you do?" Zoe demanded, shaking Willow's arm so that her hand flapped like a leaf on a tree.

Sebastian took several steps forward, planning to shake Zoe like a dog with an old towel. He pulled up short when he saw Willow's palm, which was covered in blood.

Mary had disappeared again—and it wasn't even the full moon. What she'd whispered right before she'd taken my hand, then morphed out probably explained it.

"Blood magic is the most powerful kind."

I'd been thinking that I wanted her far away from whoever had just tried to kill me. I wondered how far away she'd gone, and if we'd ever be able to get her back.

Luckily she'd already put on her jumpsuit and slippers. I'd hate to have sent her out in the night with no clothes.

I'd stepped into the shower to shut it off—Mary always forgot the simple things—then heard Dr. Frasier coming and pulled the curtain closed. I should have stuck my hand under the water. I should have done a lot of things, but my brain was firing on empty. I blame the plastic bag over my face.

Dr. Frasier paled at the sight of the blood all over my palm. Mary's blood. I doubted they'd believe me if I said she'd put it there unasked.

"What happened?" Dr. Frasier asked.

"I must have slipped and scraped myself." Let's hope they were preoccupied with Missing Mary and didn't look closely at my hand. At least until I could actually scrape myself.

"What happened to *Mary*?" Zoe shook me again.

Maybe I should just belt her in the teeth. That would make us both bleed and cause enough commingling of fluids for me not to have to explain any more.

The fingers of my free hand curled into a fist. Dr. Frasier set his over the top of it, and I stilled.

"Zoe, fetch the guards. Have them start searching."

She still held on to my wrist tightly enough to leave a bruise. "Doctor, I don't—"

"Procedure, please."

She dug her fingernails into me—hard enough to draw blood, I hoped—before she let me go and left the room to do what the doctor had ordered.

"Why did you run in here?" Dr. Frasier asked.

"I didn't hurt Mary."

"Obviously."

I was so thankful he believed me without question, I almost didn't hear the rest of his statement.

"If you had there'd be a blood trail."

"Gee, thanks," I muttered.

"I know you wouldn't," he said more gently. "But it's good to have facts to back up your statement. You want to answer my question now?"

Should I tell him the truth? Might as well. Or at least as much truth as I could give him.

"Someone put a plastic bag over my face while I was sleeping."

He blinked, frowned. His gaze lowered to my lips for some reason, and I couldn't help myself, I licked them. He peered at the ceiling. "Who?"

"No idea. I was a little busy trying not to die."

"Why did they stop?"

"No idea," I repeated. Also true. I'd heard thunder, smelled lightning, but I'd been dying. Confusion was understandable. I should probably keep the information about my fingernail tips turning to ashes to myself too. That was the kind of talk that would get me put in solitary. Though I had a feeling I wasn't going to be able to talk fast enough to stop that this time.

"Did whoever was in your room make you bleed?"

"Probably." I put my hands behind my back and

scraped my bloody hand with what was left of my thumbnail. The crescent marks Zoe had put there would be helpful as well.

"You came in here to wash off?"

"I came to warn Mary. I figured if someone wanted me dead, they might want her dead as well."

"Because?"

Talking about witches and witch hunters probably wasn't in my best interest right now. Would it ever be?

"We spend all of our time together. If I annoyed someone enough to kill me, she probably did too."

He lifted his eyebrows. I knew what he was thinking. Mary would be the one most likely to annoy someone enough to kill, not me.

"You saw no sign of her when you got here?" he asked.

"It's like she went poof."

"Not funny."

"Sorry."

He cast his gaze toward the door beyond which the sounds of a full-scale search had commenced. "Any thoughts as to where she might head this time?"

If she'd transported to the place of my last vision, which seemed to be the MO, she'd be at or near her home in Three Harbors. However, this transportation had taken place before the full moon and with the use of blood magic. Who knew what that meant? Not to mention that the vision had showed Mary defending her son and my probable sister. I probably shouldn't send anyone to fetch her before that happened.

I shook my head.

Dr. Frasier motioned me to the sinks. "Wash your hands so I can take a look."

I didn't need to be told twice. Mary's blood was start-ing to flake off my skin, a nasty sensation I wanted to stop ASAP. I shoved both hands beneath the lukewarm stream, then pumped a palm full of soap.

I knew better than to gaze at the water, so I stared into the mirror above the sinks instead. When Dr. Frasier's eyes met mine, I caught my breath. Though the room around us was institutional—nothing sexy about it—his position behind me, my position just in front, made me think again of things that hadn't yet happened. There would come a time when we would be in a bathroom—much nicer, what wasn't?—me at the sink, him just behind. He would place his hands on my hips, move my hair away from my neck, lean over and fasten his lips to my skin as he lifted my skirt, trailed his palm up my bare thigh, skated his fingertips beneath the hem of my panties and—

"Willow?"

I'd closed my eyes, remembering, and now they snapped open. In the mirror for just an instant I saw a different me—hair tumbled and curling, lips parted, skin flushed, eyes bright.

"Are you all right?"

The doctor had stepped closer, to the exact place he would one day be. It was all I could do not to arch my back and rub myself against him. But, despite my visions of us, I knew now that we could never, ever be.

"Yes." I shut off the water and reached for a paper towel at the same time he did. Our hands collided. I didn't mean for them to, but my fingers tangled with his and clung.

He tightened his around mine for just an instant before pulling the once bloody appendage close and patting it dry with the towel. I crunched the one I'd taken in my uninjured hand.

The marks Zoe had left had not even broken the skin. The ones I had welled with fresh blood.

"Not so bad," he said.

Not bad enough to cause the amount of blood that had been on my hand, but neither one of us mentioned it.

"You can probably keep pressure on that for a few minutes and it'll stop. Or we could go to my office for the first-aid kit."

"I'll be fine."

He stayed right where he was, even though the amount of commotion in the hall demanded his attention. "They aren't going to find her, are they?"

He rubbed his thumb along the inside of my wrist. I didn't want to speak and break the spell, even if I'd had anything to say to that question. Being touched felt wonderful. Being touched by him . . . both familiar and fabulous. As if I'd finally found my home.

"I'm worried," he said. "Mary's getting out somehow, which means someone could get in the same way. Now you've been attacked."

It hadn't occurred to me to consider that my attacker wasn't a patient or staff. I hadn't considered much but breathing and then finding Mary. But now that I had, it made more sense for the attack to have come from the outside than from inside. I'd been in here a while. If someone local wanted to kill me, wouldn't they have tried it before tonight?

"You should be in solitary." Dr. Frasier squeezed my hands. He seemed sad. "Not a punishment, Willow, for safety. Okay?"

"Okay," I echoed. Was he moving closer? I swayed in his direction, unable to stop myself, drawn by his heat, his scent, his—

He kissed my forehead, then seemed as surprised about doing it as I was. We stood there, staring into each other's eyes, holding hands until someone shouted, "Dr. Frasier!" right outside the door.

He released me, stepped back, seemed about to say something, then shouted, "Here!"

Deux appeared in the doorway.

"Take her to solitary," he said. "Keep her there. No one in or out until I say otherwise."

Deux blinked. "Sir?"

"Do it," Dr. Frasier snapped then left without another glance in my direction.

# Chapter 13

Sebastian felt terrible about sending Willow to solitary, but it was for her own safety. He probably should have taken her there himself, but he was afraid if he spent one more instant in her company he'd give in to the career-ending, jail-time-inducing desire to touch her in the ways he'd been dreaming of.

What was wrong with him? He was a psychiatrist. He knew that dreams weren't real and the dreamer shouldn't beat him- or herself up about having them. The subconscious was like a snarled ball of yarn—it could be unraveled, but why it was the way it was, how it had gotten to be that way, was often a mystery.

On the other hand, his dreams were pretty straightforward. He wanted Willow in ways that he shouldn't.

What he needed was to get laid. Unfortunately he was new in town, had no time to meet anyone, let alone date them enough to warrant getting naked. He wasn't going to pay for it either. Not only did the idea make him twitchy for more reasons than one—legality and the possibility of blackmail among them—but how would he even find such a place around here? He certainly wasn't going to ask one of the Toms or Justice for a recommendation.

"Doctor!"

Speak of the Tom. The first Tom, phone to his ear, motioned for Sebastian to join him at the front desk.

The man hung up. "County sheriff thought he saw a woman in the woods about two miles west of here. Lost her but he's setting up a block on the other side of that patch. Officer stationed every twenty yards. You want me to go?"

"I will."

If this escape went like the last two, Mary was going to need sedation.

I didn't sleep. By dawn I was pacing. I tried for a vision—but all I had in the way of liquid was coffee and milk. They possessed a good amount of water but not enough to show me anything without blood for a boost. As I was in solitary, the items available for self-mutilation were few. I'm sure I could manage, but I decided to wait. If I did something too drastic I'd be in this room a lot longer than originally thought.

The guard on duty would tell me nothing. I asked for Dr. Frasier and I was told he was out searching. As I doubted he'd be searching where Mary had gone, I shouldn't be worried, but I was.

I asked if Peggy was in yet and shortly thereafter, she stood outside my door. Even she couldn't get past Dr. Frasier's order of no one in, no one out.

"You rang?" Peggy asked.

"Anything new on Mary?"

She cast me a suspicious glance. "I just received a call from Three Harbors."

"What happened?"

"She tried to kill a witch."

"But—"

Peggy lifted her hand. "When I get back, we'll all talk. Maybe you can even get her to make sense, though I won't hold my breath."

\* \* \*

Sebastian spent the rest of the night and most of the morning in the forest with the county sheriff. Not a trace of Mary did they find. It wasn't until he traipsed back to the highway and his phone went buzzing nuts with missed calls and messages that he realized he had been without service the entire time he'd been shaded by the monstrous, freaky trees.

The first several messages were from Toms I and II, as well as Zoe, giving him an update on the boots-on-the-ground search.

Zilch. Zip. Nada.

The fourth was from an irate Dr. Tronsted—as he hadn't called her, someone had snitched. Number five advised him that Three Harbors PD had called the facility and the sixth was from Peggy Dalberg who was headed to Three Harbors to fetch Mary. Sebastian beckoned the sheriff and ended the search, then he got in his SUV and phoned the caseworker.

"Got her," Peggy said. "We're on our way back."

"She sedated?"

"They brought someone in to give her something right after she arrived at the jail. There was head banging."

Sebastian sighed. When wasn't there? "What happened?"

"She turned up at her house."

"That's understandable."

"I guess. What isn't is the attempted murder of a witch."

Mary thought she *was* a witch. Why would she—?

"Listen, she's coming around. I'll see if she makes any sense. If not, we'll try again when we get back."

Sebastian returned to the facility and ordered Willow released from solitary and brought to his office.

Zoe appeared in the doorway. "Shouldn't I take her to *her* psychiatrist's office?"

Sebastian looked up from his e-mail. "Shouldn't you go home?"

Zoe's eyes widened behind her thick glasses. That *had* sounded a little irritated. Probably because he was. He blamed lack of sleep, along with Zoe's constant hovering. If this kept up, he'd probably have to fire her. As she was very good at her job when she wasn't trying to advise him on his, he hated to do it. But he'd had enough.

"I'm the administrator. I don't have to explain anything."

To her. He had a sneaking suspicion Zoe had been the one to snitch to Dr. Tronsted, but he couldn't prove it.

Sebastian returned to his e-mail. "Go home."

Ten minutes later, Willow arrived.

"Sit." He waved at the chair. "Coffee?"

She nodded. He poured them both some from the pot he'd started as soon as he got back. He handed her the cup and sat on the edge of the desk.

"Peggy's bringing Mary back."

Willow took a sip of her coffee. "What did she say?"

"Mary? Or Peggy?"

"Yes."

She turned her coffee cup this way and that. Someone must have recently washed the thing since several droplets ran down the side. He hadn't spilled while pouring coffee, at least not that much. The sun sparked off the moisture. Definitely water and not coffee.

The cup fell, shattering across the floor into two dozen shards. Coffee splashed onto Sebastian's muddy boots and Willow's tennies.

Sebastian leaped to his feet, his own cup falling and breaking. He needed both hands to catch Willow as she pitched forward.

"Peggy," she said, and a single tear rolled down her cheek.

The phone began to ring.

Dr. Frasier helped me to the couch, made me lie down before he answered the phone. I could tell by the catch in his breathing that what I'd seen in the water was real.

Peggy was dead.

"What about Mary?" He listened. "All right. Thank you for calling. I'll notify her family."

Peggy's daughter. Her new granddaughter. I wasn't sure how many others would be even more devastated by this news than I was. A fountain of tears leaked from my eyes and tracked down the side of my face to further dampen my hair.

Dr. Frasier moved to my side.

"I'm sorry," I whispered.

"What did you do?"

I shook my head and tears flew like rain. I'd seen it, but not in time. Why not? Maybe because I'd avoided the water for too long. I'd been selfish, childish, and Peggy had paid the price.

"What did they say?" I asked.

Quickly he told me what I'd already seen. Mary was gone. She'd had the presence of mind to escape while the "bitch-whore" had used her athame on Peggy. To be fair, Mary had tried to warn Peggy that the woman was up to no good. Peggy hadn't listened, and she'd died for it. Luckily for Mary, Peggy had held on long enough to exonerate her and implicate the true killer. I doubted my vision would have been as convincing as Peggy's dying words.

"Would you like to talk to your psychiatrist?" Dr. Frasier murmured.

"No." There was nothing she could do now. Nothing any of us could.

"Then I'm going to send you back to solitary."

"No." I sat up. "Why?"

"Whoever tried to hurt you is still out there." His lips compressed.

I wanted to run my thumb along them until they loosened up.

"Maybe in here." He ran his fingers through his hair.

I was so jealous of those fingers.

"I can't risk it. I can't risk you."

Warmth spread through me. It was almost like he cared.

"I have to deal with Peggy."

"What about Mary?"

"The Three Harbors PD is pretty motivated to find her, considering."

"Considering what?"

"They've got some things going on there—"

I remembered what I'd seen at the house, in my vision. An upside-down pentagram on the wall. Black magic? Satanism? There'd been other things in the room my mind had shied away from.

"Are they up to it?" Mary wasn't the run-of-the-mill escapee, and what was going on there did not appear very run-of-the-mill either. What did lately?

"I hope so. We can talk more later, but right now—"

"Okay." I lifted my hand to be helped up. He took it and electricity zapped between us. We both jerked back.

I got up by myself.

The rest of that day passed, a night, then another day dawned. Then again, maybe it was two. Three? Trying to keep track of time in solitary was like trying to lasso fog.

At some point I asked about Mary. She hadn't been

found. I started to get worried. What could have happened?

I requested water; I stared into it for hours and saw nothing. I didn't have much choice.

I reopened one of my hand wounds and squeezed a drop of blood into the glass. As it spread outward, the call of the wild rose, filling the room with the howls of wolves—a lot of them.

"What the—?" The mutter of Deux, who was on duty outside my door, made me think he'd heard them too. I had no time to wonder why.

My hair stirred in a breeze that wasn't. I felt the storm.

No, I *brought* the storm. I had to.

This time the tempest did not come to me. I sent it to . . .

"Them," I whispered.

"Willow?" Deux said. "What are you doing?"

I wasn't sure what I was doing, so I ignored him.

Outside my barred window, the sun shone, but the instant I closed my eyes I saw a stormy sky. Clouds billowed—they looked like women. They looked like me, times three.

The cloud women's hair flowed from one to the next, the ends of one becoming the ends of the next. Their cloud fingers stretched toward each other, and when they met, lightning happened. Then rain tumbled down.

"Stop it," Deux shouted.

How did he know I was doing it? It was a storm. They happened all the time. Though never like this.

The earth shook. The sky went white. I smelled fire, ice, blood, earth.

Two of the cloud women merged—they were one— the third floated apart. No, the third fell backward. Next thing I knew, I was lying on the floor, clutching at

my chest, which felt as if that strange, curved knife—
an athame—had been plunged in deep.

The lights flickered—off, on—and in the instant
when the eyes flickered too, I swore I saw that knife in
my chest. But when I reached up to touch it, I touched
nothing but air.

In the distance, at war with the howl of the wolves
and the thunder that was the storm, I could have sworn
someone was laughing.

Then the darkness descended and I heard, saw, knew
nothing more.

# Chapter 14

"We have been unable to locate Mary McAllister."

Special Agent Nic Franklin had, indeed, called Sebastian. The agent was in Three Harbors. Whatever had happened to the Gilletts had also happened there. Sebastian didn't envy the man. Sounded like a hellish case.

"I heard Mary made a friend in your facility. Might she have told this friend something that would help us find her?"

"Doubtful," Sebastian said. "But I'll ask."

"Detective Hardy said that you directed him to a police report from several years ago, where a young woman attempted to kill a man she thought would stab, brand, and burn her. Can you tell me how she knew this?"

"No. Did Hardy talk to the guy?"

"He's disappeared."

That was disturbing.

"I really need to find Mary McAllister," Franklin murmured.

"She's a delusional woman wearing slippers and a jumpsuit," Sebastian said. "How hard could it be?"

"You lost her in the first place, Doctor. How'd that happen?"

As Sebastian hadn't a clue, he ignored the question and asked one of his own. "Do you know who killed my caseworker?"

"A woman who goes by the name of Mistress June."

"Catch her yet?"

"The woods are pretty deep and dense."

"So, no."

"No," the agent snapped, and hung up.

"That went well," Sebastian said.

He slept on the couch in his office that night. When he got up the next morning he appeared as if he'd been sleeping there for days. He certainly felt like it.

He filled out the massive number of reports necessary when a patient escaped, as well as the ones required for the death of an employee. He spoke with Dr. Tronsted, who'd sounded as tired of getting his calls as he was of making them.

"You're going to have to go before a board of review sooner rather than later," she said. "It would be good if you had something to tell them besides 'got me.'"

Sebastian had to agree, but it wasn't looking good.

About mid-afternoon, a storm rumbled in the distance. The wind howled so loudly Sebastian could have sworn there was a pack of wolves in the parking lot. He even went to the window and peered out. Oddly, the sun shone on the facility, though the northwestern horizon was a nasty shade of gray-green.

The power flickered. What was it with the electricity around here?

A commotion in the hall had him turning just as Deux appeared. "Dr. Frasier, there's a problem in solitary."

"Willow," Sebastian said before he could stop himself.

"How'd you know, sir?"

"She's the only patient in solitary right now." Sometimes Sebastian wondered how smart this guy was.

"Right." Deux scrubbed his hand through his hair. "She was staring out the window, kind of like you were."

"And?" Sebastian followed him down the hall at a fast clip.

"She passed out. I can't get her to wake up."

"You left her alone?"

"It's *solitary,*" Deux said, as Sebastian started to run.

Her door was locked. Sebastian peered in the window. She was there, on the floor, still unconscious. Unless she was dead. He couldn't tell if she was breathing.

Sebastian found his keys. His hand shook so much he dropped them, then he had a heck of a time getting the right one into the lock. Once he did, he shoved the door open so fast and hard the thing banged against the wall and almost smacked him in the face. Willow never moved.

Falling to his knees, Sebastian set his fingers to her wrist, let out a whoosh of relief when her pulse thudded strong and sure. "Willow?"

Not a flicker of her eye, not a movement on her face. Her chest didn't seem to rise and fall. He set his finger beneath her nose and felt not even the slightest trickle of air. Perhaps the pulse he'd felt in her wrist had merely been the echo of his own thunderous heart.

"Do you want me to call—?"

"Do you feel a pulse?"

Deux hunkered down and set his fingertips to Willow's neck. "Yeah."

"Help me get her onto the bed."

The two of them carried her there. Sebastian pulled a chair to her side then wasn't sure what to do beyond take her hand, which he did.

"What happened?" he asked.

"Like I told you, she was staring outside—for a really long time. I asked what she was doing. She didn't answer. She didn't seem to hear, then down she went. No reason at all."

Sebastian felt her head. No lumps from a fall. He checked her eyes, pupils not fixed. They responded to light. It was as if she were in a very deep sleep.

The phone began to ring at the desk, and Deux shifted. "Sir?"

"Go ahead," Sebastian said. "We'll give her a few more minutes."

If she didn't come to soon, he'd have to transfer her to the nearest hospital for a CT scan.

He squeezed her hand and memory slammed into him. So hard, so dark and painful, he gasped. He'd sat at his sister's side just like this. He'd begged her to come back to him. He'd held her hand, gotten no response. And then she'd died.

"Willow!"

She responded no better than his sister had.

Sebastian broke out in a cold sweat. He couldn't lose her. He wouldn't.

He patted her cheeks. No response. Her skin was as soft as the petals of a rose. She looked like a rose—Briar Rose. Wasn't that the name of Sleeping Beauty?

With her golden hair and her face in repose, Willow resembled that Disney princess more than anyone should. She even wore nearly the same color of blue today that the poor doomed girl had worn when she'd fallen into that deep dark sleep—though the blue in the cartoon was a gown and Willow's was a T-shirt. Nevertheless . . .

Sebastian had watched enough Disney princess movies with his sister to know these things. As children they'd been so close. He'd thought everything would be all right, but he'd screwed up somehow, and he still didn't know how. Where had he gone wrong with Emma? When had she stopped believing in fairy tales and decided to create an alternate reality of her own? Why hadn't he noticed until it was too late?

His guilt swamped him, and he let his head fall forward. He'd failed his sister. He'd been young, in school, distracted. Then he'd thought he knew so much, that his shiny new degree could save her. After she'd died he'd tried to atone by helping others, but he doubted he'd ever be able to help enough people to make up for the one he had not.

Willow's fingers moved in his. Just a little; he wasn't sure if he'd imagined it, so he held his breath and he went very still.

"Shhh."

Her eyes remained closed. Had she shushed him, or did he just want a response from her so badly he'd imagined one?

"Hush."

This time he saw her lips move as her fingers tightened. "Willow?" he asked, but she seemed to have gone back to sleep.

The really strange thing was the odd sense of peace that came over him, dissipating his guilt, removing his anger and fear. He almost felt . . . healed.

Which made no damn sense at all.


In the darkness lurked many things. Some frightening, some welcoming. Some I understood and some I did not.

There was a pyre—a woman and man tied to a stake. Considering . . . everything, I figured they were witches, or at least the dark-clad fellows surrounding them thought so. One took a ring and branded them both. His back remained to me; I could not see his face, or hear his voice, or those of the others, three of whom held infants in their arms.

The fire whooshed high; when it fell the man, the woman, and the infants were gone, their cries echoing through the ages.

That laughter I'd heard before now came at me from the dark—here, there, everywhere—before it faded. And while I was glad it was gone, I was also disturbed. *Where* had it gone? Where had *he* gone?

Sadness flowed through me, and it smelled of sun and limes. Dr. Frasier. *Sebastian*. He hurt. He ached. He was in pain. I took that pain into myself and his went away.

A gunshot. Into that darkness came a new soul. Closer and closer. I reached out, my fingers almost touched . . .

I sat up, my gasp still audible in the darkness of my room. My cheeks were wet with tears. The moon spilled through the window, across the floor. Something moved just past that silvery light.

"Mary?"

"Do you know where she is?" Dr. Frasier took the chair at my side.

"Gone." I wiped my face.

"You had us all frightened."

"Why?"

"You've been in and out of consciousness for over twenty-four hours."

I glanced at the moon. From this angle I couldn't tell if it was full but there was a kind of humming power to the light that I was beginning to recognize.

"I've consulted with several doctors at the Marshfield Clinic. If you weren't coherent by morning, I was going to take you there myself."

Sebastian didn't seem to realize that he held my hand so I remained very still, afraid he would realize and stop. The facility was quiet—solitary confinement in a mental institution in the middle of the night quiet. I should know.

"Do you know why you passed out?"

I shook my head.

"I examined you and couldn't find anything wrong."

He'd examined me? My face heated, and I was thankful for the darkness. I wanted him to examine me again.

"Did you have a vision?"

Had I? No. Not before I'd gone wherever it was I'd gone. But while I'd been gone . . .

I wasn't certain what that had been.

"You need to tell me the truth, Willow."

I remembered the storm—distant instead of here—and my feeling that I'd sent it somewhere, to someone.

"I brought the storm."

The sudden silence made me look at him. From his expression, I guess I'd said that out loud.

"*Was* there a storm?"

"Not here. Though the lights flickered. The horizon was green."

"Tornado." My heart began to beat faster. Had I brought a tornado? Hurt people? *Killed* people? Why couldn't I remember anything but the swirl of the wind, the women in the clouds, the howl of the wolves, and then darkness?

"No mention of a tornado on the news. No sirens."

That was good. Except I might have sent the thing far enough away that it wasn't on our news, and the sirens . . .

"It would have to be very close for the tornado sirens to sound."

"I'll keep that in mind." His gaze on my face said he was keeping something else in mind. Like upping my meds.

I wasn't sure if my vision—if that's what it had been—was of the future or the past. It might even be of the present.

"Is the moon full?" I asked.

"How'd you know that?"

I decided not to mention the way that it hummed. "I can count."

"Do you really think that you brought a storm?"

"No." I didn't think it; I knew it.

"When you lie, you bite your lip."

I stopped biting my lip. His fingers tightened around mine. I made the mistake of tightening mine back and he looked down, then yanked his away so fast you'd think I had Ebola.

He stood, cleared his throat and moved away. "I'd hoped you were improving, but I'm starting to wonder if you're getting worse."

I *was* improving, because I was embracing what I was, who I was, rather than fighting against it. People had been telling me I was crazy all my life, and I'd believed them. But if the visions were real, if I *did* bring the storm, if I *was* a witch, then I wasn't crazy at all. Never had been. But how did I convince a psychiatrist of that?

Telling wasn't going to do me any good. I'd have to show him.

"I'm not crazy," I said.

"All right."

My eyes narrowed. He was placating me, which only made my burgeoning annoyance burgeon. In the distance, thunder rumbled.

"I'll prove it to you." I stood, swayed a bit. I should probably eat something, but I had bigger fish to fry.

"Ha," I said.

"I feel compelled to mention that talking to yourself isn't helping."

"I know why the Gilletts were killed."

Dr. Frasier glanced at the window as the thunder grumbled both louder and closer. "Why?"

"Sadie was a witch. Malcolm was caught in the cross fire."

"I don't—"

"Peggy was killed for the same reason. I bet she was branded like Sadie, with the snarling-wolf icon."

His attention, which had been on the clouds billowing on the horizon, suddenly came back to me. "How do you know that?"

"The *Venatores Mali* are witch hunters," I began.

"From the seventeenth century!"

"You looked them up."

He shrugged.

"Their leader is Roland McHugh."

"Was," Dr. Frasier corrected. "They're all dead, Willow. Have been for a long time."

"They're back. Roland might be back too."

"When were you going to start convincing me you aren't crazy?"

"I'm in here because I stabbed a man who was going to kill me and brand me."

"So you said, but he didn't."

"Don't you find it odd that I knew about the snarling-wolf brand years before it became popular?"

"Just because you read about the *Venatores Mali* at some point and internalized the information into your delusion, doesn't mean your delusion is true."

Lightning sizzled and snapped as my temper simmered higher.

"The voice that speaks to Mary is named Roland," I said. "Not a common name."

"Doesn't mean *the* Roland is talking to her."

"What if it does?"

Dr. Frasier blinked. "Huh?"

"If he's talking to her, if the voice is real, then is she still crazy?"

"Tree in the woods, Willow."

The wind began to whistle, and tree branches rattled together like bones.

"Mary thinks she's a witch," he continued. "Why would the leader of a witch-*hunting* society talk to her from beyond?"

"I think he's been talking to a lot of people."

"Are you trying to tell me that every schizophrenic who hears voices is hearing his?"

"No. But the ones who've listened, then killed, branded, and burned witches probably are. Mary caught a clue before she went that far, which oddly makes her more sane than a lot of others."

"She didn't seem more sane to me," he muttered.

"Nevertheless . . ."

"You know how crazy this sounds, right?"

"Truth is stranger than fiction."

"I should probably get a nurse to bring you some food and your meds."

"You haven't noticed that while we've been talking, a storm's come up?"

"Lately, that happens a lot."

"The more annoyed I've gotten the closer and stronger the storm."

"Just because you think you're affecting the weather, doesn't make it so."

He was maddening.

"I transported Mary out of the facility."

"Why would you take her out and then come back in?"

"I didn't take her anywhere. I sent her. I didn't mean

to the first time. Actually, nearly every time I didn't
mean to. First it was the moon, and then it was blood.
The transportation spell was supposed to be for joy,
but—"

"You think you transported her through magic?"

"I did."

"Willow, please."

His frustration was evident, but what really got me
agitated was the tinge of fear in his voice. He thought
I'd gone over the edge, and I had. I was so done with
being looked on as crazy when I wasn't. I had to make
him see.

I crossed the distance between us and took his hands.
"Sebastian." I tightened my fingers. "Please."

Our eyes met, and the entire world stilled. The storm
hovered, still there but swirling, getting no worse, no
better, just waiting. I held my breath; he held his.

The clouds parted, the moon flowed in and over us
and I remembered this night, this moment, this kiss.

Our first.

Had he drawn me close, or had I stepped in? Had I
gone on tiptoe, or had he lowered his head, even as I
stretched upward like a flower toward the sun?

Our lips met, and the lightning flared as bright as the
moon. The earth shook; the whole world changed. This
was destined. *We* were destined. My entire life had been
leading to this, to him.

I wrapped my arms around his neck; he wrapped
his around my hips. Our mouths opened, our tongues
touched, stroked. I couldn't help it, I sucked, and then
he groaned, the sound reverberating against my chest,
my breasts.

I rubbed them against him and he gasped. Except
his mouth was still on mine; perhaps the gasp had

been in my head. We probably shouldn't be here, doing this. But I didn't want it to stop; I didn't want him to stop. So I held on to him as the rain began to tumble down.

How did I know about the rain? It took me a few seconds to understand that the rain was falling on us.

We opened our eyes at the same time, our mouths still fused, our tongues tangled. His lashes were wet. When he blinked, the droplets flicked into my face. Together we drew back and lifted our eyes as the sky spilled more rain.

The sky. Spilled rain. Onto us. We were no longer inside but outside.

We stumbled away from each other, stood a few feet apart, peering from the sky, to the trees, to the sky again. We were in a clearing, in the forest, in the night.

"Wh-wha—what happened?" Sebastian asked.

"Wait." I turned in a circle. "I know this place."

I'd seen it before.

"There'll be a man," I said. "All in black. A hat. Like—like—a Pilgrim."

"That's—"

"Shh!" I held up my hand. The trees rustled; but was it the wind, or was it him?

"He'll have an accent. A brogue, I think."

"A brogue? Where are we?"

"No idea."

"We have to—"

"Be ready. He's coming. He'll have a knife, and the moon will glint off his ring. The wolf ring."

"There's no moon," Sebastian said gently.

"There is. It's there, it's just—"

The rain stopped. The clouds parted. The moon shone down again.

The man came out of the trees, took one look at me, and pulled his knife.

"Another of you!" he exclaimed. "You're like rabbits."

"Believe me now?" I asked.

# Chapter 15

Sebastian was disoriented and dizzy. The guy *did* have a brogue—a really thick one that was hard to decipher with everything else that was going on. Namely the sudden appearance of the forest, the mud, the wet, the cold, the crazy man.

"One of you be dead and soon there'll be another," he said, and smiled.

Sebastian, who'd seen a hundred crazy smiles, was more chilled by that one than any that had come before. The guy started toward Willow, blade arcing downward, and Sebastian stepped between them.

Willow tried to push Sebastian out of the way. She only slowed him down. The knife grazed his side, and Sebastian's training took over. He planted a roundhouse kick to the guy's chest.

"Oof," the man said, but he didn't fall to the ground, and he didn't drop the knife.

He almost lost his hat. Who wore a hat anymore? Especially one like that, which was square and wide-brimmed and as Pilgrimy as Willow had predicted. Were they making a movie nearby? *Thanksgiving on Elm Street*? *Black Friday the Thirteenth*?

Fury filtered over the fellow's face, and he came at Sebastian wildly swinging.

Sebastian had to get the guy on the defensive rather than the offensive, and away from Willow at all costs, so he aimed sharp, fast strikes at the man's nose with the heel of his hand—right, left, right. He never landed a blow, but the nut did back up, so Sebastian kept doing it until they were nearly to the trees on the far side of the clearing.

Sebastian made a move to snatch the attacker's wrist, planning to twist it until he dropped the weapon, then maybe slam his head against the trees until he stopped moving, maybe even stopped breathing, but the world kind of shimmied and he nearly fell to his knees. Gritting his teeth, he hauled himself upright again.

The psychotic Pilgrim smirked. "Give me the witch and live."

Sebastian gave him the finger. That should get the point across without words, since he seemed to be having some difficulty drawing a full breath. He hadn't worked out since he'd arrived here. In his defense he'd been mighty busy with Disappearing Mary, but this fight revealed that Sebastian could not allow himself to slack off any longer. He was losing his edge.

Sebastian had figured the finger flip would anger the fellow enough that he'd charge forward, giving Sebastian the opportunity to do the wrist twist that he'd been imagining. Instead, the guy seemed more confused than furious. He began to circle, knife out, working his way toward Willow, which was something Sebastian could not allow. Unfortunately his quick movement to prevent that made him sway like a loose branch in a high wind.

Willow's cry of alarm was followed by a low, rumbling bestial snarl. Was that thunder? The wind?

His attacker's gaze flicked to Sebastian's right, and he blinked. "Prudence?" he asked, and then he ran.

The pure black wolf bounded after him.

My vision had ended at the appearance of the green-eyed wolf. Apparently her name was Prudence.

The black-clad man fled. The wolf chased. I waited for the sounds of predator on prey. I thought I might enjoy them. Then Sebastian lurched, fell, and I forgot anything else.

I reached him in an instant, tearing open his light brown shirt, now stained maroon and glistening beneath the light of the full moon. Blood pulsed from a gash in his side to the beat of his heart. I stared at it, repelled and fascinated, and the forest around us wavered.

"No!" I yanked my gaze away. I couldn't afford to lose myself in a vision now.

I pressed the lower, not yet bloodied, section of his shirt against his wound.

"Help!" I shouted. I didn't know what else to do. "Help us!"

"I don't think that's going to work."

Sebastian's eyes were open, and while he appeared far too pale, he was also lucid. For now.

"What will?"

"Cell phone? Maybe a helicopter?"

"Fresh out," I said. "How about you?"

"Left my cell in my office, and my helicopter in my alternate life."

If he was making a joke he couldn't be dying, could he? Panicked, I pushed harder on his wound, and he winced.

"Sorry!" I eased up on the pressure.

"No." He set his hands atop mine. "Harder is better. Pressure is good."

"Doesn't look like it." The shirt bandage was nearly soaked through. He struggled to sit up, and I felt a gush against my palm. "Stop that!"

"We're going to need to go somewhere else. A place with heat and light, a needle and thread."

I knew he was right. But—

"Which way?"

All around us the trees were so high and so thick that every direction appeared the same.

The undergrowth rustled. Someone was coming. I grabbed Sebastian's hand and set it on the cloth, then got to my feet and put myself between him and the rustle just as the wolf returned.

She stared at me. I stared at her. "Prudence?"

Sebastian snorted. She cast him what I thought was a disgusted glance, then dipped her snout to the ground and brought it back up. Sebastian stopped snorting.

"I guess she's Prudence," I said.

"Really?"

"Good a name as any, and we have to call her something."

"Why?"

"I think she's here to help."

She dipped her head again.

"See?"

"She probably came back because she smelled the blood, and I was easier to catch than the other guy."

Prudence lifted her lip in a snarl.

"See?" he mocked.

"She won't hurt us."

He struggled to his feet. "She tell you that?"

I grabbed his arm before he fell back down. "I've seen her before."

"How can you be sure it was her?"

"Those eyes aren't the norm."

He squinted in the wolf's direction. "They do look kind of . . ."

"Human?"

His squint became a frown. But he didn't comment. What could he say? They did.

Prudence trotted a few steps into the forest. Then she paused and glanced over her shoulder.

"She wants us to follow." I took his arm and started to.

Sebastian didn't, and since I was holding on to him, I had the choice of stopping, letting go, or dragging him along. The only real option at that point was stopping.

"Where?" he asked. "Why?"

"You got a better idea?"

"Than following a wild animal deeper into a forest?"

"We can't just sit here. You said yourself that we need to find shelter." And a needle and thread.

"You think the wolf is taking us to shelter?"

"Yes."

"Fine." He sagged against me for an instant before he pulled himself upright. "It's not like I have anything else to do."

As soon as we stepped from the clearing and into the trees, the wolf continued on. The moon, not as bright beneath the shadow of the forest as it had been in the clearing, nevertheless cast enough of a glow that we didn't run face-first into a tree trunk.

"Where did you see her?" Sebastian asked.

"When I was a child she came up to my carriage."

"When you were a child?" he repeated. "In a carriage? And you think you remember it?"

I didn't answer.

"You saw her in a vision."

At least he hadn't said I *thought* I saw her in a vision. Progress.

"I did."

"Wolves don't live that long."

"You sure?"

"I can't Google it right now, but I will."

I didn't care what he found when he searched the life

expectancy of wolves. I knew those eyes; I'd seen them three times before—the first time in a vision from my childhood, the second in a vision of tonight. But the third time was what made me think this wolf was not exactly a wolf. Because those eyes were the same brilliant green orbs as those of the woman I'd seen tied to a stake and burned for a witch.

And there was no way in hell Google was going to be able to explain that.

I'd hoped we were near a highway. Even a road would have been encouraging. No such luck.

Sebastian leaned on me more heavily with each passing moment. I wasn't going to be able to keep him upright much longer.

"You'll have to go for help," he said.

"No."

"I'm too big to carry and I'm getting weaker."

As if to illustrate, he stumbled and I cried out, tugging with all my might to keep him from falling. I only succeeded in hurting him. His indrawn breath seemed to slice through me like the knife had sliced into him. Because of me.

"I'm sorry."

"Me too. I should have ass-kicked that guy into next week. I haven't practiced enough lately. I've lost my edge."

"What edge? You're a psychiatrist."

"Who studies judo. I'm not used to weapons, but that's no excuse."

"You're blaming yourself because some crazy man stabbed you?"

"All I care about is that he didn't stab you."

Though I knew that he was only speaking as a doctor for a patient or even a big man for a smaller woman and not because of everlasting love, still his words warmed me. As much as I could be warmed while soaked to the skin and walking through a late-October midnight.

My chill wasn't the problem. Sebastian's was. Whenever I touched his skin, the ice of his flesh frightened me. He would soon be in shock if he wasn't there already.

"We should start a fire."

Not only for warmth, but maybe someone would see.

"Got a match?" he asked.

"Shit. You?"

"No."

This time when he stumbled, I couldn't keep him from going down. I went too, my knees hitting hard enough to hurt and my teeth clicked together.

Sebastian lay on the damp earth in a tangled pile. I rolled him onto his back, calling his name, patting his cheeks, begging him to answer.

"Shhh," he murmured.

I kissed him. I was so relieved.

He started at the contact. His lips were too cool, but they warmed beneath mine, so I kept kissing him. Pretty soon he was kissing me back.

I held his face between my palms, brushed one finger against his earring and he moaned. His hands were like ice on the back of my neck. I had to do something or he would die.

When I pulled away, he tried to hold on, but he wasn't strong enough to stop me, and that scared me more than anything had for a long time.

His eyes opened. His smile was dazed and not from the kiss. I wasn't that good at it. He tucked my hair behind my ear. "You have to go."

"I can't leave you. In the dark. In the woods. All alone. What if that nut comes back?"

"I'm more worried he'll find you than me."

"I'm not."

Prudence licked my cheek, then nuzzled my shoulder. I should have been terrified that a wolf was so near my face. Instead I felt comforted.

"She'll stay," I said. A wolf would be better protection than me anyway.

I started to get up, and the wolf yipped and snatched my shirt, holding me down.

"I need to find help."

She shook her head with my shirt still in her mouth, and the end tore just a little.

"Or not."

She released me, then trotted around Sebastian and sat. Lifting her snout to the moon, she howled. I waited for the answering call of a dozen wolves. What if they appeared? Instead, she waited an instant, howled again, then laid her body along Sebastian's and rested her snout on her paws.

"What was that?" Sebastian asked, eyes closed, lips barely moving.

Whatever it was, Prudence repeated it every ten minutes. If anyone was in the area, they'd hear it. But wouldn't most creatures go in the opposite direction from the call of a lone wolf?

I put my fingers into the hole that Prudence had made in my T-shirt, tearing free a strip all around the bottom, then pressed the cloth to his wound. It turned dark with blood far too quickly. Sebastian wasn't going to make it through the night.

I got to my feet. Prudence lifted her head and growled.

"I have to get help. I should have gone sooner."

A twig snapped. My neck got a nasty pain whipping in that direction. My heart got a nasty jolt when I heard a voice, ramped up when I heard more than one, then went even faster at the sight of flashlights bobbing between the trees. Someone was coming. Friend or foe?

I picked up a big stick, just in case the Pilgrim man had returned with help. Then the wolf yipped, barked, howled again, and the lights bobbed even faster in our direction.

Two men holding what appeared to be police-quality flashlights emerged from the forest. Both dark haired—one was slim with blue eyes and skin that hinted at an ancestry from places much warmer than this, wherever "this" was. The second was tall and solid, his eyes dark, his hair very short.

They stopped at the sight of us, but they stared wide-eyed at me. The last man who'd done that had led with his knife. I tightened my grip on the stick and held it up like a Louisville Slugger.

"Holy hell," the smaller man said, his voice a lilting combination of the South with an exotic foreign twist.

"Girls?" called the other man, with no accent at all. "Pru found her."

The wolf loped toward the men, but they didn't appear concerned. She galloped past them and into the trees. Two more lights bobbed like drunken ships in the darkness, then two women joined us. Their expressions went from anxious to stunned to joyful. I'm sure mine was merely stunned. They both looked exactly like me.

And when I say "exactly," I mean one had dark hair and dark eyes and the other had red hair and hazel eyes. But other than that . . . we could be twins.

I mean triplets.

"Maybe clones."

The women exchanged glances, then the redhead laughed.

The other one smiled. "It takes some getting used to."

"Willow?" Sebastian's eyes had opened.

I fell to my knees at his side, took his hand. It was still like ice. His eyes were too bright, his skin too pale.

"Hey," I said, and kissed his brow. Clammy. His eyes fell closed again. "Sebastian?"

No response.

I lifted my gaze to the others. "I don't know who you are. Right now I don't care. We need to get him to a doctor. Cell phone anyone?"

"Becca?" the dark-haired woman said, and the redhead hurried forward, kneeling at Sebastian's side and gently pulling back the bloody cloth.

"You're a doctor?" I asked.

"Mmm."

I wasn't sure if the sound was an answer to my question or a comment on the wound. She laid her palm over the still-bleeding slice.

"Isn't that un—"

The word *sanitary* froze in my throat as a spark of electricity gave an audible zap, then she lifted her hand.

All that remained was a thin red line.

# Chapter 16

"How did you do that?" I asked.

"How do you think?"

I didn't know what to say. That had been like—

"Magic." The dark-haired woman joined us.

The two men stayed with the wolf. They held themselves tense and ready, as if they were expecting an attack. When the larger man shifted so his glance could sweep the trees, I saw he was carrying concealed. On second glance, so was the other guy.

"What's going on?" I asked.

"What isn't?" Becca answered.

"Raye?" The man with the Southern accent addressed the other woman. "We should probably get out of the open."

"Where did you come from?" I demanded.

The women exchanged glances.

"Same place as you," Raye said.

"I meant tonight."

"Oh." She laughed. "Cabin about a mile to the north."

"We aren't going to be able to carry him that far."

"I can walk." Sebastian's voice was slurred, and his eyes were still too bright.

"We'll help him." The men's footsteps crunched over the fallen leaves.

"I don't think—" I began.

"Willow, is it?" the short-haired man asked and I nodded. "I'm Owen. I've served multiple tours in Afghanistan and I've never left a man behind. Don't plan to start now."

"He's huge," I said.

"Gee, thanks." Sebastian sat up. He swayed a bit, but he did look better.

"I can lend a hand," the other man said. "I'm Bobby Doucet. Raye's fiancé."

This close I saw that not only was he carrying a gun, but he wore a badge. He saw me staring at it. "Chief of Police, New Bergin."

"So we're still in Wisconsin?"

The two men hoisted Sebastian to his feet.

"Last time I checked," Bobby said.

They started north, the wolf in the lead, and the women fell in step on either side of me.

Silence reigned for a few seconds, then Becca wondered, "Where did you think you might be?"

"A better question is: How did you get here in the first place?" Raye asked.

An even better one . . . "Who are you?"

"Your sisters," Becca said, at the same time Raye blurted, "Witches."

"Baby steps, Raye," Becca muttered.

Mary had told me that I had sisters; I'd hoped it was true. But having it confirmed—by both words and the sight of them—made me a little bit dizzy. Supposedly everyone had a twin, somewhere, but I didn't think everyone had a triplet. Except me. Us.

The word *us,* the concept of it, warmed me more than it should. I was no longer alone. I had sisters. I nearly hugged them, but it was probably too soon.

"We don't have time for baby steps." Raye cast me a glance. "There are these witch hunters—"

"The *Venatores Mali*?"

"You know about them?" Becca asked.

"They're trying to kill me."

"Us," Becca corrected.

"Witches?"

"In general, yes," Raye said. "But the three of us in particular. How much do you know?"

"I'm not sure since I don't know how much there is."

"Maybe you should start by telling us where you've been." Raye waved a hand from herself to Becca. "We were found abandoned. Me on the interstate, Becca on a grave. You?"

"Beneath a black willow tree, which is how I became Willow Black."

"Original," Raye said. "And then?"

"Foster care. You?"

"Adopted."

Becca nodded, which I took to mean she'd been adopted too.

"You were in foster care all of your life?" Raye asked. "Never adopted?"

"I saw things in water, then they happened. Freaked everyone out. Got me sent back, every damn time."

Raye winced. "I was always afraid I'd be sent back."

"Why?"

"Ghosts speak to me. When I was a kid, I didn't know that I shouldn't answer them."

"I can understand where that might cause a problem." I switched my gaze to Becca. "What about you?"

"I can talk to the animals."

"Isn't that a song?"

"Mmm," she said again. "It was cute when I was three, not so much as time went on."

"Seeing things in the water was never cute. Once I understood it was bizarre, I tried to hide it, but I didn't have much luck. Then I tried to make the visions stop."

"How?"

"Drinking, pills, and . . ." I pantomimed smoking a joint, then sniffed a line off my index finger. From their expressions, they got the drift.

I don't know why I was telling virtual strangers about my past. Maybe because they not only didn't look like strangers, they didn't feel like strangers either. There'd been a connection between us from the instant we'd met. Loony? Maybe. But there it was.

"Did it help?" Raye asked.

I shook my head. "Alcohol and nonmedical pharmaceuticals tend to make visions worse, not better. I stopped but it was too late. I was already on the crazy train."

"I don't know what that means," Becca said.

"Saying I had visions, having them come true, the drugs, the fugue states created a pattern of behavior. I've been in the Northern Wisconsin Mental Health Facility for a while now."

"Being a little off doesn't land you there," Becca said. "Usually trying to kill someone, or actually doing it, does. Which one are you?"

"Tried. Failed."

"Who? Why?"

"Guy with a knife and a ring, some gasoline and a lighter."

*"Venatores Mali,"* Raye whispered.

"I didn't know that at the time. I saw him in a vision, then when I saw him for real, I stabbed him."

"Sounds like self-defense," Becca said.

"It would have been if he'd actually had the knife, or even the ring, on him. But he didn't. After that, any explanation I gave got me more antipsychotics. The medical pharmaceuticals didn't help either."

Raye and Becca took my hand on either side, and it felt so right that I let them.

"We tried to find you," Raye said.

"How long have you known about this, about us?"

"Less than a month maybe?" Raye glanced at Becca who gave a nod-shrug. "I did a location spell to find you, but I didn't see anything."

"Do you know why it didn't work?"

"I'm new at the craft. Kind of fumbling along. I did read that a spell of protection might prevent location. Did you do one?"

"Not me. My caseworker at the facility practiced Wicca. She showed us a few things. A friend of mine was concerned about safety so Peggy did a protection spell."

"Peggy Dalberg?" Becca asked. Before I could answer she continued, "Your friend— What's her name?"

"Mary."

"McAllister?"

"How'd you know?" I repeated.

"I'm engaged to her son." Becca pointed at the former soldier, who was practically carrying Sebastian now.

"Owen," I said. He'd told me that, but I hadn't been thinking about anything but Sebastian, and what were the odds I'd meet *the* Owen, Mary's Owen, in the middle of Godforsaken, USA?

"I saw her," I blurted. "And you, Becca, and—" I shook my head. "She was at a house, her house." I squinted trying to see it again. "She had a knife. Did she hurt someone? Is she all right?" My voice wavered.

Becca's fingers tightened on mine. "She didn't hurt anyone."

My sisters' eyes met, and I realized they'd only answered the first question.

"What happened?" I asked.

"Mary gave her life trying to save mine," Becca said.

My eyes burned. Tears spilled. "She was my only friend."

Silence descended as I tried to control my grief. My chest hurt. My throat too. This was all my fault.

"I didn't think Mary had friends," Becca continued. "I'm glad she had you."

"With me she was better." And now she'd never be better again. "I got her killed."

"No." Raye squeezed my hand. "The *Venatores Mali* are responsible, not you."

"She'd have been safe if I hadn't sent her after them."

"We're almost to the cabin." Raye pointed at a light playing hide-and-seek with the trees. "We've got wine and food and a fireplace. We'll get your guy settled, and then you can explain how, exactly, you sent her."

"He's not my guy." And I had to keep it that way.

"Who is he?" Becca asked.

"The administrator of the mental health facility."

"You know who the girl is?" Raye asked.

"What girl?"

"He's got a ghost." She kept her gaze on Sebastian. "Never leaves his side."

Sebastian heard the women talking behind them, but not what they said. Especially once the men started asking him questions.

At first just the basics—name, occupation. Then they moved on to the specifics.

"Who stabbed you?" This from Bobby, the police chief.

"Guy came out of the woods. Took one glance at Willow . . ."

*Another of you!*

"He seemed to know her. Maybe he's seen the other two."

"Maybe," Owen agreed. "Did you get in the way?"

"In the way?" Sebastian echoed.

"If he knew Willow, wouldn't he be more inclined to stab her than you?"

"Why stab anyone?"

"What did this guy look like?" Bobby again—typical cop question.

"Dark hair, dark eyes, dark clothes. He seemed to be on his way to a dress-up Thanksgiving party. Except for the knife."

The two men exchanged glances.

"Did he have a black hat and talk like an escapee from the set of *Braveheart*?" Owen asked.

"How'd you know?"

"Roland," Bobby said.

"McHugh?" Sebastian blurted.

"How'd *you* know?" Bobby demanded.

"Long story. Lots of patient privacy issues involved. Although I have to wonder why you think a centuries-dead witch hunter stabbed me."

"Because he did?" Owen said.

"All righty then," Sebastian muttered.

"You should probably tell us exactly what happened and everything the guy said."

As a police chief was asking, Sebastian did his best. But he had no answer for how they'd gotten into the woods in the first place beyond shared psychosis, and he thought he'd keep that to himself.

"Roland thinks Becca is still dead," Owen murmured.

"Still?"

The man waved a hand, dismissing what Sebastian thought was a very reasonable question. Of course, reason was in short supply around here, considering they believed the man who'd stabbed Sebastian was *the* Roland McHugh.

Sebastian could understand that there might be a group of witch hunters who'd taken the name of the old one, along with their mission statement. He could even see someone appropriating the name of the group's originator. But that didn't make him the actual originator. Nothing could.

They reached their destination at last—a log cabin in the center of a clearing. Sebastian still felt weak. Blood loss will do that. But he didn't feel worse, and considering how far they'd walked, he should. He didn't remember who'd bandaged him, but whoever it had been they'd done a great job. As far as he could tell there wasn't any fresh bleeding. Maybe the injury wasn't as bad as it had appeared with only the moon for light.

The cabin was spacious and modern on the inside, falsely rustic on the outside. From the unpacked luggage and grocery bags, the two couples had recently arrived.

They deposited Sebastian on the couch. The wolf, which had walked right inside like the family dog, curled on the rug in front of the fireplace. Owen began to lay a fire.

Willow hurried to Sebastian's side. "You want to lie down?"

"Here?" He'd take up the whole couch.

"You can have the far bedroom." Raye pointed. "There are two empty, but that's the biggest. The smaller bed isn't made up either."

"I should probably get back to the facility." The place had to be in chaos.

"Not tonight," Willow said. "You should rest."

Because he was tired, and a coward—how would he explain disappearing from the facility with a patient?—he agreed. But he didn't go to the bedroom. He wanted to hear what they said. He'd go in a minute, then he'd examine his wound too. Right now his head was too heavy to do anything but sit on the couch and watch Owen light a fire.

Bobby poured wine for the girls, grabbed a few beers for the boys—Sebastian declined, he was dizzy enough—while Becca and Raye made sandwiches. Eventually everyone had a drink, some food, and a seat. Raye started the story; Becca chimed in. Every so often, Bobby and Owen would add a line or two. Sebastian felt as if he were listening to a fairy tale, but they all believed it was true.

*Once upon a time in seventeenth-century Scotland, there lived two witches—Henry and Prudence Taggart.*

Sebastian eyed Prudence the wolf. She eyed him back. In fact, those eerie, green, not at all wolflike eyes rarely left him—or maybe she was staring at Willow, who didn't leave him either.

*Prudence was a healer, a midwife. She was very, very good. Supernaturally good. Unfortunately, some things cannot be healed even with such powers. One of Pru's patients died in childbirth along with her child. That Pru was delivered of three healthy girls soon after created suspicion. That the dead woman and child belonged to the chief witch hunter of King James led to a great big pyre.*

*Her husband, Henry, a powerful witch in his own right, had seen this coming and prepared. He knew that running was not an option with three infants. Pru's powers were significantly drained by the births. So he did the only thing he could do.*

*Blood magic.*

"It's the most powerful kind." Becca, Raye, and Willow said the words as one. Which was almost as creepy as the story and the way the girls told it—like they were detailing personal history and not fiction.

*As the flames took their lives, Henry cast a spell to transport their daughters to a time where no one believed in witches anymore. The triplets disappeared, never to be found again.*

"Until now," Raye said.

"I saw that." Willow licked her lips. "The pyre. The babies. The black-clad zealots. One of them—I couldn't see his face—branded the man and the woman with his ring."

"The brand remains after death." Becca ruffled her fingers through the wolf's black fur, revealing a circle of white at the neck. "Henry's got it too, even in ghost form."

"The guy who did that . . ." Willow pointed at Pru's neck. "Was the same guy who did that." She pointed at Sebastian's side.

"You know that's impossible," Sebastian said.

"That I saw it? That it happened? That he's here? Now?"

"Yes."

"That's it." She yanked up his shirt. "How do you think this happened?"

He lowered his gaze. His skin was stained with dried blood. A lot of it, but not enough to obscure his wound.

Where was his wound?

"The guy stabbed me." He looked at Willow. "Didn't he?"

"He did," Willow agreed. "Then Becca healed you."

Sebastian laughed. No one else did.

"Obviously, he just scratched me." He found a thin, red line. "Here. See?"

"A scratch doesn't make you bleed that much."

She was right, but still . . .

"That's crazy."

"That's magic," Becca said. "All my life those around me have healed faster. Once Raye and I met, my power increased even more."

"Power," Sebastian echoed. He felt light-headed and dopey. Probably from blood loss, except he shouldn't have had any blood loss when he'd only been scratched.

"We seem to have inherited the abilities of our parents," Raye continued. "Witches born to the craft are magic."

Sebastian refrained from snorting. Barely. From the expressions of everyone in the room, even the wolf, they believed this. He should probably remain silent so he could discover the extent of this shared delusion.

"Witches born are elementals—air, fire, water, and earth," Raye said. "Henry and Pru were very powerful, rare witches who possessed dual elements. I inherited Henry's telekinesis and his affinity for ghosts. I'm an air witch."

"I received Pru's affinity for animals, particularly wolves, and the healing." Becca wiggled her fingers. "I'm a fire witch. Since Willow has visions, she's a water witch."

"Did I get that from Henry or Pru?" Willow asked.

The wolf yipped.

"Pru," Raye said. "The touch of a water witch can cleanse. Around them, people feel better—less stressed, less tired, less crazy."

"Mary," Willow murmured. "She was always better when she was with me."

She had been but that didn't mean Willow had made her that way. Right now, Sebastian was feeling a lot *more* tired, stressed, and crazy.

Raye stared at the shadowy corner of the dining area. "Henry says Pru had visions, but it wasn't one of her strengths. Not like you, Willow."

"Henry's here?" Willow's voice was full of awe.

"His affinity for ghosts has made him one."

"That's ridiculous," Sebastian snapped. Willow was so desperate to find a family she believed every insane thing these women said. "There's no such thing as ghosts."

A book flipped off the end table, slapping against the floor with a sharp crack.

"Knock that off, Henry," Raye said.

Sebastian rolled his eyes.

"Who is she?" Raye asked.

Sebastian thought she was talking to invisible Henry and didn't answer at first. When he noticed everyone, including Raye, was staring at him, he spread his hands. "She who?"

"You have a ghost, Dr. Frasier. She's been at your side since I met you. She won't speak to me."

"'Cause she isn't there."

"You've never felt haunted?"

He'd been haunted since the day his sister died, but not the way she meant.

"No," he said shortly.

"She's in her early twenties. Long, dark hair. Too thin. Big blue eyes. Same earrings." Raye's gaze flicked to Sebastian's ear. "Earring."

She'd just described Emma. How could she?

"I don't know anyone like that," he managed.

"Now you've made her cry."

"Stop it!" The words were too loud, a bit panicked.

Willow took his hand. "Just breathe."

He took her advice. Couldn't hurt. And if he was concentrating on breathing, he wasn't thinking about his dead little sister.

"I was like you," Bobby said. "I thought Raye was playing me when she talked about my ghosts. Figured she'd do a séance, tell me what I wanted to hear, then take me for everything I had."

"But you believe her now?"

"I've seen enough to believe. I think you have, too, you just don't want to admit it yet."

"I haven't—" Sebastian began.

"How'd you get here, Doctor?"

"Walked."

"Not here." Bobby pointed at the floor. "How'd you end up in the woods, in the night? No road. No car. No parachute. You're dripping like you got caught in that downpour earlier, which came out of nowhere."

"What are you trying to say?"

"There are a few powers left that neither Raye nor Becca have. One is bringing the storm."

Sebastian glanced at Willow. "Just because she thinks she can make it rain doesn't mean she can."

"The other is transportation," Bobby continued as if Sebastian hadn't spoken at all.

"Plane, train, automobile?"

"Magic. Henry transported the girls from one place and time to another. It was one of his lesser powers as well, which was why he had to boost it with blood magic. But since Willow is a water witch, transportation is one of her gifts. I'd bet my next paycheck that you and Willow started out in one place and in a blink you were somewhere else."

"That's how Mary got out," Willow said. "I wanted to tell you but I knew how insane it would sound."

"How insane it *does* sound," Sebastian corrected. Problem was . . . He *had* blinked and been somewhere else.

"He's a 'have to see it to believe it' kind of guy," Owen said. "So was I once. My mom's being a lunatic made me a bit skeptical about crazy talk."

"Your mom," Sebastian repeated. "You're Owen *McAllister*?"

Owen nodded.

Sebastian shouldn't be surprised, but he was. First of all the guy was supposed to be in Afghanistan. Second of all, there was coincidence and there was . . . whatever this was.

"You can see why having the woman I love tell me she's a witch freaked me out," Owen said.

"I can. About your mother—"

Owen stiffened, and Becca scooted closer to him on the floor in front of the fire.

Willow laid her hand on Sebastian's arm. "Leave Mary for later."

He didn't like the sound of that, but he let it go. For now. He'd need to have Mary in hand, or an answer as to why he didn't before he went back to the facility tomorrow. Dr. Tronsted was going to flay him alive as it was.

"What did you see that turned you into a believer?" Sebastian asked.

Owen considered. "I think when Raye tossed a *Venatores Mali* off a cliff from a hundred yards away."

"You're sure the creep didn't just fall?"

"He kind of flew up into the air and hung there a second and then . . ." Owen lifted his hand high and then dropped it down to the ground to illustrate.

"You expect me to believe that?"

"No. I'm sure you're going to have to see it too. Raye?"

The dark-haired Willow clone stood, lifted her arms to the side, and then levitated until her head brushed the ceiling.

# Chapter 17

"Cool," I said.

Sebastian leaped to his feet. "How is she doing that?"

Becca spread her hands. "Air witch."

"Where are the pullies?" Sebastian demanded. "Fishing line?"

"Come on down, baby." Bobby beckoned, and Raye floated gently to the floor.

Sebastian whooshed his hand above her head, frowned.

"Satisfied?" Bobby returned to his chair and pulled Raye into his lap.

Sebastian swayed. I grabbed his arm, not that I'd be of any use if he decided to pass out.

"You really did transport us, didn't you?"

I nodded.

"I think I need to lie down."

I led him toward the bedroom Raye had earlier indicated. Halfway across the room the air felt like ice. I stopped, glanced at the windows—closed—the door—also closed.

"What's wrong?" Sebastian asked.

"You feel that chill?"

He shook his head.

"You walked through Henry," Becca said.

"Did you ever feel him like that?" Raye asked Becca.

"No."

"Hmm," Raye said.

I wanted to find out what that meant, but right now I had bigger things to worry about. I tugged Sebastian into the bedroom, shut the door. "Lie down before you fall down."

He stared at the pristine white bedspread and sheets, then lifted his bloodstained hands. "I should probably shower first."

"You need help?"

"Not since I was four." He made an ushering movement toward the door with gory hands. "I'll shout if I fall and can't get up."

He disappeared into the bathroom, and I waited, but when all I heard was water running, no thud and cry, I returned to the others. If I continued to stand there I'd first begin to imagine him naked beneath the water, and then I might go inside so I could see him naked beneath the water.

Bad idea.

Raye and Becca sat in front of the fire with Pru. Bobby and Owen were gone.

"They thought we needed some girl time." Raye offered me my glass of red wine, which had been refilled.

I took it and joined them. Pru put her head on my knee.

"She says she loves you." Raye tapped her glass to mine. "We all do."

"You don't even know me."

"Blood is thicker than water. Didn't you feel all your life as though you were part of something you hadn't yet found?"

"I was abandoned, why wouldn't I feel like that?"

"Even Becca, who didn't know she was adopted until I showed up, felt that way."

I sipped my wine and considered her words. I'd thought the way I felt—alone, part of something larger, which I only needed to find—was just me longing for a family. All system kids felt that way. Some imagined they were the love children of movie stars or princesses. That someday their parents would come for them and it would be amazing.

I'd never imagined I was one of three time-traveling witch triplets. Who would? But I had hoped for something, someone. Anyone.

When the visions of Sebastian had begun, I'd figured he was my answer. If I didn't have a family, I'd make one. With him. Kind of sad, a little pathetic. But I was.

"The instant Becca and I met," Raye continued, "I felt less alone. As if the part of me that was empty had begun to fill. But that hole couldn't completely go away until we found you."

"I had parents, brothers and a sister, no knowledge of any of this, but somehow I knew there was more. As soon as Raye arrived . . ." Becca touched her chest. "That ache began to fade."

I did feel less alone since they'd walked into that clearing . . . had it only been a few hours before?

"Now that we've found each other, our powers will get stronger," Raye said. "When I was alone, I could move things. Once Becca and I were together, I could toss people and levitate. Becca's healing increased to epic levels. Have you noticed any changes recently?"

"I never transported anyone until Mary." Quickly I explained how I'd done it, each incident being different and somehow "more."

"And the last time, last night, you transported yourself *and* Sebastian," Raye murmured.

"Yeah," I agreed. "What was that?"

"Practice makes perfect," Becca said. "The moon adds a boost. Full moon even more so. So does blood."

"And we got here yesterday." Raye indicated the

cabin. "This place is only a few miles from the mental health facility."

"Why here?" I asked.

The two exchanged glances.

"We scried for your location," Raye said. "I'd tried before and gotten nothing. But the two of us together saw this place. It was conveniently available for rent, and considering the *Venatores Mali* had already found both of us, we thought we should all get out of Dodge."

"You were just going to hang out until I showed up?"

Raye shrugged. "We didn't plan that far."

"Roland was pretty close. How'd that happen?"

"How'd he wind up in the same forest?" Becca asked. "No clue. How'd he wind up in the twenty-first century and not in hell?" She glanced at Raye. "You should probably explain that."

"Roland's been whispering to a lot of people from beyond the grave."

"Like Mary."

"Like Mary," Raye agreed. "I'm not sure why they're listening to a voice that tells them to kill, brand, and burn witches, but they are."

"Roland's got his own serial killer club," Becca muttered.

"The *Venatores Mali*," I said.

My sisters nodded.

"Until Roland returned," Raye continued, "the leader of the *Venatores Mali* was the one with the most witch kills."

"Exactly how did he return?"

"The first time they tried to raise him it was blood of a witch, shed by the leader of the *Venatores Mali,* as worthy believers chanted skyclad beneath the moon."

"The first time," I repeated. The rest was kind of gibberish.

"They used my blood. Didn't work. He . . ." Raye waved at the air above her. "Pushed against the sky. Nearly made it, but didn't."

"Then another nut job had delusions of grandeur," Becca continued. "He killed their leader, Mistress June, and became the new boss. Did the ritual, killed me. Voilà. Roland is free."

"Killed you?" I glanced at Raye, wondered momentarily if Becca was a ghost, but I couldn't see them. Raye smiled as if she could read my mind, then shook her head. Maybe she could read minds, though she hadn't mentioned that in her list of witchy-powers.

"I'm alive," Becca said, "thanks to the power of two—"

"Maybe three," Raye interrupted. "Remember that storm?"

They both looked at me, and I knew instinctively what they meant. There was some kind of triplet telepathy going on here that felt both strange and wonderful, and weirdly, completely normal.

"I had a vision of clouds that were women." The third woman falling, the pain in my chest. "You were stabbed."

"Yes," Becca answered.

"I felt it."

They lifted their eyebrows at the exact same time. Pru, who lay with her snout on her paws, gaze flicking to each of us as we spoke, growled low.

"And you sent the storm," Raye said.

"I did. It was the first time I sent one instead of bringing one. I never controlled it before."

"It helped. We merged—Becca and I. I healed her, but Roland was already out."

"Now what?" I asked.

"Now—" Raye offered her hands. Becca did the same.

I set down the wineglass I'd continued to hold though I hadn't taken another sip, and put my palms against theirs. A low hum filled the air. I'd have thought I imagined it, except our hair lifted and began to swirl together just like the cloud sisters' hair had in my vision.

"Now, we put him back," Raye said. "Any ideas on how?"

"Me?" I was so startled I let their hands go. Our hair fell back to our shoulders the instant we stopped touching.

Pru, who'd been watching our hair swirl with the avidness of a wolf watching a rabbit, yipped. I really wished I could understand her. While I was at it, I wished I could see Henry.

"You're the one with the visions," Raye said.

"I never had much control over them—when they came, how they came, what I saw. But I've gotten better at it."

Becca's head turned toward the corner. "Henry says—"

"Wait a second," I interrupted. "I thought Raye saw ghosts and you talked to animals."

"That instant when we merged, our powers merged," Raye explained. "But not completely. I can understand Pru, but no other animals. Becca can see Henry, but no other ghosts."

"Make it so I can too."

Pru growled.

"Hush," Raye said. "I know."

"What?"

"Becca died. I did what I had to do to save her, but it was dangerous. We can't do it again and risk losing one of us. Only together will we have enough power to end this. To end him."

"Says the woman who can see her father and understand her mother."

That I believed I had a ghost for a father and a wolf for a mother was something I didn't pause to dissect. They were my parents. I knew that as surely as I knew these women were my sisters and that Sebastian was my soul mate. I loved them all with a strength and surety that some might call wrong, if not insane, but that I knew to be as right and sane as anything I'd ever felt before.

Pru set her head on my knee again, and I ran my palm over her fur.

"She saw you once," Becca said.

"In my carriage, in the park."

"Right. But then she could never locate you again."

"How'd she locate me that time?"

"She's a wolf, but she's also a witch. Her senses are much sharper than any wolf alive. She tracked your scent."

"If that was the first, the only time she ever saw me, then how did she have my scent?"

"She had ours," Becca said. "Close enough."

"Bobby did a search for abandoned babies around the time I was found and got no hits but me," Raye continued. "Why didn't he find you?"

"Foster system didn't have the best records back then." I wasn't sure they had the best records now. "He didn't find any mention of Becca either?"

"I was never formally adopted, nor reported as found." Becca shook her head. "Long story. Where did you go after the park/carriage incident? Why couldn't Mom ever find you again?"

"I don't—" I began, and then I remembered the candles, the tub, the chant. "Protection spell."

"You did a protection spell from the cradle?"

"No, my foster mother was a witch. After she saw a wolf with its head in my carriage, she cast a spell of protection."

"A very good one," Raye said. "I'd like to talk to her."

"She's dead."

"Doesn't usually keep me from talking to people. What happened?"

"Tortured, murdered, branded, and burned."

"Hell."

"Pretty much."

"Is that why you didn't stay with them?"

"They sent me back. When you foam at the mouth every time you take a bath, people get twitchy." At their identical expressions of concern, I lifted a hand. "Kidding. I did scream, thrash, and freak out, but there was no actual mouth foaming."

"If your foster mother was a witch," Raye said, "you'd think she would understand."

"You'd think."

"Maybe she was trying to protect you. Figured you'd be safer away from her."

"Safe from what? How long have the *Venatores Mali* been back?"

"As far as we know, only a year or so. Then again, who's to say Roland hasn't been trying to get his club going since we arrived."

"Do you know how a spell of protection can be removed?" I asked.

"Why would you want to remove it?" Raye asked.

Same question Peggy had asked. She'd cast a spell of

protection around the facility, and us, yet she was dead, just like Sadie.

"I just wonder how Sadie—my witch foster mother—and her husband got dead. Same thing with Peggy Dalberg. They both did spells of protection."

"I don't—" Raye paused when Pru lurched to her feet, staring at Becca.

"She says that a protection spell can be weakened by a location spell. Shit." Becca's gaze flicked to Raye. "We got Peggy killed. First Raye tried to locate you and couldn't. So we tried again later, together, and probably melted the magic away like wax. Mom says it's always a good idea to renew a protection spell every so often, just in case they've been weakened."

"They died because of me," I said.

"A protection spell isn't going to stop a knife," Raye insisted.

"No." Becca sighed. "But if we hadn't weakened it, Mistress June probably wouldn't have been able to find Peggy."

"Mistress June. Big woman. Long hair?"

My sisters nodded.

"She's dead now?"

Another dual nod.

I shouldn't be glad, but I was. I'd seen her do some terrible things.

"We're sorry," Raye said. "We just wanted to find you."

"How could you know that searching for me would lead to people dying?" I asked.

"We are flying blind," Raye agreed. "But that doesn't make Sadie or Peggy any less dead. They aren't haunting you. If they were pissed about it, they would be."

Well, goody. No vengeful ghosts on my heels—one less thing.

"Couldn't the *Venatores Mali* do a location spell and find us?" I asked.

"They aren't witches," Becca said. "They're witch hunters."

"They seem pretty witchy to me," I muttered.

"She's right," Raye said. "Raising Roland was magic—black magic, but still magic. Back in the day he was righteous, he never would have stooped to fighting fire with fire—" She rolled her eyes. "So to speak. But once his family died, he lost his teeny-tiny mind. Being unable to have his revenge sent him over the edge. He went to the dark side. He'll do anything, including magic, to kill us. We should probably recast the protection spell every night, just to be sure."

"Works for me," I said. "Do you have . . ." I tried to remember what Peggy had used. It would have been a good idea to bring along her *Book of Shadows*. I wondered where it was now. "Peppermint, lavender, chamomile . . ."

My sisters looked at each other, then at me.

"Why?" Becca asked.

"That's what Peggy used."

"Every witch has a different way."

I had a flash of the roses floating in the bathtub at Sadie's and carnations in a pot at the facility.

"Okay," I said. "What's yours?"

"Ours," Raye said. "The protection spell of the Taggart family."

She tilted her head as if listening, and from the way Pru stared at the nearest corner, I knew she was listening to Henry. Our father.

It gave me a both a tingle and a chill to hear myself referred to as a Taggart. A tingle because I had always wanted to belong to something, to someone. A chill because being a Taggart had marked me. At least it hadn't marked *only* me. There was power in numbers. There was power in us.

"I am air." Raye's hair fluttered in a breeze that couldn't be since every window and door was closed. She offered her hand to Becca, who took it.

"I am fire," Becca said, and the fire in the fireplace whooshed upward, reminiscent of the way the pyre had whooshed upward and obscured Henry and Pru all those centuries ago.

Becca offered her hand to me at the same time Raye offered hers.

"I don't—" I began.

They took my hands in theirs and suddenly I did understand.

"I am water," I said, and outside, rain began to fall.

"Protect," Raye whispered.

"Us," Becca murmured.

"All," I finished.

Lightning flared. Thunder crashed. The wind howled, or maybe it was wolves. Then the fire went out.

"That oughta do it," Raye said.

# Chapter 18

"We'll start fresh in the morning." Raye's gaze drifted to door number one, behind which Bobby Doucet waited. I could understand her eagerness.

"Start what?" I asked.

"Looking for Roland." Becca's gaze was equally captured by door number two and the promise of Owen McAllister.

"Locator spell?" My own gaze flicked to door number three.

"Henry wants to set a trap," Raye said.

My eyes flicked back. "He thinks Roland's going to fall for a trap?"

"If it's baited right."

"Ah." I knew exactly what bait they meant. *Us.*

"We'll be fine." Becca set her hand on my arm. "Owen's a marine. Just because he was in K-9 Corps doesn't mean he can't shoot a gun."

"We're going to shoot Roland?"

"Not we," Becca said. "Owen and/or Bobby."

"Bobby's a pretty good shot," Raye continued. "Saved my life."

Could it be that simple? Could we dangle ourselves as bait, then shoot the bad guy and end it all? I had my doubts. But I was too tired to voice them, and what did I know? I was late to this party.

"Grab what you want out of my bag." Raye indicated an overnight case in the dining area.

"Or mine." Becca pointed to a duffel nearby.

I guess we *were* all the same size, or close enough.

"Here." Raye offered me a clear bottle half filled with green flecks.

I frowned and didn't take it. "I gave that up."

At her confusion, I mimed smoking a joint.

"I'm a kindergarten teacher!"

"That would be a good enough reason for me."

She shook the jar. "Rosemary. Put a line across your threshold. It keeps the ghosts out."

"I don't—"

She pressed the cool glass container into my palm. "You want his sister watching what goes on in that bedroom? Or Henry?" She held up her own container and Becca did the same. "We learned early on to ward the bedroom before Dad saw something he couldn't unsee."

"I'm not—"

"Night." Raye's door closed.

"See you in the morning." Becca's followed.

Jealousy flared. It was the couch for me. I tucked the jar into my pocket, then went searching for PJs, not only because I'd be sleeping out here, where anyone could see, but my clothes were muddy and bloody. They had to go.

I found an oversized T-shirt in Raye's case that appeared big enough to reach to my knees. Perfect. I hated to borrow underwear, but I didn't have much choice. I snatched a pair and went into the half bath off the living area. There I undressed, then washed up and changed into the clean garments before taking my stained things to the utility area where I'd seen a stacked washer/dryer. Someone had tossed Sebastian's in at some point, and I moved his to the dryer, then retrieved the rosemary jar before I threw my stuff in, set the machine on "soiled" and pushed "start."

I grabbed an afghan and turned toward the couch.
Pru lay all over it. Unless I wanted to shove a wolf over,
hunt for bedding and make a bed, or sleep sitting up, I
was going to have to . . .

My gaze went to door number three again. "I should
probably check on him."

Pru snorted.

"You could move."

She stretched out farther and showed me her teeth.

"Not very motherly."

She closed her eyes and ignored me. I tossed the afghan back where I'd found it and headed for the bedroom.

The TV was on, though the sound was off. The flicker-
ing light cast just enough shadow to reveal that Sebastian
was asleep. And naked—at least from the waist up. His
hair was wild and curly from the shower, his earring
flashed silver-blue. I wanted to chase it with my fingers
through those damp strands the way I'd done in nearly
every vision. His chest was big and broad, taut; his arms
were too. I wanted to lick him all over.

I opened the rosemary jar and sprinkled a line across
the door.

He shifted. His skin twitched, and he set his hand on
the slice that Roland had made. Concerned, I hurried
over. The thin red line had faded to pink. In this light I
couldn't tell if the color indicated festering or fine. Becca
had healed his flesh, but that didn't mean there couldn't
be something nasty lurking beneath. What if Roland had
used a poison blade? Which sounded exactly like something he would do. Bastard.

I set my hand atop the mark, terrified it would be hot
to the touch, but it wasn't. Just to be sure, I touched him
several other places.

All good. In fact, they were so good, I ran my fingertips over them more than I should have. I would have

felt uncomfortable about stroking him when he was unaware, except my touch calmed him. The twitching and
shifting stopped, and he appeared to have slipped into
a deep, restful slumber.

I should wrestle Pru for a piece of the couch, sleep
by the fire or maybe in a chair. But what if Sebastian
began to thrash again during the night? What if he began to run a fever? What could it hurt to lie at his side
and make sure everything was all right? It would hurt
more if I didn't and something bad happened. The way
things were going lately, bad was more likely than not.

I reclined on top of the quilt, feeling righteous—until
the chill stole in. Then I crept beneath the covers and
listened to him breathe. The in and out sounded natural, but what did I know?

I set my hand on his chest, and the steady up and
down lulled me to sleep, too.


After his shower, which he'd had to cut short because
the heat—or the blood loss, or the weirdness—had made
him light-headed, Sebastian wrapped a dry towel around
his waist. His bloody clothes had disappeared. He hoped
someone was washing them. He couldn't very well return to the facility in blood-drenched clothes.

Sebastian wasn't sure how he was going to return to
the facility at all and what he would say if he did, but
he shoved those thoughts aside for now. He was too
tired to deal with them.

He opened the door a crack, saw Willow, Raye, and
Becca by the fire with the wolf—weirdness again—and
shut it. He turned on the TV, muted the sound, then
crawled under the covers. Easier than trying to make
sure his towel pants were where they belonged.

He must have slept, because he dreamed. First of the
dark man—Roland—looming from the forest, right

after Willow had predicted he would. She was right too often to ignore, even though he wanted to. Just like he wanted to forget about Raye floating to the ceiling and Becca apparently touching a gaping wound and making it close without stitches. He definitely wasn't going to think about Raye describing his sister, right down to the earrings she wore—one of which now resided in his own ear. How could she know that?

He turned, uneasy, and the movement pulled something where his wound had been—faded but not forgotten. The room was too warm, or maybe he was. He shifted, then he caught the scent of Willow. Even though it was different now—no longer institutional soap and shampoo—he recognized her. She smelled like fresh snow, heat lightning, and mint.

She touched him, and the heat receded; the pain eased and peace flowed into his soul. The emptiness that had been there since his parents died, since Emma had died, receded. He could fill that emptiness with . . .

*Her.*

She curled against his side, her skin so soft, herself so fragile and fey—like one of those little people his mother had told him about. She wasn't really small, but next to him, everyone was. He wanted to protect her, to save her. He wanted to love her. Which was crazy talk, but he was used to it. Though not usually from himself.

Her breath brushed his skin, made him tingle and shiver. Her hair drifted over his chest. It tickled. He liked it. He set his cheek atop her head and slept ever deeper. It had been so long since he'd held a woman, and he'd never held one who'd felt as though his arms had been waiting forever just for her.

When she kissed him, he kissed her back. Why not? He was a psychiatrist. He knew that sometimes dreams meant something and sometimes they didn't. This one meant he hadn't been laid in eons, and Willow smelled like heaven on a stick. She kissed like heaven, too, or maybe it was hell. Because he was burning, down low where fire like that belonged, and it felt so good, he ignored the ding-ding of warning as his hand cupped her ass and his fingertips grazed the soft skin where her thigh began.

Her moan rumbled against his mouth. His tongue slipped through those sweet-sweet lips and stroked hers. Since this was a dream—the *best* dream—he rolled her onto her back, settled between her thighs. With only a wisp of her panties between them, he nearly came like a kid.

His biceps bunched to keep his full weight from crushing her. Her palms curled around them, her thumbs stroked, then her fingernails bit as she arched. Her breath caught. He knew that sound. He could swear he felt her clitoris swelling against him. Then she wrapped her ankles around his and a soft "oh!" escaped her before she shuddered.

She continued to tremble in his arms. He kissed her harder. She nipped his lip. The dual pleasure and pain had his eyes opening, displeasure at the end of the dream a growl in the center of his chest.

Willow smiled—her eyes sleepy, her hair tousled, her lips swollen. Then she reached up and brushed her thumb against his earring. "I always wondered how that would be."

He blinked. She was still there. "Oh, God."

"I know," she agreed.

Sebastian scrambled out of bed. Morning sunlight through a crack in the curtains lit her with a soft pink glow. Or maybe it was afterglow.

Her gaze lowered. His followed. He was naked and

fully aroused. He scrambled back into bed. His bare leg brushed hers. Memories flickered. She reached for him.

"Whoa!" He held up a hand between them like a crossing guard. They were so close his palm brushed one breast, the erect nipple sliding enticingly on the other side of a T-shirt so old it was nearly transparent.

The dream hadn't been a dream.

He was going to hell. Right after he went to prison.

He looked around for the towel he'd had last night. Found it on the floor close enough to snatch and snatched it, then slid out from beneath the covers as he slid the cloth around his waist.

Hurt flickered in her eyes, across her face. "Sebastian?"

"We didn't—" he began. Had they? "I didn't—" Had he? "You. Dammit." He rubbed his face and gave up.

She lifted her chin. "I did. And thank you. I never had before. It was lovely."

"Lovely?" he repeated like the moron he was.

"Fantastic. Mind-blowing. Life-altering. What do you want me to say, Doctor?"

He certainly didn't want her to call him "Doctor."

"Willow, I'm s—"

She held up her hand as he had. The universal sign for "Halt!" or perhaps "Shut the fuck up!"

"Do *not* say you're sorry."

"But—"

"Zip it," she ordered. "My fault. I shouldn't have slept here. I was worried you were getting a fever and—" She glanced away. "Let's pretend it never happened."

"Just so we're clear . . . *what* happened?"

"You made me come. First time ever. Woo-hoo."

Her voice didn't sound very woo-hoo. He didn't feel very woo-hoo either.

"We didn't—I didn't—um—"

"Take my virginity?"

He winced. This was getting worse by the second, and he hadn't thought that was possible.

"You didn't." Her lips tightened.

Did that mean he hadn't taken it or that she wasn't a virgin? And how did one ask such a thing? Considering the way she was glaring at him . . . one didn't.

"Forget it," she said. "Please."

He didn't think he could. From her expression, he didn't think she could either. He sighed. They were going to have to talk about this.

His gaze landed on the TV, which he'd turned on last night in an attempt to make the unfamiliar room more familiar. He often fell asleep to the flicker of the television. It was something you could count on nearly everywhere you slept, and he'd gotten used to drifting off to the muted silvery-blue light The sound was off, but he didn't need it to know what was going on.

The camera panned back to show the Northern Wisconsin Mental Health Facility. In front of it, Zoe and Deux. Cop cars filled the parking lot. On the steps stood Dr. Tronsted, arms akimbo, scowling at the spectacle. At the bottom of the screen blared a headline.

*New Director of NWMHF Helps Patient/s Escape!*

He cursed, then found the remote and turned on the sound.

"I saw him kissing her." Zoe's lip curled. "He was always around her, touching her. Very inappropriate."

"Bitch," Willow muttered.

Sebastian had to agree.

"Things have pretty much gone downhill since he came," Deux added.

The reporter turned to the camera. "According to reports, one inmate . . ."

"Patient," Sebastian corrected.

". . . Has escaped several times. A caseworker is dead and a second inmate has disappeared with Dr. Sebastian Frasier. Be on the lookout for—"

His photo appeared between one of Willow and one of Mary. From this angle, they all appeared as desperate as he felt.

"I need to find Mary," he said. If he returned with the missing patients, he might keep his license. His job was already toast. Probably had been for a while now. Dr. Tronsted had been very tolerant, but her expression as she'd surveyed the fiasco from the top of the steps hadn't been tolerant any longer.

"About Mary—" Willow began, and licked her lips.

Sebastian was distracted by memories of how those lips tasted. Sweet. Warm. Heaven. Hell! He yanked his gaze to her eyes, which were troubled. "What about her?"

"She's . . . uh . . . a little dead."

He thought she was kidding, except what was funny about that, then tears replaced the trouble. The two had been friends. Or as friendly as anyone got with Mary McAllister.

"How? When? Why? Are you sure?"

"I don't know the how, except by *Venatores Mali*. Since she was alive a few days ago, the when is recently. The why—she was trying to save Becca. Am I sure?" She shrugged. "I don't know why my sisters would lie."

Sebastian wasn't certain if a dead, escaped inmate—*patient*, he reminded himself—was better than one who was in the wind or not. It definitely wasn't better for Mary.

He was such an ass, worrying about his job when the poor woman was dead. Still, he should probably take her back with him.

"Her body?"

The glance Willow cast his way made Sebastian feel the same way Zoe's curled lip had. "You'll have to ask Owen."

Well, that was a conversation he couldn't wait to have. Right up there with the one he hadn't had yet with Willow.

"This isn't your fault." He indicated the tousled bed with an awkward hand wave. "I'm your psychiatrist."

"No," she said. "You aren't. And after what happened last night—" He tensed, and she cast him that disgusted glance again. "*Before* this—all that you saw, what I did, what they did. I don't think I need a psychiatrist anymore. I didn't need one in the first place."

"Willow, you—"

"I'm *not* crazy, Doctor. I never was."

She got up and went into the bathroom, the long, smooth line of her bare legs giving him flashbacks. The slam of the door gave him a chest pain.

He sat on the bed and put his head in his hands.


Why had I thought what had happened between us was real?

I turned on the shower as hot as I could stand, tossed the T-shirt and panties on the floor and got in.

Because I wanted it to be so badly. For me, Sebastian was familiar. I knew the scent of his skin, the feel of his hands, the taste of his mouth. When he'd touched me in the night, it had been a dream come true, literally.

But for him that dream had turned into a nightmare even before Zoe and Deux had appeared on the TV screen. He thought of me as a patient not a woman, someone he'd taken advantage of because I was less

than. How could he ever fall in love with me if he believed that? How could I ever fall in love with him?

Problem was, I already had.

Tears burned, not only for all I'd hoped and dreamed
but for Mary. She was a casualty in a war that had started
centuries ago. She'd been eager to fight. According to
Becca, she'd died a hero. That didn't make me miss her
any less. Mary had been like me in ways no one else
could ever be, not even my triplet sisters.

I'd cried for my friend a little last night, but this morning I cried a lot—both for the loss of her and for the
loss of a dream.

The water had cooled as my tears petered out. I'd just
grabbed a towel when someone knocked.

"I've got your clothes," Becca called, saving me the
trouble, and the embarrassment, of telling Sebastian to
do something anatomically impossible.

I wrapped the towel around me and unlocked the
door, cracking it a few inches to reveal my redheaded
sister and an empty bedroom. She must have brought
Sebastian's clothes too and given him a chance to put
them on. I wondered if he'd already run back to the facility to try and fix things.

"We're having a powwow at breakfast," Becca said.

I took my clothes, still warm from the dryer someone had put them in. In the stack was also a pair of jeans
and a sweatshirt, which would be less obvious than
scrubs and a T-shirt that advertised the mental health
facility I'd escaped from, not to mention warmer.

"Thanks," I said. "Be there in five."

I found a new toothbrush, travel toothpaste, deodor-
ant, a small hairbrush next to the sink. Either someone
had visited Walmart or had come prepared for guests. I
adored that someone either way.

My relief at the sight of Sebastian at the kitchen table with the others annoyed me. I had more important things to worry about than my pathetic, unrequited feelings for my former psychiatrist.

He leaped up. I waited for him to say good-bye and run away. Instead he offered me his chair. I took it—and his coffee too. He got another without comment, then sat on the edge of the couch—in the room, yet apart from everyone in it.

"I'm sorry for your loss, Owen," he said.

"Thank you." Owen set a box of doughnuts on the table.

I pounced. Nothing like fried dough to soothe a broken heart.

"I lost my mom years ago."

Owen and Becca joined hands. The soft smile on her face, the adoration on his made the doughnut in my mouth hard to swallow past the lump in my throat. I wanted what they had so badly I ached with it.

"Truthfully, I never really had her in the first place," he continued. "The craziness did."

"I wish I could have helped her more," Sebastian said.

"Me too. Peggy told us she'd made a friend." Owen glanced at me. "I take it that was you?"

"I got her killed."

"No—" Becca began.

"She was safe in the facility. I sent her out to the places I'd envisioned, to the people I saw in them. I didn't mean to, not at first."

"Then later?" Owen asked.

I swallowed again, had equal difficulty even though the doughnut was gone, drank some coffee and sucked it up. I owed him the truth. "Later, I sent her on purpose."

Sebastian shifted uneasily, but he didn't argue about my ability to transport people. How could he?

"She convinced me that I wouldn't have seen what I had if she wasn't meant to stop them."

"She tried," Owen said. "Her death is on the *Venatores Mali,* not on you."

He seemed to believe that. I wished that I could.

"Making them pay, sending Roland back is all we can do." Raye set her hand on my shoulder and squeezed. "And we'll do it."

"Where is Mary now?" Sebastian asked.

"Gone." Owen bit into a doughnut and chewed as if he were crunching nails.

"I know she's gone," Sebastian said in his best Dr. Frasier voice. "But her remains?"

"Gone," Owen repeated.

"Buried at sea? In the earth? Cremated?" Sebastian asked.

"Poof?" For that I earned a scowl from Sebastian and a giggle from Becca, with a snort from Raye.

"You'll have to ask the FBI," Owen said. "They took care of it."

"The FBI," Sebastian repeated. "Why would they care?"

"All these murders are connected," Bobby said. "That's how I got involved. I was a New Orleans homicide detective. We thought we had a serial killer."

"But you didn't."

"We had more than one. A lot more."

"Witches are people, too," Raye murmured.

Sebastian's brow furrowed. "What does the FBI think about serial killers who are being controlled from beyond the grave?"

"Not anymore," Bobby said. "Roland is corporeal enough to have stabbed you."

"I still find it hard to believe that the FBI is on board with time travel, witchcraft, and whatever the hell else this is."

"The FBI, per se, probably wouldn't be. But Nic Franklin—"

"He called me—" Sebastian interrupted. "He was looking for Mary. Wasn't very friendly."

"The FBI is funny that way," Bobby said.

"He's not really FBI." Becca got up and began to re-fill everyone's coffee.

"Yes he is." Bobby took a doughnut, but he didn't eat it. "He's also a *Jäger-Sucher*."

Sebastian glanced at me, and I shrugged. "My Latin is better than my German." My German was nonexistent.

"Translates to hunter-searchers," Raye explained. "They're a monster-hunting unit that's been around since the Second World War."

"Monster hunters?" Sebastian repeated. "Seriously?"

"There are more things in heaven and earth than are dreamt of." Raye shrugged. "Shakespeare always says it best."

"Anything strange that comes to the FBI gets routed to Nic," Bobby continued. "He's been helpful."

"Cassandra too." Becca spread her hands. "Voodoo priestess."

"Sheesh," Sebastian said.

If he hadn't put a crack in my heart, I might feel sorry for the guy.

"We need to talk about the trap," Bobby said. "The sooner we get 'er done, the better."

"What trap?" Sebastian asked.

"You don't need to be involved," I said. "Run along."

My sisters cast me confused, concerned glances, which I ignored.

"What trap?" Sebastian repeated.

All eyes turned to me.

"He shouldn't be involved."

"I'm already involved."

"You didn't mean to be. You don't want to be. I understand."

And I did. He was attracted to me, but he didn't love me. How could he? Why would he? To sign on with something like this required more than a few illicit kisses. It required a lifetime commitment—or at least the commitment of a life, because one or more of us might be losing ours. I didn't want it to be him.

"You need to go back to the facility," I said.

"If I go back to the facility without you and Mary, I think I'm gonna be arrested. I'll pass."

"Dr. Frasier—" I began.

"We're way past 'Dr. Frasier,'" he said.

# Chapter 19

"I'm staying." Sebastian crossed his arms over his chest.

Willow scowled. Her sisters beamed. Their significant others had expressions somewhere in between.

What choice did he have? The idea of leaving Willow behind when someone—a lot of someones—wanted to kill her was an idea he hated almost as much as the idea of going back to the facility. He wasn't sure what he'd do about his job, his license, his life, but he'd worry about that once the time-traveling crazy man was gone. Wherever it was that time-traveling crazy people went. Except . . . was Roland really time-traveling if he'd been dead and now he wasn't?

Sebastian's head hurt a little. He drank more coffee.

"You look like you can handle yourself," Owen said.

"Except for the stabbing," Bobby pointed out.

"He was doing great until I tried to pull him out of the way," Willow said. "He knows judo."

Owen considered him. "That might be useful. I doubt Roland does."

"If it comes down to hand-to-hand, maybe." Bobby shrugged. "I'd rather it didn't. You know how to shoot a gun?"

Sebastian had never been a fan of guns. Hence the judo. He shook his head.

"We aren't going to need him to shoot a gun when you and I are both pretty good at it," Owen put in. "Roland comes from a time of knives and sticks."

"And fire," Becca said.

"He brings any one of those things to a gunfight"—Owen spread his hands—"we win."

"How do we get him to come to the gunfight?" Sebastian asked.

"I wish Reggie was here," Owen muttered. "He'd *voran* the stuffing out of that guy."

"Who's Reggie and what does *voran* mean?" Sebastian considered the doughnuts. All that was left were jelly filled. He took one. It was better than he thought it would be. The jelly tasted homemade.

"Reggie was my MWD."

Sebastian spread his hands and managed to drop jelly on his lap. As his jeans still had bloodstains despite being washed, it didn't matter.

"Military working dog," Owen translated. "If I told him to *voran*—or do what he's supposed to do—to Roland, he'd *bringen*—in Reggie-speak, fetch him—and drag him back to me."

"He might leave a few holes," Becca said.

"That would be the best part."

"Where is he?" Sebastian hoped the dog was okay. Military working dogs were closer to the action than anyone.

"I sent him back to Afghanistan." Owen seemed bummed about it. Why wouldn't he be?

"Sorry," Sebastian said.

"Reggie lives to sniff out bombs and *bringen* insurgents. He's happier there."

"And safer," Becca said.

"In Afghanistan?" Sebastian asked.

"No magic there."

"And no Henry," Raye put in.

"What does a ghost have to do with the safety of a dog?"

"Reggie had a serious crush on Pru. Henry wasn't amused."

"Henry wouldn't hurt anyone," Becca protested.

Raye's head tilted. Her mouth twitched. "Don't be so sure."

"Reggie belongs to the Marines," Owen continued. "I didn't have much to say about where he went. But finding Roland might take us longer than we'd like without him."

"We shouldn't need to search for Roland," Willow said. "Isn't he searching for us?"

"He is," Raye agreed. "We'll let him find us when we want him to."

"Hold on." Sebastian frowned. "You plan to be bait?"

"Got a better idea?" Raye asked.

Pru, who'd been lying next to Becca's chair, lifted her head and yipped.

Becca's gaze went to Willow. It seemed troubled. "You okay?"

Willow wasn't listening to them or even looking at them. She seemed transfixed by the window.

Sebastian followed her gaze and understood why. It had rained more during the night. Droplets sparked on the glass, and from Willow's expression—dazed, dazzled—she'd seen something within.

"Vision." He set his coffee on the table, then caught her as she fell out of her chair.

The others jumped up as both he and Willow went down. The world around them shimmered, fading away as another took its place.

"Touch her," he managed before he was pulled along with Willow to another place, perhaps another time.

As the others appeared—bing, bing, bing—next to him, he assumed they'd done what he said.

\* \* \*

One minute I was listening to my sisters and the men discuss a trap for Roland, the next an innocent glance toward the sun shining through the window sent me somewhere else.

Dark and dank, below the earth. For a minute I thought I was buried, and I struggled, tried to scream, could not. I hated when that happened.

Then a faint light bobbed in the darkness, growing stronger, larger as it came closer. A hag appeared holding a torch, two others followed behind.

"How *Macbeth* can you get?"

Raye's voice. Everyone was in the cave—which explained the damp and the dark and the creepy, closed-in feeling. I'd had company before in a vision. I'd thought because Mary was more magical than I'd known. But the magic had been mine, and as my sisters had predicted, it was growing.

The crones came toward us, then walked through us. One of them frowned, seemed to stare right at me, but when one of the others clucked at her, she continued to the flat-topped rock. Upon it lay a book, open to a page labeled: *Evocation*.

"What's that mean?" I asked.

"Not now," Becca said. "Watch."

She was right. I wouldn't be seeing this, they wouldn't be—though how they were I would save for later as well—if we didn't need to know it.

From behind the rock, a hag drew a bowl and set it upon the altar. Another produced a double-edged knife from her voluminous, tattered clothes; the third began to chant.

"Come to us. We summon thee, master."

Scottish accent. More *Macbeth*-ish by the instant.

The athame wielder snapped her fingers and the other two offered their wrists. I stifled my outcry as she slashed them, then her own. The blood of all three mingled in the bowl.

The one not chanting or slashing lowered the torch and the blood caught on fire. Could that happen? It had. When the flame died, smoke plumed upward—and within that smoke, I saw a face. That face turned toward us, saw us, and contorted into something horrible, ghoulish, and inhuman.

I gasped, the sound cut through the cave, broke the spell, and I sat up, back in the cabin, in Sebastian's arms, with the rest of them all around—each touching me, my sisters holding my hands. I nearly clipped Sebastian on the chin, managed, barely, to stop my upward movement before I did.

He kissed me—on the forehead—but still . . . I liked it.

"Where was that?" Bobby asked.

"Who was that?" Owen countered.

"Why was that?" Sebastian pulled me closer as the others moved away, taking their chairs, rubbing their eyes.

"You were with me," I said.

"Have you ever done that before?" Raye asked.

"Shared a vision?" I nodded. "With Mary."

"We knew our powers got stronger with proximity," Raye murmured. "Maybe stronger still the longer we're together."

Made sense to me. Especially since I'd just taken five people along on a vision quest.

"What's an evocation?" I asked.

"Invoking someone or something," Becca answered.

I guess I'd already known that, considering.

"Everyone gather around the table," Raye ordered.

"Willow's exhausted, she needs to—" Sebastian began.

"Now!"

Raye's voice left no room for disobedience. I got up.

When I swayed, Sebastian scooped me off my feet, which only made the world spin faster. He set me in a chair at the table and took the one next to me, then scooted his so close our legs, our shoulders, brushed. I could lean on him if I needed to. But I knew that already.

"Join hands," Raye ordered.

We did.

"Holy shit," Bobby said.

"Sir!" Owen straightened as if poked in the butt with a cattle prod.

The handsome young man I'd seen in my vision, who'd died on a pyre in Scotland centuries ago to save me, now stood in the kitchen with his hand on the head of our mother, the wolf.

"Henry," I said at the exact same time Becca and Raye did.

The plurality of the word seemed to make him more corporeal. I hadn't even realized he wasn't completely solid, until he became so.

*"Mo chlann,"* he whispered. "My children."

His dark eyes glistened. Raye's eyes, I saw. Becca had Pru's, though they were more hazel than green. What did I have that marked me as theirs? The storm. My visions. Transporting. I still felt left out. Not only because of my blue eyes and blond hair, but I'd actually *been* left out. Henry had been with Raye and Pru with Becca since arriving in this time. I'd only had myself. Spilled milk, but I still would have liked to have my mother's hair, my father's presence, or vice versa.

"How is this happening?" I asked.

"It's you, *mo leanabh,*" Henry said.

My *something,* I guessed. Didn't matter. I just liked

the way he said it. Henry had a brogue, both like Roland, and also nothing like him. Because Henry's voice was filled with love, not hate.

*My child.*

The voice was female and in my head.

"Who was that?"

"Pru," Becca answered. "I hear her by telepathy."

"Now we can too," Bobby said.

*The three of you, together, are doing this. For now, you can see your father, hear me.*

"My hair was just that shade as a child." Henry smiled. "Or so my mother told me. To go from light to dark was cause for constant comment, and back then, some suspicion." His head tilted. "You have her eyes."

I'd just wished for that connection and there it was. Mind reading? Magic? Or just fate and family?

"I'm glad."

"As am I," Henry said. "But I must tell you what you need to know before I become ghostly again. Your vision, Willow, was of a grimoire, a book that contains the instructions for summoning evil spirits."

The face in the smoke had definitely looked evil.

"That's dark magic," Becca said.

"To summon darkness, darkness is needed. I wish it wasn't so, but it is."

"Wait a second," Raye said. "I know the spell to summon spirits, both good and evil. Good are summoned with the breath of a witch and evil with the blood of one."

"If she knows how already, why the vision?" I asked. I could have done without the head rush.

"Because Roland is no longer spirit but flesh."

"What does that mean?"

*You misspoke, darling.*

Henry smoothed his hand over Pru's head. The love

they had for each other was so clear in their eyes, their mannerisms, and their voices that I got misty again.

"I did," he agreed. "An evil spirit become flesh is a demon, and the spell that you saw—blood of three witches, fire, smoke—is used to summon one."

"Roland is a demon now?" Raye asked.

"*Mo leanabh,* he always was."

Sebastian was having a difficult time not breaking free of the circle and running until he couldn't run anymore. But he wouldn't leave Willow. Not when there was a demon after her. And that he believed such a thing only made him want to run all over again. However, he couldn't deny what he'd seen, and the only explanation for it was magic. Or psychosis.

He much preferred magic. Who wouldn't?

"The chief witch hunter of King James was a demon?" Raye asked.

*Not technically, no.*

Hearing the wolf's thoughts in his head was kind of freaking Sebastian out.

"In my opinion anyone who is that evil is a demon," Henry said. "But your mother is right, he wasn't truly a demon until he was evil spirit become form."

"What if a good spirit becomes form?" Becca asked.

"Angel."

For a minute Sebastian thought Henry was merely using another endearment for his wolf-wife. Then he understood the man-ghost had actually meant *angel*.

"There are angels among us?"

"Have you ever heard the phrase 'you may entertain angels unaware'?"

"Old Testament."

"Yet it still applies."

Sebastian's headache became worse.

"Never mind that now." Willow's fingers tightened around his.

His headache faded in response to her touch. Had that really happened or did he just wish it had? Did it matter? His headache was almost gone and his chest, which had been tight with nerves, disbelief, and fear, loosened. He could suddenly breathe much better.

Sebastian was so focused on her, on him, on their hands together and how good it felt, how right and soothing and warm, that when he lifted his gaze and saw the man standing behind Bobby's chair, he thought the fellow had walked in when he wasn't paying attention.

Then he saw Mary McAllister with her hand on Owen's shoulder. She leaned over and kissed the top of his marine-styled dark hair, and Owen smiled.

"What the—" Sebastian began, and someone touched his shoulder.

*Bass.*

He couldn't breathe again. Only his sister had ever called him that.

He leaped up. Willow and Raye, who held his other hand, yanked him back down.

"Do not break this circle, Doctor," Raye snapped.

"But—but—"

"There are ghosts here," Raye continued. "I know. They're with me. Or rather, I guess, with the ones they haunt."

"Why?"

"First things first. The plan for Roland McHugh."

He should turn his head and see Emma. How many times since he'd lost her had he wished he could see her, speak to her, just one more time. But he discovered he couldn't. He was frozen with both horror and hope. He wasn't sure what he'd do if he saw her. Probably flee like the coward he was, and right now he had to stay; they had to finish what they'd started. What if he broke the bond and they couldn't get Henry and Pru back? Willow might die; they might all die. And then what?

"Okay," he said. "I'm okay."

Something—*someone*—touched his hair. *You are. You always were. You always will be.*

He wasn't okay. Not really. But he could pretend long enough to do what needed to be done. In truth, the brush of Emma's fingers and the whisper of her voice had made the panic fade a bit. The warmth of Willow's hand helped too.

"Go on, sir." He met Henry's gaze. "Please."

The ghost studied Sebastian for an instant, then went on. "Summon Roland to a place of your choosing."

"Owen and I can scout the best location for an ambush around here." Bobby glanced at Owen who nodded.

"Then the girls will do the spell at that location." Henry spread his hands. "And voila. Roland will appear."

"Poof?" Willow asked.

"Now that he is flesh, I am not sure how."

"It doesn't matter." Bobby's eyes hardened. He was a cop all right. "We'll be ready."

*The girls are fatigued.* Pru sounded very motherly. *Break the circle; let them rest.*

Owen withdrew his hands just as Sebastian threw a glance over his shoulder. Emma wasn't there. How could she be? Of course, now that the circle was broken, why would she be?

Owen brushed his fingertips across Becca's cheek. "You're too pale."

"I'm always pale. I have red hair."

She *did* look exhausted. So did the other two.

"All three of you take a nap," Bobby ordered. "You were channeling enough power to light up Las Vegas. We'll scout a location for this trap."

"Who do you mean by 'we'?" Willow asked.

"All of us men." Bobby puffed out his chest and grunted like a beast.

Everyone but Willow laughed or smiled. "What if Roland attacks?"

"We did the protection spell, remember?" Raye indicated the area in front of the fireplace where Sebastian had seen them last night.

They'd been doing more than getting to know each other. Or maybe that was how witches got to know each other, by casting spells and sharing power. Sebastian's headache threatened again.

"How far does a protection spell reach?" Sebastian asked.

"Anyone within the charmed circle is protected."

Pru trotted to the door and glanced back. Apparently the wolf was going with them.

Sebastian hesitated. "Maybe Pru should stand guard here. The girls will be sleeping."

"We'll be fine." Raye made an upward motion with her hand and a vase levitated off the table.

"I don't see—" he began.

"Imagine that's Roland." She made a slapping motion. The vase smacked against the wall and shattered into a gazillion pieces.

"If that doesn't work," Becca said, "I could always . . ." She cupped her palm and a ball of fire appeared.

"That's new," Owen murmured, and she grinned.

"But very fun and very handy."

"I guess I could transport him to death," Willow muttered.

"Except you'd have to touch him," Sebastian said. "And that ain't happening."

Becca closed her palm, and the fire went out, leaving the scent of doused flames behind. "Maybe we should just summon him here now and set him on fire."

"Or summon him to a cliff and toss him off," Raye said.

"The three of you are as pale as one of your ghosts, Raye." Owen's face reflected the worry Sebastian felt. "Once you summon him, you might not have enough juice left to end him."

"Listen to the man." Bobby stroked his gun. "Besides, I really, really want to shoot the guy."

"They're probably right," Becca said.

"And even if they're not, we should let them have their fun," Raye agreed.

No one had asked Willow's opinion, which might be why she was scowling. Sebastian hoped that was why she was scowling.

"You see any problems with the plan?" he asked.

Willow shook her head, but she didn't stop scowling. She waved him toward the door. He could refuse to go, but then what would he do? Stare at her while she slept? Or stare at her until she couldn't sleep. He knew he wouldn't be able to with someone hovering over him.

He left with the guys, resisting the temptation to kiss Willow good-bye when Owen kissed Becca and Bobby kissed Raye. The only way he was able to stop himself was because Willow spun on her heel, walked into the bedroom and shut the door behind her.

They climbed into the Suburban parked outside— Sebastian in the back seat, Bobby at the wheel, Owen riding shotgun. Pru leaped into the rear cargo area and sat with her nose to the window. Nothing was going to sneak up on them with her there.

They bounced down what looked like an old deer trail.

"We probably need a map," Sebastian said.

"Got one." Owen tapped his forehead. "I Googled local topography."

"I heard Google, blah-blah-blah."

Owen ignored Bobby. "There's a ridge behind my house that would be perfect for this maneuver but we can't use it, because Becca's family farm is on the other side."

"And we don't want Roland anywhere near them," Bobby said.

"Exactly. So I examined the topography of that ridge and found one ten miles from here that is almost the same. Actually better because the area around it is flat not forest."

"There's flat and not forest around here?" Sebastian asked.

"Not much, but according to Google, just enough. We'll make sure. That way we'll know if Roland is bringing minions. In a forest, that'd be difficult to see."

"What if he does?" Sebastian asked.

"I'd like to shoot 'em all," Bobby said. "But I suppose I shouldn't."

"If Roland knows we're there with guns," Owen continued, "he'll leave."

"Can he leave if he's been summoned?" Sebastian wondered. "For that matter, if he's summoned, will he have time to gather minions?"

"I don't know," Owen admitted. "But if we blow this chance, we might not get another. We save our shots for the demon, okay?"

"Okay." Bobby didn't sound happy about it.

"And if he arrives with others, what do we do?"

"Maybe there's a spell to keep anyone but Roland from arriving," Owen said.

"Maybe the spell keeps anyone *but* him from arriving."

Bobby cast Sebastian a glance. "That would be awesome."

Silence settled between them as they continued to bounce along the glorified deer trail, he hoped on their way to a real road. Pru continued to stare out the back window. Since she didn't bark, growl, or snarl, they must still be alone.

"So," Sebastian said. "About those ghosts."

Bobby sighed. "They freaked me out at first too."

"Not anymore?"

"No, they still freak me out."

"You saw them?" Sebastian asked.

"I saw yours," Bobby said. "Felt mine behind me, but then I always kind of did." At Sebastian's frown he continued, "I'm sensitive to them. Had a voodoo queen in my family tree."

Sebastian turned his gaze toward Owen. "And you?"

"No voodoo queen in my tree. Never felt a ghost in my life."

"Not even today?"

"Didn't need to *feel* anything. I saw yours and his." He jerked his head at Bobby.

Bobby and Sebastian exchanged a glance.

"What?" Owen asked.

"Your mom—" Sebastian said at the same time Bobby said, "Dude."

"She was there?"

"She kissed your head." Sebastian lifted one shoulder, lowered it. "You smiled. I thought—"

"Shit. I was hoping she'd gone on. She deserves some peace."

"Why is she here?" Sebastian asked. "Why are any of them here?"

"Unfinished business," Bobby said. "Either their own or ours. A ghost might hang around because their murder went unnoticed or unsolved, or they didn't say what they needed to say, which is their unfinished business. But they might also haunt someone who can't let them go."

Sebastian winced.

"Yeah," Bobby agreed. "I felt the same way."

Silence returned but not for long.

"Now that you're with Willow—" Owen began.

"I'm not *with* Willow."

Owen snorted.

Bobby appeared as if he wanted to. "If you aren't now, you will be."

"I can't, she's—" He paused. She wasn't his patient, and she wasn't crazy.

"Exactly," Bobby said as if Sebastian had finished the sentence. "I know what a Taggart woman in love looks like. She loves you."

"She doesn't even know me."

"Did you ever think that maybe she's known you most of her life?"

"What does that mean?"

"Visions."

Sebastian remembered the first thing she'd ever said to him.

*It's you.*

As if she knew him. As if she'd always known him.

"If you're with Willow now," Bobby continued, "maybe you can let that other girl go."

"She's my sister."

"Oh. Well, that's different then. Though you still need to let her go."

"How?" Sebastian asked.

"That's something you'll have to figure out on your own." Bobby met his gaze in the rearview mirror before he returned it to the road. "Like I did."

The stark pain in his eyes and in his voice did not invite questions about who and how and why, so Sebastian didn't ask them.

"Figure it out after we off Roland, okay?" The car shot out of the trees and onto a road. Owen pointed north and Bobby accelerated.

"If we murder Roland, won't he be hanging around haunting us rather than going back wherever it is he escaped from?"

"How can we murder what was already dead?" Owen asked.

# Chapter 20

When I awoke the bedside clock read noon. I'd been sleeping for over two hours. I felt rested, revved, ready. I hoped Raye and Becca were the same.

A door closed somewhere in the house and I tensed, but when I heard Sebastian's voice, followed by Owen's and Bobby's, I relaxed. They sounded calm, almost happy. Female voices joined them, asking questions, being answered. I wanted to be part of that conversation.

The instant I emerged from the bedroom, Sebastian's gaze went to me. I wasn't sure what I saw in it. Something new. Would I have time to discover what?

"They found the perfect place," Raye said. "We should do the spell today."

Guess not.

"I'd like to get this over with before another darkness falls." Becca glanced at me with a lift of her eyebrows.

I had to agree that ending Roland before another sun set sounded like a great idea; I nodded.

"Shouldn't you practice or something?" Sebastian asked.

"There is no practice with a spell," Raye said. "There is only do or do not."

"Sometimes she channels Yoda." Becca shrugged, which made me laugh.

It would have been nice to grow up together. I liked them.

Raye rolled her eyes as I imagined a big sister might. No one had ever told us our birth order, but I knew she had been born first, Becca next, and then myself as surely as I knew we were sisters at all.

"If we cast a spell," she said, "we've cast the spell. So we need to do it where we want it done."

"You really want to go now?" Bobby asked, but he was already checking his service weapon.

"Yep." Owen pulled two rifles from the closet, handed one to Sebastian, who held it like a smelly diaper, then proceeded to pull out boxes of ammunition and stuff them into an empty duffel bag.

"I'm not going to be any good with one of these." Sebastian handed the rifle back to Owen.

"Okay." Owen tossed the rifle to Bobby.

He caught it with one hand. "I'll give you my pistol, just in case."

"Just in case what?" I asked.

"In case he kicks Roland's ass and he gets back up. You okay with shooting the creep then, Doc?"

"I'm okay with shooting him now," Sebastian said. "I just want to make sure I don't miss."

"If he gets past us, he's gonna be close enough so there's no way you can miss. But we'll do a few practice shots out back just for the hell of it."

"Maybe you should stay here," I said. The last time Roland had been that close, Sebastian had gotten stabbed.

"No." Sebastian didn't even look at me, though everyone else did.

"But—"

"No," he repeated, this time meeting my eyes. I wasn't going to change his mind; I saw that as clearly as I saw him. "I'm not letting you out of my sight, and you can't make me."

"She could transport you to Delaware," Bobby said.

I hadn't thought of that. Could I? Should I?

"Don't. You. Dare." From the sound of the words, and the set of his jaw, Sebastian was grinding his teeth.

Pru yipped, and Becca held up her hand. "She says we need him. He's part of this, and Willow knows it."

Everyone looked at me again.

"I haven't caught a glimpse of this showdown. Not yet anyway."

Suddenly Sebastian was close enough to touch, looming over me—so big and strong and solid. "What have you had a vision of?"

Did he suspect how many times I'd had a vision of him? Of me? Of us? Together.

"Willow?"

The way he said my name didn't help me to stop remembering things that, right now, I shouldn't. I closed my eyes, shutting him out. It was the only way I could think straight.

"I saw you before I met you. I knew you were important, but I didn't know why. That you would keep me safe, that you would save me. But I didn't know from what."

"That's informative."

I opened my eyes, shrugged. It was what it was.

"Good enough for me," Raye said. "Sebastian comes along."

I could have argued, maybe I should have. But the truth was, I wanted him there. He made me feel strong and whole, and while I'd risk my life to keep him safe, was it fair to risk everyone else's?

"I'll be fine." Sebastian brushed my fingers with his. I managed, barely, not to grab onto them and cling.

"Roland isn't going to have time to do anything to any

of us before he's barbecuing his nuts back in Hades,"
Bobby said.

"Or having his nuts barbecued for him," Owen
agreed. "I kind of like that image."

"I like the image of using his own athame to cast the
spell that begins his end." Becca held up the curved
knife with the wolf head carved into the hilt that I'd seen
in my visions.

"Why would a witch hunter use the magical instrument of a fire witch?" I asked.

"Christians have been appropriating pagan symbols
and holidays for centuries." Becca put the knife into a
shopping bag, along with a stainless-steel bowl from the
kitchen. I nearly suggested a first-aid kit, then remembered that Becca could heal us quicker than we could
open one up.

"For that guy to call himself Christian is stretching
it," I said.

"Preaching to the choir, sister." Becca winked.

"What about the wolf carved into the hilt?" I asked.
"It looks just like the ring Roland used to brand Henry
and Pru."

"We don't know for sure, but we think Roland or
one of his minions snatched a fire witch, appropriated
her athame, and carved the symbol in it to make it
theirs."

I suddenly liked the idea of using that particular item
to end him too.

An hour later we stood on top of a ridge.

"This is great," Becca said.

"Perfect," Raye agreed.

The land around us was flat. We could see what was
coming for several hundred yards in all directions. A

small grove of trees stood nearby, spaced far enough
apart that it would be hard to hide within.

Owen indicated the grove. "He won't suspect anyone's there."

"Sebastian's not going to fit behind one of those tree
trunks," I said. From the size of Owen's shoulders he
wouldn't either. Bobby might, but barely.

"We'll be in the trees." Bobby pointed to the branches.
"Higher ground is the best offensive position."

"There's a reason taking a hill is so damn hard,"
Owen said, "and why a lot of battles are won because
of the terrain."

He should know. I liked the idea of Sebastian hidden
*in* a tree so much better than the idea of him hidden
*behind* a tree.

"Ready?" Bobby asked.

Everyone broke into couples. Even Pru sat with her
back to us, staring at the air, head tilted. I assumed
Henry was professing his everlasting love. I hoped so.
On the one hand it was nice that they were still together
after all these years. On the other, it kind of sucked that
they couldn't touch, kiss, or otherwise engage.

Sebastian held Bobby's service pistol. Before we'd
left the cabin, he'd fired at a can a few times and hit it.
There'd been a lot of backslapping and congratulations.
I did not point out that hitting a nonmoving can was a
lot different from hitting a moving demon. Right now,
confidence might be our best weapon. It certainly
couldn't hurt.

"Please be c—"

Sebastian kissed me and not on the forehead. He
planted one smack on my lips, and he used his tongue.
Best kiss ever. I never wanted it to end. I clasped my
fingers around his neck and held on.

He put one arm around my waist and pulled me

against him. He was so warm, so solid and real. He tasted like midnight and the heat of the sun. The scent of lime was faint, but his. A little tequila and a sprinkle of salt would explain the dizzy euphoria that came over me.

Someone cleared his or her throat. We broke apart, our eyes caught. Together we smiled.

A hand came between us and the fingers snapped. I met Raye's gaze.

"Let's kill the creepy demon now, okay?"

I nodded. I didn't trust myself to speak just yet.

"Did we ever decide what we'd do if he brings minions?" Sebastian asked.

I hadn't thought of that.

"The instant I see McHugh, I'll shoot him," Bobby said. "The minions will scatter, they always do."

"If they don't?"

Pru growled.

"According to Mom," Becca said, "the spell will bring him. He shouldn't have time to collect anyone else, and if he does, Dad will take care of them."

"What's a ghost going to do?" Sebastian wondered.

"He's the ghost of a powerful witch." Raye indicated a good-sized boulder that was now hovering in thin air. It dropped, smacking into the ground so hard a puff of dry dirt lifted up then sifted down.

"Okay, then," Bobby said. "Any more questions?"

The men strode toward the trees. Pru glanced back and forth between them and us. Raye pointed after the men, so did Becca. She went with them and I was glad. We had magic to protect us; at least they had a wolf.

Raye led us to the center of the ridge. "Becca, find a flat rock." She held her hands about a foot apart. "At least this big."

Becca moved off, gaze on the ground as she searched.

"What's that for?" I asked.

"Natural altar. The crones had one in the vision, we need one too." Raye pulled the athame and the bowl from the bag and handed me the latter, for which I was glad. I didn't mind the idea of the athame being used for blood magic, but I didn't want to be the one letting the blood.

Becca returned with the flat rock and set it on the ground. Raye dropped down, sitting cross-legged next to it. Becca and I did the same. Raye pointed with the knife to the bowl in my hand, then tapped the top of the rock. I set it there.

"Okay. We chant, then we bleed, then the fire."

My heart was beating so loudly her words seemed faint, or maybe her voice was. She looked as pale as I felt.

"We didn't bring a match or a candle," I said.

"Don't need one." Becca traced her finger through the air and flame followed.

That also explained why Raye was using the athame when it was the magical instrument of a fire witch; Becca had to bring the fire.

"Right. Sorry."

"I'm not used to it yet either," she said.

"I'll do the chant first." Raye glanced at me and Becca in turn. "Then you repeat."

"They called their master," I pointed out.

"I am not calling anyone 'master,'" Becca snapped.

"I've summoned a spirit before."

"Henry," Becca said.

"Yes. Names have power. We'll use his. Summon Roland McHugh. Everyone ready?"

She was getting impatient. Couldn't blame her. The sooner this was over, the sooner we . . . I had no idea. But I still wanted it over.

"Come to us. We summon thee, Roland McHugh."

On the second round, Becca and I joined in. The wind stirred. I swore it whispered along with us.

Raye snapped her fingers. Becca offered her arm. I did too. We continued to chant as she cut Becca, then me, then herself. It didn't even hurt, or maybe I was just too distracted by what happened when our blood merged together in the bowl.

It swirled on its own. No one was touching it, and the wind wasn't strong enough to cause that much movement. In the center, I saw McHugh. He'd changed from his Pilgrim outfit into jeans and a black button-down. Expensive athletic shoes had replaced his ancient, handmade footwear. He stood in front of a group of people. From the expressions on their faces—rapt, worshipful—they were minions. He lifted his arms. They fell to their knees, bowed their heads.

We continued to chant. This time when we said his name, he stiffened, glanced over his shoulder. His eyes widened. He seemed to see us. I heard the crackle of flames an instant before Becca zapped the bowl of blood with fire. We said "Roland McHugh" a final time.

The flames shot up, dancing and crackling. When they died, Roland was close enough to touch. The three of us scrambled to our feet.

"I killed you." He glared at Becca.

"Not good enough."

His coat fit funny. It wasn't until he pulled out the concealed weapon that I understood why.

"I'll get it right this time." He pointed the gun at her.

Becca growled and burst into flames.

The gunshot made me cry out. But Roland jerked and turned toward the trees. A second shot made him jerk again. I waited for him to fall, but he didn't.

The flames around, in, through Becca died. A wolf the shade of cinnamon, with Becca's eyes—more green than hazel now—had taken her place.

Roland shot her, and she staggered, fell. An instant later he flew through the air and landed several feet away with a good, solid thud; the gun skidded over the cliff.

Raye and I fell to the ground at Becca's side. She was still breathing. Thank God. How were we going to heal her when she was the one with the power of healing?

"What was that?" I asked.

"Which *what* are you talking about?" Raye returned. "The one where the demon asshole didn't die? Or the what where our sister became fire and then a wolf?"

"Yes," I said.

She laid her hand on that wolf and motioned for me to do the same. The instant I did, the bullet that had gone into Becca popped out. She sprang up as if she'd never fallen down, then loped after Roland, who must have gotten up while we were occupied with Becca. Not surprising that being slam-dunked by a ghost hadn't hurt him any more than being shot twice.

Pru joined her and the three of them went over the ridge. Raye and I stood so we could see them racing across the open expanse of flat land all around us.

Then Roland disappeared. One second his tennies were being nipped at by our mother, and the next he was nowhere to be seen.

"Holy shit." Bobby dropped out of the tree and started to run.

"This is not good." Owen landed and sprinted after him.

"Do you think we should have used silver bullets?" Bobby asked.

"Those were silver bullets," Owen answered.

Sebastian followed without comment. What could he say? Disappearing demons. Silver bullets. A woman who burst into flame, then turned into a wolf. He was pretty much out of words at the moment.

They reached the two remaining women, who were bleeding more than Sebastian liked. He snatched the bloody athame and used it to slice the bottom third of his shirt into strips for bandages.

"A first-aid kit would have been useful." He tied the strips around their wrists.

"Becca was supposed to heal us." Willow sounded as dazed as she looked.

"Then she ran off on four paws before that happened." Raye sounded a bit better. She'd been doing this longer than Willow had.

"Did you know she could shape-shift?" Willow asked.

Raye shook her head. "It's one of the powers of a fire witch, but she insisted she didn't have it."

"She does now," Sebastian said.

"Problem is . . ." Raye frowned as the wolves returned and stood between Bobby and Owen. "Does she have the power to turn back?"

Becca whined, twitched, pawed the ground. She did not become a woman again.

"Can you hear Becca like you hear Pru?" Owen asked.

Raye shook her head. Owen cursed.

"Pru," Raye said, "help her."

Pru huffed.

"Dammit." Raye kicked the grass.

"What?" Owen sounded a little panicked.

Sebastian didn't blame him. It was going to be difficult to have a life with a wolf, though Henry had managed it. Then again, he didn't have a life with her, he was having his death with her.

"Pru's not a werewolf." Raye lifted one shoulder. "So she can't help."

"Becca's not a werewolf," Owen snapped.

"Edward would beg to differ," Raye said. "She was shot and she didn't die."

Bobby picked up the bullet that still lay on the ground. "Not silver."

"Not helping." Owen snatched it from Bobby's hand. "Becca can heal. That's a witch trait, not a wolf one."

"Having people eyes in the face of a wolf is very werewolfy," Raye said.

"Pru has the same."

"Pru didn't change from a woman to a wolf."

"Yeah, she did," Owen muttered.

Technically Pru had died and been reborn a wolf, but Sebastian decided not to point that out. Owen was upset enough.

"Who's Edward?" he asked.

"Someone who can't see her like this." Owen went to his knees and put his arms around Becca's neck. She whined and licked his cheek. "He'll kill her."

"What?" Sebastian blurted. "Why?"

"Edward Mandenauer is the leader of the *Jäger-Suchers,* and the greatest werewolf hunter of all time," Bobby said. "He shoots first, finds out if he should have later."

"He shot Pru," Raye said.

"And he's still breathing?" Sebastian asked.

Raye's lips twitched. "Barely. In his defense, she does look like a werewolf, and he's seen a million—give or take. He knows better now."

"About Pru," Owen said. "Not Becca."

Bobby pulled out his phone. "I'll call Franklin. Tell him the skinny. See what he can do."

"No Edward," Owen said.

"No Edward," Bobby agreed.

# Chapter 21

I felt dazed—whether from the aftereffects of the spell, the blood loss, the shift in Becca—ha-ha—or the realization that our plan was toast, I didn't know. Whatever it was, when Sebastian put his arm around my shoulders, I leaned in not only because I wanted to, but because I had to.

Bobby ended his call with Special Agent Franklin. "He's on his way."

"Alone?" Owen asked.

"He's bringing his wife. She's some kind of werewolf expert."

Owen threw up his hands. "Becca is *not* a werewolf. What did he say about Edward?"

"Not coming. At least not yet. He's with Cassandra."

"Where?"

Bobby frowned. "New Orleans."

"Is that a problem?" I asked.

"I hope not."

I glanced at Raye, who shrugged, then shook her head. I didn't have to read her mind to know what she meant. We had enough problems of our own without bringing in new ones. If there was an issue in New Orleans, the folks in New Orleans would have to handle it. Bobby was no longer NOPD.

"Let's get back to the cabin where I can clean those wounds," Sebastian said.

No one argued. I think we all wanted to get out of the open.

In the Suburban I almost stopped Bobby from driving off. One of the seats was empty. Who were we missing?

Then I remembered Becca wasn't using a seat anymore. She was in the back, staring out the window with Pru. As I watched, the black wolf turned her head and nuzzled the red one. Envy spiked, so sharp it was painful. Raye took my hand. She was watching them too.

"How did Roland disappear?" Sebastian asked.

"Magic," Raye said. "Had to be. His followers were chanting, so was he. One or the other or both of them together did something funky."

Bobby's fingers tightened on the steering wheel. "Hypocritical asshole."

"Redundant." Raye tilted her head and gazed at the empty seat that should have been Becca's. "Henry says a demon isn't human."

"Ya think?" Owen murmured.

"Roland now has supernatural powers," Raye continued.

"Like not dying by bullets?" Bobby asked.

Owen smacked his fist against his knee. "Would have been handy to know that before we shot him."

"Ya think?" Raye echoed. "None of us have dealt with a demon before. We're kind of making this up as we go along. We need a new plan."

"Is there a spell to contain a demon?" I asked.

"Contain how?"

"If we evoke him again, we're going to need to hold him in place or he'll just disappear—be it by his own demonic power, or with a little minion black magic. I'd love to nail his feet to the ground, but only if it works."

Owen stared out the window. "I'd like to do it just for fun."

"We need more information." Raye's face was stark, paler than I'd ever seen it. I had no doubt mine was the same. "While we're researching containment, we should find out how to kill a demon. You'd think a silver bullet would at least slow him down, but noooo."

"How to kill a demon might be something the *Jäger-Suchers* know." Bobby turned onto the main road.

"Nothing's ever that easy," Raye said.

Silence settled over the car for the remainder of the drive. It seemed to take longer to get back than it had taken to get there. Wasn't that always the way?

We reached the cabin; everyone piled out. Owen opened the rear hatch for the wolves. Not having opposable thumbs must really be an ass pain, though having fangs and claws might make up for it. Especially when Roland was around. I wished he hadn't gone poof before Becca and Pru had caught up with him. We wouldn't be in this mess. Then again, if a bullet—make that two—hadn't killed him, would wolves have been able to?

Raye and I sat at the table. Bobby and Owen went into the kitchen and started pulling out bread, cheese, cold cuts. We'd missed lunch. Soon night would fall. The idea of darkness all around and Roland out there in it, looking for us, maybe using black magic to find us, made me want to be anywhere but here. However, I wouldn't leave my sisters. I couldn't.

Sebastian went searching for first-aid supplies. We removed the now bloody strips of shirt. My cut began to well again. Raye's did too. Becca's paw appeared good as new—probably because it *was* new.

"Do you think you could have sliced a little less deeply?" Sebastian sat between us. "These might need stitches."

"A bowl of blood doesn't come about by drip-drops," Raye said.

Becca appeared at my side. She tugged on my shirt-sleeve with her teeth, pulling my arm to the edge of the table. Before I could figure out what she planned, she licked my wound. I gasped as a sharp pain shot through me. I peered at my wrist.

"It's gone."

Sebastian, who'd been digging out antiseptic cream, glanced up. "What's gone?"

"The wound. All better."

He reached for my hand. I put mine in it. His eyes widened. "Hold on."

Becca, who had already moved around my chair toward Raye, lifted her lip in a silent snarl.

"Calm down. I just want to watch."

She licked Raye's wound, and the slice seemed to evaporate between one second and the next.

"At least she still has healing powers in this form," I said.

"Why wouldn't she?" Raye asked.

"I don't know," I said. "I just got here."

"Henry is a telekinetic ghost." Raye continued to stare at her miraculously healed wrist. I was having a hard time keeping my eyes off my own.

"Can Pru still heal others?" I asked.

"No. Not all their powers remain. Henry hasn't been able to affect the weather. Pru can still call in the wolves."

"Not much of a 'power' for a wolf," I pointed out.

"It must have been nice when she was human."

Pru yipped. Apparently it had been.

"She can communicate telepathically with Henry and Becca—and now me. She can understand us. She's not a normal wolf."

"Never said she was. What about her visions?"

Pru shook her head.

"That bites."

Pru huffed.

"You should eat." Bobby set a hand on Raye's shoulder. "Both of you. You're too pale."

"Blood loss and shock." Raye got to her feet. "Cheapest high in the world."

"I feel fine." Though I *was* pretty hungry.

"I don't," Sebastian said. He was pale too.

"You okay?" I asked.

He gave me a dirty look, went into the bedroom and shut the door.

"What did I do?"

"You scared him," Bobby said.

"Me?"

"He had the same heart attack both Owen and I had. When that bastard didn't die, and then he pulled a gun and pointed it at you."

"He pointed it at Becca."

"From where we stood, we thought he was going to shoot all three of you. Bing. Bang. Boom." He punctuated the final three words with a gun finger pointed at me, Raye, and Becca in turn.

"I guess it would be pretty hard for Sebastian to explain two dead patients."

"Considering that kiss earlier, I don't think that's what he's upset about."

"Me either," Raye said.

The two of them went into the kitchen and filled their plates. Owen sat on the floor, feeding Becca and Pru pieces of roast beef. Now that I thought about it I'd never seen Pru eat before. I assumed she was hunting when she took her outdoor jaunts, and she must have been. I wondered how long it would be before Becca started to become more wolf and less woman. Hopefully we'd never have to find out.

"When will Franklin and his wife get here?" Owen asked.

"Morning at the earliest." Bobby took a bite of his sandwich.

"You think she can put Becca back the way she was?"

Both Becca and Pru swung their great, furry heads in our direction. They cocked them in the exact same way, but in different directions. It was both freaky and kind of sweet.

"I think that if anyone knows who to call it's Nic Franklin."

The *Ghostbusters* theme song began to play in my head. Great. Now I wasn't ever going to get it out.

"If he says his wife is the best person to bring," Bobby continued, "then she's the best person to bring."

Owen didn't look convinced; he looked terrified. And for a man who'd hunted IEDs with his dog in a place most of us feared to tread, that was saying a lot.

"Good enough for me." I hoped my cheery, upbeat agreement would help Owen feel better. I don't think it did. Nothing short of Becca without a tail probably would.

I made a sandwich, glanced at the closed door again, then made another. "Should we recast the protection spell?"

Raye looked first at me, then at Becca. "I'll do it."

"I can—"

"She can't. Besides, I'm just boosting it." She waved her hand at the door. "Run along. You know you want to."

And since I did, I did.

Sebastian sat on the bed, his back to the door. When I came into the room, he didn't even glance my way.

Which gave me time to sprinkle the rosemary. I didn't want his sister, or anyone else who might be floating around, to hear this.

"I brought you supper."

Nothing.

I approached with the plate held out as an offering. "You need to eat."

"So do you."

At least he was talking, though he still wasn't looking at me.

"I will if you will."

He snatched the sandwich from the plate and took a bite so huge he couldn't speak, even if he'd wanted to. Which he obviously did not.

I sat next to him and took a much smaller bite. We remained side by side, silent except for the chewing, until both of us were done. Then I took his plate, set it on mine, and placed them both on the nightstand. I had to lean past him to reach it, and when I leaned back my forearm brushed his stomach, bared by the strips of material he'd chopped off to make bandages.

I froze as my skin prickled with awareness. He stilled as his breath caught.

"I was so scared," he said.

I set my hand on his thigh. "I'm all right."

"For now."

"Sebastian."

He turned to me at last.

"Now might be all we have."

He took my shoulders, and I thought he'd kiss me. I even puckered up. Instead, he pulled me against his chest, wrapped his arms around me and held on. I slipped my hands around his waist. He seemed to be trembling.

"Hush," I whispered. "Hush."

I listened to the beat of his heart. Steady and sure against my cheek, it was familiar in a way that it shouldn't be. I wished I could give him the same comfort, but I wasn't sure how.

"Did you dream of me?" he asked.

"Sometimes."

Once I'd begun to have visions of him, the dreams had soon followed. I'd been a young girl—I still was—with no one, nothing but the promise of him.

Though I wanted nothing more than to continue to listen to his heart, hold him and have him hold me, the time had come for the truth. All of it.

I pulled back. His hands slid down my arms, his fingers tangled with mine.

"My first vision of you came fifteen years ago. You were big and strong. I knew you'd protect me. That you would save me."

"From this?"

"What else?"

"You're the psychic," he said.

"You'll save all of us, Sebastian."

His shoulders slumped. "How?"

"I don't know. But you will."

He let out a breath, then lifted his gaze to mine. "The first time we met you said 'It's you,' then you fainted."

"I'd been waiting forever, and there you were. Just like I'd imagined."

"You didn't imagine. You knew. You'd seen."

I tightened my fingers around his. I hadn't realized how wonderful it would be to have him believe.

"I had, but until you arrived, how could I be sure?"

"You knew about the *Venatores Mali*?"

"No. I'd seen the guy I stabbed—the ring, his knife. But I didn't know what that meant. Especially after he showed up and he didn't have either one of them.

Visions can be like a puzzle. Or maybe a movie with holes in it. I see pieces and flashes. Not the entire thing. Sometimes it starts late, or ends early. There are feelings and premonitions. There are even scenes that I don't remember I've seen until an instant before they happen."

"That has to be difficult."

"There's a reason I was in a psychiatric facility."

"I'm sorry."

"It wasn't your fault. It wasn't anyone's fault. I sounded crazy. I acted crazy."

"But you weren't crazy. You aren't crazy."

"Thank you."

He stared at our joined hands, rubbing his thumb over my palm. I wanted him to rub his thumb everywhere else. From my visions, I knew that eventually he would, but I wasn't sure when. Our first time was in a room lit only by the moon, which made it pretty hard to identify, even if I could remember much beyond the taste of his skin and the shape of his biceps beneath my palms.

"I feel as if I know you," he said. "Better than I *can* know you. Like I've always known you. Like we were . . . destined."

"We were."

He shook his head, and my chest began to ache. He was going to deny this, deny us, and then what would I do?

"This is . . ." His lips tightened. "I want to say insane, but it's . . . not. What would be insane would be to continue to refute everything I've seen, all that we've done. All that I feel."

"I've been waiting for you," I said.

"I didn't know it, but I was waiting for you too."

He drew me closer, kissed my nose, my cheeks, my

chin. I held my breath, hoping he would kiss my lips. And then he did. Gentle at first, as if he wanted just a taste, our mouths met, his tongue tickled mine. Gooseflesh erupted all over, and I shivered.

"Willow?" he whispered.

"Shh." I nipped his lip.

His eyes flared. His tongue shot out to lave the tiny hurt. Then he cupped my face with his big hands, tilted my head and kissed me until everything but the taste of his mouth went away.

Since this wasn't the right place, the right time—the room was too bright and where was the moon?—I wasn't nervous, thinking about sex and condoms and virginity. I wasn't thinking about anything but him, and that was as it should be.

I sucked on his tongue, tasted his teeth. He nibbled my lip, my chin, rubbed a thumb along the underside of my breast. I arched into that touch, and he cupped me with his huge palm, then rubbed that thumb across my peak.

At first I thought the wail of the wind was merely my blood pumping through my veins to the beat of my wildly excited heart. Then something thudded against the wall on the other side of the curtains and I jumped. Why were there curtains over a wall?

"Just the wind," he said as he sucked on my ear.

"Wind," I repeated. There was something about the wind I should remember.

Then there was a *zzzt*, a thunk, and the lights went out.

Sebastian was testing his teeth on my collarbone. I had my fingers in his hair. He lifted his head, which I only knew because I felt him move. I couldn't see a thing.

"Hold on." He got up.

I wanted to yank him back down, but he was fast for such a big man and he slipped away.

The sound of curtain rungs across a rod sliced through the wail of the wind, and I understood why there were curtains on a wall. The wall was a window, through which the moon spilled down, casting the room, the man, the bed, and me in silver shadows.

I'd seen this before. I knew what would happen, what we would say, how it would feel, how I would feel. Pain and passion, both novelty and memory, nothing to be afraid of. Everything would be all right.

It would be better than all right. For both of us.

"I thought it might be a storm." Sebastian stared out the window.

"Wasn't me."

"It's just wind. The sky's clear or it wouldn't be so bright." He reached for the curtain.

"Don't."

His arm fell back to his side.

"I want to see you." I moved up behind him and slid my hands around his waist, settling my palms on his solid stomach. "All of you." I flicked the button on his jeans, slid down the zipper. The sound seemed to drown out the wind. I dipped my fingers beneath the waistband of both his jeans and his skivvies and touched him there for the first time.

Except it wasn't the first time. I knew every step. I didn't feel like a virgin. I wasn't unsure. I took him in my hand. He was hot; he was hard and yet so soft. I curled my palm around him, then used my thumb across his tip. The added slide of his bare waist across my inner arm was nearly as arousing as the solid feel of him in my hand.

"Take off your shirt," I said.

He started to pull away, and I tightened my fingers. His breath hissed in—pain or pleasure? Perhaps both.

"You can take it off without me taking this off." I pumped my hand just once. He took off his shirt.

He had a beautiful back, big and smooth and ripply with muscle. Beneath the moon he sparkled silver-gray. The trees still rustled, casting spidery shadows over his skin, which I traced with the fingers of my free hand. When he got gooseflesh, I used my teeth.

He cursed and grabbed my wrist, pulled it free, spun. "If you keep that up, we'll be done before we start."

I smiled because he'd said exactly what he had in my vision. I felt like I'd finally come home.

Holding my gaze, moving slowly as if he were afraid he'd spook me, he drew my shirt over my head. Then he traced a finger down the curve of my waist. My nipples tightened, a sharp spike against my bra. His eyes flicked there as if drawn by a wire. Then he lifted his hand and drew his fingernail along the clearly visible bud beneath the padded cotton.

I let him until I couldn't stand it a second longer, then opened the clasp and my breasts sprang free. He stooped and took my entire breast into his mouth. Probably the first time I was ever glad to be so slight. I was sure it wouldn't be the last.

My legs wobbled. He lifted his head.

"Don't stop."

He scooped me into his arms and deposited me on the bed. Then he stood with the moon at his back. I couldn't see his face. For a minute he was an outline, a stranger, whose shape, scent, and taste were so familiar. He was the man I'd been waiting for. I'd never been afraid of him. I'd always known that with him, I didn't have to be.

He finished undressing me. The brush of his fingers, his nails, his palms made me shiver.

"Now you." I still wanted to see all of him.

I thought he'd argue, but he lost the rest of his clothes as quickly as he'd gotten rid of mine. The twin thuds of his shoes excited me almost as much as the sheen of his skin in the silver light.

I beckoned, but he didn't join me. Instead he stayed where he was, a shadow lover—fiction until he became fact.

"I want to remember you just like this. Your hair is silver. Your skin is alabaster." He tilted his head. "Maybe. I've never seen alabaster. More like ice."

I beckoned again. "I won't melt."

He put his palm around my ankle, ran it up my calf, my thigh, my flank, my hip. The bed dipped as he reclined at my side. "You don't feel like ice." He leaned over and suckled my breast. "You don't taste like ice either."

"Maybe I will melt."

He chuckled and the puff of his breath along the dampness left by his mouth made my breath catch. I set my hand against his chest and pushed. "Let me touch you."

He lay flat on the bed. "Your wish is my command."

I liked the sound of that.

I kissed his chin, which was rough with a late-in-the-day beard, making me recall the first time I'd seen him in the flesh, fresh off a motorcycle trip, scruffy and windblown, wearing black leather and that earring. No wonder I'd fainted. I rubbed my cheek along his, relishing the contrast between man and woman.

"Careful." He placed his big hand against the small of my back. His fingertips curved around my waist on one side, his thumb nearly reached to the other. "I'll leave a mark on your skin."

"Maybe later." My lips curved. "And lower."

Speaking of lower, I was fascinated by the sprinkling of dark hair across his chest and belly. I kissed his pecs—springy, a bit coarse. I rubbed my nose against his belly.

"Mmm." That was so soft I wanted to—

I rubbed my lips there too.

His penis leaped, and he groaned.

I sat up. "Did I hurt you?"

He tangled his hand in my hair and drew me back down. "Hurt me again."

He allowed me to explore any way that I wanted to, and there were many ways—with lips and teeth and tongue, fingers, palms, the back of my hand. I rediscovered every line, every curve and dip, the slide of skin, the spike of bone. I didn't want to stop. Wouldn't have except fair was fair, and he wanted to explore too.

I couldn't stay still like he had. I arched; I squirmed; I begged.

"Shh," he murmured against my stomach. His beard scraped my hip. I rubbed myself against him. I itched—everywhere. His breath brushed between my thighs, then his fingers did.

"Oh," I said, then, "Oh!"

He laughed and kissed me there too. "Shh," he repeated. "They'll think I'm doing something in here that I shouldn't."

I lifted my hand to his cheek. "You should."

He kissed my palm, then moved away from me and I clung. He came back and kissed me quick, on the nose. "Condom," he said, and found his pants, rustled a bit and returned.

For an instant it bothered me that he had one—maybe more—available. It meant he'd been with other women. But I'd known that, and the only thing that mattered was that now he would be with me.

I welcomed him with open arms, open eyes. I wanted to see his face in the night, shadowed by the moon. That was how I'd seen him first—in my mind, then accepted him into my heart. Now I welcomed him into my body.

The pain was brief. I'd known it would come, exactly how it would feel. Which made it not a surprise but the fulfillment of a promise I'd been expecting all along.

My breath caught and he stilled. "I don't want to hurt you. Did I hurt you?"

"Hush," I whispered as if he were the one who was hurt. "Show me." I pressed upward, taking him deeper. There was no more pain. "Show me now."

"Just . . ." He pressed his forehead to mine. "Just a second, I need a second."

I tried to hold on, but I couldn't. There was something fantastic on the other side of stillness. This was both my first time, and *not* my first time, the situation playing out with a duality I knew too well. I'd been here before, in my mind, but until I was here in body too, I didn't really know. I couldn't. Certainly he'd made me come last night, but this was different in ways I wanted it to be very badly.

I clasped his buttocks in my palms and pulled him tighter. He cursed and gave in to the storm.

# Chapter 22

Sebastian lay with Willow's head on his shoulder, the greatest peace he'd ever known washing over him. Which was damn strange, considering.

Certainly he no longer believed she was crazy, nor that she should be a patient of a mental health facility. Still, he shouldn't have touched her. But after he'd nearly lost her, he'd known that touching her was inevitable. Even before she'd shared that it was.

As wonderful as being with her had been, he was still bothered by *how* it had been. He watched the moon sparkle across the sheets, across her, across them.

"You seem . . ." He paused. He hadn't meant to speak. Why had he? "Never mind. It's not appropriate."

"I think that ship has sailed."

Sebastian winced.

"I meant you can tell me anything." She lifted her head, a frown marring her beautiful face. "I thought we were past the patient/doctor thing."

"I am. We are. Though the world isn't going to be."

"The world will be lucky if we save its ass," she muttered.

"I know."

"But they won't understand. People who matter to you, your job, your life." She stroked his chest. "And we won't be able to explain why they're wrong."

He nearly said no one mattered but her, which felt very real, but it was too soon for that. Or maybe it wasn't.

"If we tell them the truth," he said, "we'll both end up in the loony bin."

"I wish I knew how to fix this for you, but I don't."

"We have enough to worry about without my problems. Let's put out one fire at a time—biggest fire first, which is the insane, demonic, unkillable witch hunter that's been raised from the dead."

"Good plan," she said.

"I wish we had a plan."

"Me too." She laid her head back on his shoulder. Silence fell over them, as cool and navy blue as the night. "You wanted to ask me something?"

"No."

"Sebastian, you're thinking so loudly I can't fall asleep. Just ask."

He let out a long breath. "I don't want you asking me about my past with women, so it isn't fair for me to ask you—"

She leaned back so she could see his face. "I have no past with men. Unless you count the past I have with you."

"That's not the kind of past I'm talking about."

"I've seen this, seen us, together. Many times."

That might explain it. "You said you'd never . . ." And he knew that was so. He'd felt her virginity, taken it as he'd never taken anyone else's. But still . . . "It seemed like you had."

Her eagerness, her passion had inflamed him. He hadn't been as gentle as he should have been. Then again, she hadn't seemed to mind.

"The visions feel very real, even though they aren't. I can't explain—"

"You don't have to." He pulled her closer, rubbed his cheek against her hair. "It must seem odd to know me but not know me."

"*Odd* isn't the word I'd use."

"What is?"

"Both comforting and exciting. I know you. You'll never hurt me. But I also don't know you. Every touch is both a memory and a surprise."

"How can it be a surprise if you've seen us, seen this, seen everything before?"

"Not everything. Not all of it. Time changes what happens. People think they'll say one thing, instead they say another. Visions aren't exact."

He thought of the crones and the spell. "More's the pity."

She made a muffled sound of agreement and cuddled closer. He wanted to hold her like this forever. He was terrified he'd lose her. She was both a stranger and a part of him as no one else had ever been. Willow had lived with that duality all her life. That she *wasn't* crazy was a miracle.

"Can I ask you something?"

He pressed his lips to her hair. "Of course."

"Your sister—"

He tensed.

"If you don't want to tell me, I understand."

"No." He didn't want to, but he should. "She died." He let out a short, sharp breath. "Obviously." Hence the ghost.

"What happened?"

"My parents were killed in a boating accident."

Now she tensed. "Water is dangerous."

"Yes," he answered. Though, as her former psychiatrist, he should probably tell her it wasn't. But they were beyond that foolishness. Water *was* dangerous. It was also life-giving—in more ways than one. "I was twenty and my sister, Emma, was fifteen. I took care of her. But not well enough."

Her arms tightened around him, but she remained silent. She didn't argue that it hadn't been his fault, and because of that he told her everything.

"It was probably the worst possible time for a girl to lose her mother."

"I don't think there's a good time for that. Lost mine four hundred years ago and it still sucks."

"You're right, of course. Emma was devastated. I tried to help. I thought I was so smart. I was studying psychology."

"You were in college *and* responsible for your sister?"

"Yes," he said. "Well, no. I mean, legally I was, but I wasn't very responsible. I believed she was exhibiting typical teenage behavior. I talked *at* her instead of *with* her. I thought I was getting through, but she just told me what I wanted to hear so I'd go away. I left her on her own too much. She needed something I didn't give her."

Attention? Time? Love? Discipline? All of them and more.

"She made new friends. I was happy she had something to do, people to hang with. But these kids . . ." He shook his head. "I should have checked them out. I didn't. They weren't the kind of kids anyone should hang with. Ever. She overdosed. I didn't even know she was on drugs."

Or maybe he just hadn't wanted to know. Hadn't wanted to see. He'd been such a fool.

"I was taking exams when it happened. They couldn't reach me. I got to the hospital just in time to watch her—" His voice broke. "I begged her not to go, but—"

A tear dripped from Willow's face onto his chest. Sebastian kissed her hair again. It kind of helped. The tightness around his heart loosened.

"That's why she's haunting you."

"I don't blame her."

She leaned back to see his face. Her eyes were luminous. They seemed to shimmer silver in the light from the moon. "Not because she blames you, but because *you* blame you."

"Why wouldn't I blame me? It was my fault."

"That's not true."

"I wasn't able to help her and I should have been. I should have been able to help you too."

"You did help me. You're still helping me."

"I'm no good for you. You should stay away from me." *He* should stay from *her*. He'd be of no more help with what was going on here than he'd been with what had been going on with Emma. He couldn't bear it if Willow was hurt because he was an idiot.

"I'm not even going to address that stupidity."

He wasn't sure which stupidity she meant, but she didn't give him a chance to ask.

"Your sister loves you. I saw that as clearly as I saw her. She doesn't blame you, but she can't go on until you let her."

"I'm not sure how."

She laid her head back on his shoulder. "You will be."

She sounded so certain, he almost was too.

"Sebastian?"

"Mmm?"

"I think I've loved you all my life."

He wasn't sure what to say to that. He'd told her his most profound shame, and she'd made it less shameful. He'd admitted his shortcomings, and she'd insisted they weren't shortcomings at all. He'd suggested she leave him; she'd stayed right where she was and admitted that she loved him.

Luckily he didn't have to say anything as her breathing evened out; her body went heavy against his, and she slept.

For a long time, he stared into the moonlight and listened to her breathe. He'd do anything to be able to listen to her breathe every night for the rest of his life. He knew that with a certainty that both comforted and confused him.

But there were worse things to do anything for than love.

I awoke to the sun shining across the bed. When I'd fallen asleep it had been the moon. The sharp contrast between silver-tinged night and golden-bright light would have made me think I'd dreamed the first, except there was a man in my bed.

*The* man.

Had I told him I loved him? That seemed dreamy too. If I had, I was glad. If I hadn't, I would. He needed to know. I needed him to know.

He'd shared his deepest pain with me. I hoped that sharing it had helped. I couldn't believe he'd carried that guilt for so long. After we finished sending Roland back where he belonged, we'd work on sending Emma—on sending all the ghosts that haunted us back where they belonged.

I kissed Sebastian's scruffy chin. I liked him with a beard. I liked him without one. I just liked him. Almost as much as I loved him.

He didn't stir. Someone had worn him out.

I slid from the bed with a smile. I wanted badly to wear him out again.

After a long hot shower, I dressed in more of my sisters' clothes and slipped from the room, intent on coffee. As soon as I opened the door, the line of rosemary across the threshold scattered. I kicked it all over just in case Sebastian saw it. I didn't want to explain what it had been for and bring up thoughts of his sister again. We needed to concentrate on one supernatural entity at a time. Demons first.

Pru lifted her head from her paws and watched me as I put on coffee. I couldn't wait for the entire pot to brew, so I stuck a cup beneath the stream and, when it was full, put the carafe back where it belonged.

What would today bring? I hoped a better plan than yesterday's.

I went to the window. The sun sparked off the dew that trembled atop the grass. The world seemed to wobble. I had just enough time to set the coffee cup down before I wobbled too. Pru began to howl.

The crones were back. Or maybe they'd always been there but I was back. Same cave, same rock, same grimoire. Different page. This one said—

"Banishment."

Raye stood next to me. The cave rippled and Becca appeared. She was still a wolf. Bummer.

*We join together the power of blood-linked elemental witches.*

Each crone set an item on the stone, one of them—who looked different somehow, but I couldn't figure out how—set down two.

Athame. Wand. Pentacle. Chalice.

*He comes.*

The whisper swirled from the air, the shadows, the dark—three voices as one. They lifted the items, then chanted.

*Go back from whence you came. Banished. Now and forever.*

A shadow loomed in the doorway—the hulking figure of a man flickered to the hunched shape of a beast. Hooves one instant, feet the next. Horns to head. A tail, there and then gone. I didn't want to see whatever that was when it stepped from the darkness and into the light.

The crones didn't either. They tapped the four items together and *zzzzt,* a bright beam flared. The man-thing shrieked, and his shadow was pulled backward away from the women, the fire, the light.

*He is gone.*

The crones set down the objects and smiled toothless smiles. I found myself smiling too. We had a new plan.

The next instant I was in the living room again, on the floor, with Raye holding one hand and Becca with her paw planted firmly on the other. Pru sat right behind her. Sebastian, Owen, and Bobby hovered nearby.

I sat up. "Sorry."

"Why?" Raye helped me to my feet. "That was awesome."

"Being scared awake by a wolf first howling and then scratching down the door isn't my idea of awesome." Sebastian's pants were zipped but his shirt was inside out. As it was a whole shirt and not a ripped mess, he'd borrowed another at some point.

"Ditto." Bobby frowned at the bedroom doors; which seemed to have been mauled by a mad dog. "We're gonna have to pay for that."

"What did you see?" Sebastian asked.

"Act Two of the crones saga. Page two of the grimoire."

"There was a second page?" Owen sat on the floor and put his arm around Becca. She licked his chin.

Pru yipped at an empty corner, which, considering Raye's head tilt, wasn't that empty.

"Henry says grimoires contain information on both the summoning and the banishing of demons."

"That would have been good to know before we summoned one," Sebastian muttered.

I took his hand. It seemed to help.

"Spilled milk," Raye said. "Let's move on."

Quickly she related what we'd seen to those who hadn't shared my vision.

"The banishment of a demon requires combining the powers of blood-linked elemental witches," she finished. "That's us."

"We need all the items," I said.

"We have three." Raye lifted one finger. "Asshole's athame." She lifted another. "My wand." She drew a necklace from beneath her shirt. "The pentacle of an earth witch."

"Where'd you get that?" I asked.

"I yanked it off Mistress June. She'd stolen it from an earth witch she killed."

"We need a chalice," I said.

"*You* need a chalice—the mystical item for water, your element."

"Can I buy one in the chalice section of the nearest big-box store?"

"Very funny." Raye didn't appear amused. "There's a Wiccan shop in Madison that carries them."

"We need something closer," Bobby said.

"Wiccan shops are a little scarce in northern Wisconsin."

"What about an antiques shop?" Sebastian asked.

Raye cast him an appreciative glance. "Good call. There are a ton of those on the outskirts of every tourist town around. It can't hurt to try."

"What if we don't find one?" I wondered.

"There's always eBay."

An hour and a half later we rolled into the parking lot of the first antiques store on our list. As Raye had said, there were a ton and they all seemed to have a Web page, which was both weird and wonderful. Weird because since they sold antiques, you'd think the owners would be anti-Internet. But wonderful because that made them so easy to find.

Some were in restored barns, others in not-so-restored sheds. By noon, I felt like we were filming a new reality show: *American Pickers Goes Wicca.*

"I wonder if we could cast a spell that brings a chalice to us," Raye said, as we left yet another shop—*shop* being very generous as it had been housed in a root cellar.

"If we don't find what we need in the next two or three places"—I spread my hands—"I'm down with that."

We found it in the third place. I was glad I'd insisted on "just one more," because the chalice was mine. I knew it as soon as I walked in the door. I felt pulled to the back of the store—an actual store this time, what a novelty.

"Willow?" Sebastian followed in my wake. He'd been hovering since this morning. It was kind of nice.

"I'm okay." Though I wasn't sure if that were true. "Does anyone else hear water?"

The sound of a brook babbled somewhere out of sight. It was irresistible. I had to see it. Now.

"No," Raye said.

Sebastian caught at my arm. I dodged him and scooted around a huge stack of shiny hubcaps. The brook babbled louder.

We'd had to leave Pru and Becca at the house. How would we explain two wolves in the rear of the SUV? Better to not have to try. Owen refused to leave Becca, so we made a party of four, all of whom hurried after me.

Sebastian bumped into me when I stopped, then grabbed my hips to keep me from falling on my face.

When Sebastian bumped into someone of my size, they flew.

"Do you see it?" I asked.

"Yes." Raye stood at my side.

"Good." I was afraid I was having another vision. In the past, sometimes it had been hard to tell.

As they hadn't heard the water, I doubted that the others saw the halo that glowed around the chalice. They probably would have mentioned it.

The cup was tarnished and old. I was sure if I found some silver cleaner I could make it shine. As soon as I picked it up, the brook stopped babbling; the chalice stopped glowing. I felt something engraved on the side, rubbed at it, then turned the cup so that everyone could see the pentacle carved there.

"Let's go banish an evil spirit," I said.

"I'm gonna put some gas in the tank."

Bobby and Sebastian stood a few feet from the girls as they haggled over the cost of the chalice. The owner had quoted a ridiculous price. He must have seen the way they all ogled it.

"Let me." Sebastian held out his hand for the keys. "I'd rather you stayed with them."

Doucet had a gun, and he knew how to use it.

He appeared ready to argue, then his phone chimed and he glanced at the caller ID. "Office," he said, and handed over the keys.

He seemed to be running the police department by remote. Sebastian doubted there was that much going on in New Bergin, Wisconsin. Now that Raye wasn't there.

When Willow glanced over her shoulder, Sebastian lifted the keys, pantomimed filling a gas tank. She nodded and returned to the negotiations.

Sebastian drove the Suburban across the street. He had no idea what town this was—or if it even was a town. Besides the antiques store there was a gas station, two taverns, and a church. Period.

He nearly used his credit card before he reconsidered. The police were probably searching for him. All he needed was for them to find him. If he weren't arrested, he'd at least have to answer questions. Until this was over, he didn't want anything taking him away from Willow. He definitely didn't want Willow hauled back and locked up.

He was certain both Bobby and Owen could protect her. He was certain the three girls could protect themselves—with a little help from their ghost father and his wolf-wife. Nevertheless, he wanted to be there for her in any way that he could.

Sebastian counted his cash. He might have enough to fill the tank. He eyed the size of the vehicle. Then again, maybe not.

He started the pump, keeping a close eye on the cost. Too close, because he never heard anyone come up behind him.

The sting on his neck had him slapping his palm against it. The spike of pain was sharper than a bug bite. He immediately felt woozy. He turned his head.

"What are you doing here?" he asked, or tried to.

The words came out garbled at best, and then darkness closed in.

# Chapter 23

"Sebastian!" Bobby shouted, and I looked up from my dazzled contemplation of the chalice.

The Suburban was parked at the gas pumps. No sign of Sebastian anywhere.

"He probably went inside to pay or pee." Bobby glanced both ways and beckoned us across the street.

The pump was still in the gas tank. The heart-stopping cost of a full tank glared from the dial.

"I'll go in and see what's what," Bobby said. "Maybe he didn't have enough money."

I followed. I wasn't sure why. Probably because Sebastian had been out of my sight long enough to miss him.

No one was inside but the attendant—twenty or so, tall, skinny, all Adam's apple and big brown eyes. He was on the phone. He held up a finger. "One sec. Gotta call the cops. Dude took off and never paid."

He indicated the Suburban. Bobby and I exchanged glances. He pulled out his badge. "Hang up."

The kid blinked, did. "That was fast. I never even got a person on the line."

"Yeah, we aim to please. How could the dude take off if his car's still here?"

"I know, right?"

I wished Raye hadn't stayed outside so that she could toss this guy, at least hold him off the ground until he got to the point.

"What happened?"

He cast me a glance—had I shouted? "He was there, and then he wasn't."

I wasn't sure what to say to that. In our world, such a thing might actually happen.

"Where were you?"

There was a reason Bobby was a cop. He knew all the good questions.

"I had to fill the paper towels in the men's room. When I came back the car was still here, but the guy was gone. I waited a bit. But that's a lot of money he put in that tank. I couldn't wait forever. Why would someone fill a tank and leave the car?"

"He wouldn't." I was starting to panic.

"How did you know you needed to fill the towels?" Bobby asked.

"The guy told me."

"Which guy?"

"Big."

"Tall?"

"Not really." He spanned his hands wide.

"Hair?"

"Yes."

Bobby's eyes narrowed and the kid shrugged. "Short. Brown. Eyes too."

"Car?" Before the kid could say yes again, Bobby snapped, "Make? Model? Color?"

"Didn't see it. He parked on the side. Came in for cigs and the bathroom. Told me about the paper towels. I think he used about a zillion himself 'cause I checked them not more than an hour before he showed up. Anyway, when I came out he was gone."

"Security cameras?"

"Here?" The kid shook his head. "We're in the middle of nowhere. Nothing ever happens here."

Until today anyway.

"Anything else?" Bobby asked.

The attendant began to shake his head, and stopped mid-movement. "The ring."

I got a nasty chill. "What ring?"

"Big-ass one. He kept tapping the thing on the counter. Thought it was for a state championship or something, but it had an animal head on it and nothing else. Snarling dog maybe?"

I must have made a soft sound of distress because the attendant glanced at me, uneasy. Or maybe it was the rumble of thunder that seemed to shake the earth. Though why would he blame me?

I ran out the door as Bobby tossed twenties on the counter.

"They took him," I blurted as soon as I saw Raye.

"They who?"

*"Venatores Mali."* Bobby removed the gas pump that still dangled from the tank. "Get in."

I didn't have to be told twice.

He accelerated in the direction of the cabin.

"Wait! We have to look for him."

"How do you suggest we do that?" Bobby glanced at me in the rearview mirror. "We have no clue who took him or how or where."

"That doesn't mean we just drive off and leave him behind." I tried to open the back door, even though we were going forty miles per hour already, but Bobby had engaged the childproof locks.

"Of course not," Raye soothed. "But we need Becca and a plan."

"How can we plan? We don't know what, where, how—" My voice broke.

Raye took my hand. "That's why we have you."

*     *     *

I intended to rush into the cabin, turn on the nearest faucet, and stare at the water until I saw what I needed to. I'd add blood if necessary.

And I would have, if there hadn't been a car in the yard and people I'd never seen before getting out. I might have even done it anyway, except several things happened at once.

The front door opened. Pru and Becca rushed out, hackles raised. The man, dark haired with flecks of gray, wore an equally dark suit and dark shoes. He stepped in front of the woman, who was as light as he was dark. She wore killer heels the shade of a fire engine and a striped primary-colored dress, which hugged a body that deserved to be hugged.

She swept him aside. Since he flew off his feet and onto the hood of the navy blue sedan, I didn't think she was human, even before she changed.

I'd seen Becca become a wolf, but it wasn't the same. There'd been blood and fire then fur. This time there was crunching and shifting. Then fur.

Her clothes erupted outward as she went from two feet to four. Hands became paws, feet too, hair sprouted from her pores. Her nose and mouth expanded into a snout. Ears grew. Last but not least came the tail.

It took me longer to describe her change than her change took to happen. In no more than a blink or two, a white wolf lifted her lip and showed her impressive fangs to Pru. Then, when the deep blue, human eyes of the werewolf shifted to Becca, the black wolf stepped between them and snarled back.

"Elise, what the hell?" The man clambered off the hood of the car.

She didn't spare him a glance. I didn't blame her. My mom was pissed.

"Franklin." Bobby approached with a nod that both

welcomed the man and indicated the wolf-woman. "Your wife, I presume?"

Special Agent Nic Franklin, *Jäger-Sucher,* frowned and twitched one shoulder. "She doesn't usually do that in mixed company."

"Mixed how?"

"The werewolf-uninitiated." He looked at Raye, then me, then back at the wolves, who'd put away their fangs but kept their ruffs up. "I guess, considering, you really aren't uninitiated."

"Why did she shift?" I asked.

"No idea," Franklin answered. "She has people brain and wolf body, but she can't answer that until she shifts back."

"No telepathy?" Raye asked.

"Not with me."

"What about you, Mom?"

Pru shook her head and snorted.

"I guess not." Raye continued to stare at Pru, obviously hearing what the rest of us couldn't. "Elise is communicating with Becca but Mom can't quite get it. She—"

Suddenly the white wolf bounded into the trees. Becca followed. With a huff that was very motherly, Pru sprinted after.

Owen leaped off the porch, took several steps toward the woods and stopped. "They're long gone."

"They'll be back," Franklin said.

"Unless someone shoots them," Owen snapped.

"You need a permit to shoot wolves, don't you?" Bobby asked.

"Only if someone sees you," Owen replied.

"I don't think that's in the rules."

"Most people who shoot wolves don't play by the rules. You have met Edward, haven't you?"

"Yeah." Bobby rubbed between his eyes as if they pained him.

"All three of them are more than wolves," Franklin said. "They can outsmart any varmint hunter around."

"It isn't the varmint hunters I'm worried about," Owen muttered.

"Edward wouldn't shoot his own granddaughter. And Elise wouldn't let him shoot Becca."

"Hold on," I said. "Heap big werewolf hunter has a granddaughter who is one?"

The fed slammed the gaping passenger door on his sedan. "Did I not mention that?"

"We knew," Raye said.

It would have been nice if someone had told me, although I'm not sure what I might have done with the information except been amazed by it.

"Edward's still in New Orleans anyway," Franklin continued. "Some issue with your partner, Doucet."

"Sullivan?"

"You have more than one partner?"

"I don't have him anymore. I'm no longer NOPD."

"Edward and Cass will handle him."

"Handle him how?" Bobby said warily. "What did he do? What did he see?"

"What he shouldn't."

Bobby cursed. "He'd better be in the same huge, single Irish piece he was when I left him."

"He will be."

From the expression on Bobby's face he wasn't sure if that was comforting or not.

"This has been fun, but I've got places to go, visions to have, lovers to find and wrest from the jaws of creepy people." I started for the house.

"Huh?" Franklin asked.

"Tell him." I flapped my hand at the man, including

Owen in the gesture since he'd been here with the wolves and not with us. Raye followed me inside. I heard Bobby explaining who I was—just in case Special Agent Franklin was blind—then what had gone down, followed by a few curses from Owen and questions from the agent.

I headed for the kitchen faucet, but my sister snatched my elbow, hanging on when I tried to shrug her off.

"Sit somewhere," Raye said. "I'll bring you the water."

"No time."

"If you fall into the vision and crack your head, Becca isn't here to make it go away." She shoved me toward the living area. "Couch or table. Take your pick, but if I have to I'll levitate you until you behave."

Raye had certainly taken to being a bullying big sister with no trouble at all. Considering the only one of us who'd *had* brothers and sisters was Becca, I found this interesting. Not only did having sisters feel right, being the youngest did too.

I sat on the couch and scowled at Raye the entire time she filled a bowl with water and brought it to me.

"You know I'm right." She set the bowl in my lap. "Quit pouting."

I didn't bother to answer. As previously stated—no time. I lowered my gaze to the rippling surface of the water. Saw nothing. Squinted. Cursed.

"Get a knife," I said. Blood magic was dangerous, but it worked.

"Let's try this first." Raye took my hand, and the earth shifted.

The center of the water began to swirl like an inverted cyclone, or maybe a portal, just as the blood had earlier on the ridge. Everything shimmied. I felt like I was falling down that hole; I even smelled the water all around me. Raye said something I couldn't make out. I closed my eyes for a second, hoping maybe then I'd "see," and there Sebastian was bound to a chair. His face was bruised and bleeding.

"No," I whispered. I heard the water begin to bubble and boil. The vision did too.

"Calm down." Raye tightened her grip on my hand. "Breathe."

It was hard to breathe when my chest hurt this much, but I tried. After a minute or so, the vision smoothed out.

Sebastian was alone in a huge, abandoned building. The windows were grimy, the floor—concrete—wasn't much better. Empty shelves lined one brick wall.

"Where?" I asked.

A door opened, and light flowed in; from the angle, I thought it was late in the day. The future by a few hours, I hoped. I didn't want this to be another day, another week. I had to find him. Soon.

"Just the man I wanted to see." Roland McHugh's distinctive Scottish accent made me jerk so hard the water sloshed across my thighs. It was hot enough for me to be glad I wore jeans.

A shadow spread across the floor. For an instant it resembled the hooved and tailed beast we'd seen in the cave of the crones before it solidified into a man.

"I knew some Frasiers once," McHugh said. "They did not join me."

"I'm glad to know my ancestors had some sense."

"I had no need of their help. There were plenty of others. There still are. Now we'll wait right here until the Taggarts come for you."

"They won't come."

"Of course they will. Mendolson Road and old County Highway B. The abandoned cheese factory."

"Do. Not. Come."

Sebastian was speaking to me. He knew I'd force a vision—that I'd see and hear and come. So did Roland.

"Be here by midnight, lassies." He rotated his wrist and a switchblade snapped clear. "Or I'll gut him like a deer."

I stood, dumping the water onto the floor and racing onto the porch. "Roland's at the abandoned cheese factory. Mendolson Road and old County Highway B."

"That's eighty miles away," Owen said.

"Then we'd better hurry." I lifted my gaze to the fading sun. If we left now, we'd get there right on time.

Bobby touched my arm. "You know it's a trap, right?"

"Yes." I didn't care. Sebastian had stayed with me, risking his career and his life. Even if I hadn't loved him, I could do no less.

"I don't think Roland realizes his trap is going to snap closed right on him." Raye held the athame in one hand and the wand in the other. The pentacle around her neck seemed to catch the sun and glow like lava.

"Don't you need Becca?" Bobby asked.

"You got her."

The voice came from the forest—Becca's voice. Owen rushed into the trees. They came out together with Becca wearing his shirt. Pru trailed after.

"Where's Elise?" Franklin asked.

"Waiting for you to bring me a blanket." Shrubbery at the edge of the yard waggled.

He snatched said blanket from the back seat of his sedan—they'd obviously been down this road before—then disappeared into the foliage, emerging a minute later.

Except for some twigs in her long red hair, Becca looked no worse for her ordeal. Her eyes still appeared greener than before but I decided not to mention it.

"How did you change back?" I asked.

"My mind was a jumble of human thoughts and wolf instincts and senses. I couldn't focus, until Elise showed me how." Becca reached for Elise's arm, and Franklin made a move to stop her, but too late, her palm curled around the other woman's wrist.

"Happy to help." Elise covered Becca's hand with her free one. Hand hug.

"Guess she isn't a werewolf," Franklin said.

"I keep telling you that." Without a shirt Owen appeared even bigger than before. His Marine-style physique should be on a military romance novel cover.

"Since they can touch without getting a mutual migraine, I believe you." Franklin shrugged. "When werewolves touch skin to skin . . ."

"Supreme ice cream headache," Elise finished. "I don't know what you are, Becca, but it isn't a lycanthrope."

"According to Cassandra, a fire witch is a djinn with fire in the veins instead of blood." Becca tugged at the hem of Owen's shirt, which hit her mid-thigh. "There was also something about shape-shifting."

"Cassandra would know," Elise said.

"What's a djinn?" Owen asked.

"I think it's a genie."

"I'm not a genie," Becca muttered.

"Magic and fire and shape-shifting sounds like a genie to me." Elise went to the car and pulled out an overnight bag.

"Did you watch *I Dream of Jeannie*?" Becca asked. "No wolves, no fire."

"No demons or witches either. But she blinked and magic happened. She turned into smoke." Elise started toward the cabin. "And where there's smoke—"

"There's fire," Becca finished. "Shit. I'm a genie."

"That's great." I shoved her after Elise the way I thought a little sister would. "Put on some clothes. We have a demon to banish."

Sebastian was furious with himself. He was trussed like a turkey, being offered as the proverbial lamb. A lot of animal imagery. At least it passed the time.

The girls had to know this was a trap. Would that keep them from coming? Probably not. It wouldn't have stopped him.

How could he have let himself be taken? To be fair, *let* wasn't the right word. He'd been drugged—probably with a syringe and meds right from his own facility. He'd figured that out the instant he'd come to and seen Zoe and Deux.

"Which one of you tried to kill Willow?"

The guard, who looked a lot younger and smaller wearing jeans and not his uniform, jerked a thumb at Zoe. "I told her not to. The master wanted to use Willow as bait for the other two."

"She annoyed me."

Oddly Zoe appeared older out of uniform—probably all of eighteen.

"Annoyed you how? She was a patient. You're a nurse."

"Zoe has a thing for you," Deux said.

Willow had intimated the same, but attempted murder was going a bit far for a crush, wasn't it?

"Is that why you told the police I'd done something I shouldn't?" Sebastian asked.

"You *did* do something you shouldn't. I saw you kiss her. She was a patient," Zoe mimicked. "You're a doctor. Though you won't be for long."

As he probably wouldn't be alive for long, Sebastian wasn't going to worry about his career right now.

"I called the police and the TV station," Deux continued. "I figured someone would see you and report it. They did."

"The antiques shops," Sebastian said.

"Rookie move, Doc. You were going right down the line, south to north, junk store to junk store."

"How'd you get there so fast?" If "someone" had called the cops or the news, wouldn't the cops or the news have arrived before Deux?

"There are *Venatores Mali* everywhere. One of them informed me."

Sebastian still didn't see how that had worked, but Deux had gotten to him before anyone else had. No denying that.

"What do you care about witches?"

"I don't. Roland does."

"Why do you care about him?"

"He came back from the dead."

Sebastian waited, but Deux seemed to think that was an explanation.

"Zoe?" Sebastian asked. "What about you?"

"Same reason."

Sebastian gave up. "*What* reason?"

"He conquered death. We can too."

"You think he's going to raise you from the dead?"

"He promised," Zoe said, a touch of whine in her voice.

"You're twelve. You're really worrying about death?"

"He promised her he'd fix her up—give her a better body, better face, eyes that don't need Coke-bottle glasses."

"He can do that?"

Deux shrugged. "Guess we'll see."

"He's a demon," Sebastian said. "He lies for a living."

"You think he's a demon?" Deux asked.

"You think he isn't?"

For a minute they appeared uncertain, a little confused. Then the guard laughed and shook his head. "That's crazy."

"You're a member of a serial-killing witch-hunting society that believes its leader is going to raise you from the dead. Who's crazy now?"

Confusion flickered in the man's eyes.

"Quit listening to him and do what you're supposed to do." Zoe was obviously the brains of this outfit. Wasn't much of a contest.

"What's he supposed to do?" Sebastian asked.

He didn't see the first fist coming. Pain exploded under his eye, then across his jaw on the backswing. His teeth cut his lip, and he tasted blood.

"Good enough?" Deux asked.

Zoe smirked. "Not even close."

Hours passed. The two left. Roland came in and issued a threat. He'd gut Sebastian like a deer. More animal imagery. At least they were on the same page.

Sebastian thought the guard might have given him a concussion. He'd had them before, and he'd always felt a little removed from the world—just like this.

Zoe and Deux returned. They stayed in the shadows, both awed and a little cowed by Roland McHugh.

The man didn't look like a demon. He looked like someone who'd spent most of his life in the wind and cold. His face was weathered but very white, as if every element but the sun had battered him. His hair was unruly, straggling to his shoulders—dark and misted with gray. He was tall and thin, gaunt—very Ebenezer Scrooge.

Sebastian considered the worn Levi's, flannel shirt, and boots. Hadn't McHugh been hoofing around in expensive athletic shoes the last time they'd seen him?

"Did you rob a construction worker?" Sebastian asked.

"If you like."

From the man's expression, Sebastian deduced he'd *killed* a construction worker.

"You'd better hope they come," Roland said.

"I hope they don't."

"I *will* kill you."

"Better than your killing them."

McHugh's brow creased. "Why wouldn't you value your life over theirs? You barely know them."

"I barely know you, but I still want you dead."

"You don't understand what they did to me."

"They were infants. They couldn't do more than puke or pee on you."

The demon's lip curled in disgust.

"Grow a pair," Sebastian ordered.

Roland's eyes flared, flames seemed to leap in their center. "My wife died screaming. My child never drew breath. Because of that witch."

"No. They died because of you. Because *you* didn't get help in time."

For an instant, sympathy flickered. Sebastian understood what guilt could do to a man. How losing someone you loved could make you think crazy things. However, it had made Roland McHugh do evil things and entice others to do them too. Charles Manson had never been proven a murderer, only an instigator of it. Yet still he rotted behind bars and always would. McHugh deserved no less; he deserved more.

A wolf howled—so close all of them jumped except the demon. He smiled. "Prudence."

That smile gave Sebastian the heebie-jeebies. There was lust in that smile—whether for the woman she'd been or the death he planned for the wolf she had become, it didn't matter. The expression was as nasty as he was.

Someone banged on the door. Roland jabbed a bony finger in that direction, and Deux disappeared into the encroaching darkness. The door opened. Silence descended. Both Roland and Zoe frowned.

"Deux?" Zoe called.

Nothing.

"Go," Roland ordered.

Zoe hesitated.

"Haven't I promised you beauty, wealth, and life everlasting?"

The guy was a real piece of work.

"You are safe," he said, his voice that of a TV evangelist. "Have no fear."

Zoe went. The silence deepened.

"You should probably have brought along more than two minions."

Shouts rang out, then shots.

Roland grinned as wide as the Grinch. "I did."


We circled around, came in from the forest and not the highway, sent the wolves ahead to scout.

"He's got an army positioned all around that factory." Elise stood behind a tree. She'd shift back as soon as we had a plan. A werewolf was a better weapon than a virologist. She couldn't throw theorems at them, but she could tear them into several smaller pieces. I wish I could watch.

"How are we going to get in?" Franklin asked.

"You aren't." I lifted the chalice. "We are."

My sisters held their items—wand for Raye, athame for Becca.

Raye's gaze lit on the pentacle carved into my chalice. She pulled the necklace over her head and offered it to me. "You should have this."

"You sure?"

"In the vision, the crone with the chalice also had the pentacle."

She had. There'd also been something about her that bothered me, but I still couldn't get my mind around what it was. I took the necklace.

Bobby, Owen, and Franklin held sniper rifles. Franklin had brought an impressive arsenal in the trunk of his sedan.

"How are we going to keep them occupied so you can slip into the factory without catching a stray bullet?" Franklin asked.

I lifted my gaze to the moon just peeking over the tree line and tucked my chalice into the waistband of my jeans. Raye and Becca did the same with their magical items. Then I held my hands out to my sisters.

"No need," I said, and when they touched me we disappeared.

# Chapter 24

We knew the spell. We had the items. We'd seen the lay of the land. What we hadn't seen was Zoe and Deux.

The instant we transported into the most shadowed, remote corner of the factory, I stifled a curse at the sight of them. What were they doing here?

Visions weren't exact. They changed depending upon the situation and the people involved in it. What they did. How others reacted to it.

I'd also brought about the vision of Sebastian on my own rather than receiving it from wherever it was the images came. I might have seen the situation before I was meant to, and then it was altered after the fact.

Nevertheless, they were here, and we had to do something about them. It was going to be difficult enough to perform the spell, which would require speech, and keep Roland off our necks long enough to finish. We weren't going to be able to deal with all three of them and cast the spell at the same time.

Raye tapped me on the shoulder, leaned in and whispered: "Send me outside. I'll take care of them."

If we waited too long there might be more of Roland's followers than we could handle. I had to trust that Raye knew what she was doing.

I touched her, thought of the outside of the building, and she was gone. I was getting really good at transportation. I hoped we were all getting very good at spells.

Things went quickly from that point on—Raye

knocked. Deux answered. Silence followed, then so did Zoe. I listened with half an ear to Sebastian and Roland converse. At least Sebastian was conscious, and he sounded coherent.

Roland seemed to think that his army was a secret. Excellent. Every little bit helped.

Raye returned, slipping silently through the shadows. I spread my hands in question. She flicked hers in answer. She'd tossed them far, far away. I hoped they landed in Afghanistan or maybe an Ebola-ridden African nation.

One of them had tried to smother me—I figured on Zoe, she was the type. But both of them had pretended to be caregivers, and considering where we'd just found them, their only care was murder and mayhem.

We waited for Roland to go after his missing minions. He wouldn't be gone long, but we'd get as much of the spell done as we could before he came back and found us. Then he was all Henry's. Our father had been waiting centuries to ass-kick this guy.

Except Roland didn't leave. That was the trouble with minions. It didn't matter if you misplaced a few, there were always a whole lot more.

I motioned to Becca, who'd found and brought along a flat stone similar to the one we'd used on the ridge as an altar. She set it down.

"We join together the power of blood-linked elemental witches."

We whispered the spell, yet still Roland heard. We'd known that he would.

"You need to run," Sebastian shouted.

Roland punched him in the jaw as he went past, and Sebastian slumped.

I cried out and Raye cut me a glance. "Focus. Start again."

"We join together the power of blood-linked elemental witches."

We set our items atop the stone. Athame. Wand. Pentacle. Chalice.

"He comes," we murmured as one.

Raye's eyes cut in a direction where there was nothing. When Roland flew backward and smacked into the far wall then landed on the cement, I knew that empty space held Henry.

Despite hitting brick and then falling onto concrete, Roland got up. We lifted our items, one for each of them, two for me. The chalice seemed to buzz with power against my palm, but from the pentacle I felt nothing.

"Go back from whence you came. Banished." Our joined voices rose, louder and stronger with every word. "Now and forever."

The three of us waited for Roland to start screaming as he was pulled into hell. Instead, he began to laugh. "You think magic will work on me? I'm immortal. I'll be here until the end of time."

Outside, gunfire erupted.

"And I'll never run out of fools willing to listen. My army will multiply. Eventually the *Venatores Mali* will overrun the world." He started toward us.

This time Becca shot fire from her fingertips. It hit him and rolled off like rain.

I took a step in his direction, thinking I'd send him to that Ebola-ridden country. Not that disease would hurt him either, but at least he wouldn't be here.

"No," Sebastian croaked. "Do not touch him."

Did he know something I didn't? What if I tried to transport Roland, and he ended up transporting me, or dragging me with him? I didn't know what kind of powers he had, but as I didn't want to touch him—at all, ever—I hesitated.

Raye swept her hand upward, lifting Roland off the ground. He dangled in the air, legs pumping, arms flailing. I wished for a convenient cliff to drop him from, but that probably wouldn't kill him either.

"Go," she said. "Get Sebastian out of here."

"We aren't leaving you." Becca glanced at me for confirmation, and I nodded.

"I'll transport him to the others." I hurried to Sebastian's side, started tugging on the ropes, got really dizzy and nearly fell on my face.

"Willow? You okay?"

I opened my eyes. My cheek was against his knee. I wasn't sure how that had happened.

"You've done too much." Becca was there, helping me untie Sebastian. "We all have. Magic drains energy. We're gonna have to regroup, recharge."

"You're going to have to do more than that," Roland said.

I tried to ignore him, but he was right. The spell hadn't worked. What were we going to do now?

Becca and I helped Sebastian to his feet. He was wobbly. So was I. Becca looked pale enough to wobble too.

"I'll be right behind you." Raye's eyes narrowed on the demon. "As soon as I drop him on his head."

"That won't do a damn thing," I said.

"It'll amuse the hell out of me," Raye muttered.

Outside, the moon poured down. The gunfire had petered off, though a shot sounded in the distance. As no bullets winged our way, I had to think that all the minions had been drawn elsewhere or killed.

A cry from Raye had us pausing mid-drag. Before I could say "Go" Becca growled, burst into flames, and became a wolf. She was getting really good at that too.

Sebastian's knee buckled, but he managed to get it

back under him and not drag us to the ground. Becca disappeared into the factory. I considered propping Sebastian against a wall and following her, then a white wolf and a black bounded inside too. Snarling and slavering ensued.

Raye emerged and took Becca's place with Sebastian. "I think Mom's enjoying tearing pieces out of him a little too much."

"That's impossible." There couldn't be too much enjoyment in that.

Headlights careened around the bend, and the Suburban skidded to a stop. Owen and Franklin spilled free, took Sebastian between them and hauled him toward the tailgate.

"Is he gone?" Franklin asked.

I lifted my eyebrows at Raye. If a bullet hadn't ended Roland McHugh, I doubted wolves could.

She shook her head.

We piled into the truck and sped away.


Sebastian lay in the cargo area, trying to catch his breath. From the sharp pain that caused, he thought Deux might have broken a few ribs.

"You shouldn't have come."

Willow, who had climbed into the back along with him, touched his cheek very gently. "He would have killed you."

"Better me than you."

"Shh." She traced her thumb across his fat lip.

"He isn't going to stop."

"Neither are we."

"From now on we stay together," Franklin ordered.

"No argument here," Sebastian said.

"What happened?" Bobby asked.

Raye told him. It didn't take long. Nevertheless,

Sebastian shut his eyes—they hurt—and then he drifted along on pain and his concussion as he listened.

"What happened with you guys?" Raye asked when she finished. "We heard shots."

"Pru wandered off and someone saw her," Bobby said.

"I doubt my mother wandered off. She was probably scouting the perimeter."

"Whatever. When all hell broke loose, she ran toward the factory and Elise followed."

"I can't believe neither one of them got shot."

"A black wolf is going to be pretty hard to hit in the dark," Franklin said. "And Elise isn't going to die unless someone was packing silver bullets."

"What would happen if they were?" Sebastian asked, curious.

"Great balls of fire."

Bobby slammed on the brakes. Everyone gasped. Sebastian sat up, wincing. If Roland McHugh stood in the road, surrounded by a halo of headlights, ready to kill them all, Sebastian didn't want to be lying flat on his back like an invalid.

However, the headlights revealed three wolves—black, white, cinnamon. They all glistened as if they were wet. It wasn't until they jumped into the cargo area too that Sebastian smelled the blood.

"Dead?" Raye asked.

Pru shook her head. Becca snorted. Elise just sat there being exquisite.

"I guess they tore him up pretty good before he went poof."

"How is he doing that?" Willow asked.

"Demon with black magic minions," Raye answered.

"I wish I knew more about them."

"No, you don't," Franklin said. "They're icky."

"Icky," Willow repeated. "Is that an FBI term?"

"Yes."

Sebastian laughed, then stopped when his ribs shrieked. He lay back down in a hurry.

"Becca." Willow's expression reflected her concern. "Can you do something for him?"

The cinnamon wolf swung her snout in Sebastian's direction. It was an odd feeling to have those fangs so close to his face, but the familiar eyes of Becca were gentle and kind. She licked his forehead and the blistering headache and some of the dizziness faded.

"Only the worst of it now," Raye warned. "Or you won't have the energy to shift back."

"But—" Willow began.

"I'm okay," Sebastian said.

"You are so far from okay it isn't even funny."

"I never said it was funny."

Willow yanked up his shirt. Her indrawn breath told him that he was right about the ribs. They must be bruised pretty badly. He decided not to look.

Becca licked him right where it hurt, and suddenly it didn't anymore.

"Thank you," he said.

She flopped down next to him. Her fur tickled his skin. Her warmth felt really good. With the steady hum of the tires on the highway like a lullaby, Sebastian drifted off.

He awoke when the Suburban stopped. They were back at the cabin.

The wolves jumped out the instant the cargo door went up. Pru shot into the forest. The other two did not. For an instant Sebastian wondered why Elise and Becca hadn't changed back, then he remembered they'd have naked issues.

"Everyone get some rest," Raye said. "Morning

powwow." She flicked a glance at Willow. "Maybe we'll know something new by then."

"What we knew before wasn't good enough." Willow scooted to the edge of the SUV and hopped off. "Why have a vision if it isn't going to work?"

It was a good question. One that no one had the answer to since they all trudged into the house. Except for Franklin and Elise, who started for their car.

"Where do you think you're going?" Willow asked.

"Hotel."

"Not." Willow pointed at the cabin. "There's an extra room."

The fed hesitated.

"And a protection spell," Sebastian added.

"Sold." Franklin and the white wolf followed the others inside.

"Are you hungry?" Willow asked, and Sebastian shook his head. From the appearance of the empty living area and closed bedroom doors, no one else was hungry either.

Sebastian and Willow went into their room and closed the door. She took one step away, and he couldn't help himself, he pulled her into his arms.

"I told you not to come." He pressed his aching face against her hair.

"Did you think that would work?"

"I hoped."

"Would you have left me there?"

"Of course not!"

"There you go."

She went into the bathroom. Water ran for long enough that he leaned against the dresser and closed his eyes. When he opened them she knelt by the door, sprinkling something from a glass jar in a line right in front of it.

"Rosemary," she said, when she saw him watching. "Bars the ghosts."

"Have you done that before?" He certainly hoped so. The idea of his sister—or her father—seeing what had gone on here—

"Of course." She came to him and pressed a warm washcloth to his lips, chin, nose, and cheek. It felt almost as good as her touch. The pain and the steadily pinkening washcloth should have turned off his libido. They didn't.

She tossed the cloth onto the dresser, then slid her arms around his waist and held on. "I was so afraid."

He remembered what she'd looked like as she'd done the spell. She hadn't looked afraid; she'd looked magnificent.

He pressed his lips to her temple. She brushed hers against his throat. He felt her tongue snake out and taste the curve of his neck. His body tightened, and he stepped away. "We need to rest."

She put her hand against the front of his pants. "This doesn't feel very restful." Her fingertip traced his length and he leaped. "More restless."

He should turn away, perhaps run away, lock himself in the bathroom like a frightened virgin. He *was* frightened—of what he felt, what he knew, what he'd seen and what he hadn't. This could end badly. For all of them.

"You're thinking too loudly." She continued to stroke him. He wasn't strong enough to make her stop. What if they never had another night beyond tonight?

It was that last very loud thought that convinced him. Life was too short and theirs might be even shorter. He couldn't go forward with any kind of strength and courage unless he gave in to his weakness for her.

He buried his fingers in her hair, the soft strands spilling over his wrists, caressing the backs of his arms. He felt her smile when he took her mouth, tasted it too—oranges and snow, cherries and firelight, lemons and a summer rain.

They lost their clothes, moved to the bed where he took his time, worshipping every inch of her with his lips and hands and tongue. He rose onto his knees. All she wore was the necklace—a five-pointed star within a circle.

"Isn't that Raye's?"

"It belonged to an earth witch. We needed the four elemental items." She frowned, thinking too hard.

"Okay." He brushed his nail across it and got a shock, which made her frown harder. He started to take the necklace off and she shook her head.

"I think I need to keep it on."

"Why?"

"I'm not sure."

A week ago, he would have questioned that kind of talk as obsessive or compulsive or delusional. But now he knew better. He left the pentacle right where it was and lay at her side. He brushed at the frown lines on her brow with his thumb. When they didn't go away, he used his mouth until they did. Then he used his mouth everywhere else.

When she was gasping his name, grasping his arms, begging, bucking, he slid home.

*She* was home, and she always would be.

Electricity seemed to spark along his skin, causing every hair on his body to lift. Her hair stirred in an invisible wind. It wrapped around his neck, pulled him closer. When he kissed her, every vision she'd had of them through the years spilled into his mind. Her. Him. Them. Us. We. He felt her fall in love with him. More importantly he felt himself fall in love with her.

At first he thought her soft gasp was completion, then

he saw the wonder in her eyes. She felt it too, the connection between them that went deeper than any he'd ever had before, or ever would have again.

"I love you," they said as one.

Her body contracted; he came in a rush that dizzied him. He kissed her, drinking her cries, tasting the joy.

Outside, rain began to fall. Gently. Peacefully. No thunder. No lightning. No wind.

When it was over, he held her close and listened to the patter of the drops against the window. He had a nagging feeling that he'd forgotten something, but what? Everything he'd needed was in her.

"You're thinking too loudly again." She stroked his stomach. "Go to sleep."

Her voice, her touch, her love, soothed him. When his parents had died, he'd lost a home. When his sister did, he'd lost faith in himself. He'd given up any hope of family. Now he'd found all three in her.

"I'll do anything to keep you safe."

"Me too."

In the depths of the night, something woke him. Willow lay in his arms. He tightened them, and she whispered his name. He tried to open his eyes but they were sore, swollen, and he could only crack one a bit.

The room seemed to glow—not silver with moonlight, how could it? The rain still fell—but golden and warm, like the sun. It was nice.

He turned his face toward that warmth, that glow.

Toward her.


The pentacle was glowing—throbbing, humming, heating. The energy I'd felt from the chalice now flowed from it too. I had no idea what had happened while we slept, but the object had changed somehow. I needed to tell my sisters.

I slid from Sebastian's arms. Then stood at the side of the bed just looking at him. His poor face. I never wanted him near Roland McHugh again.

I put on my clothes and brought my chalice with me into the living room. I could see every nook and cranny clearly since the pentacle was still throwing off light like a beacon. No Pru. I wondered if she was searching the forest for a trace of Roland, or just out being a wolf.

Two bedroom doors opened, and my sisters came out. Becca had feet and hands again. She'd need them.

Their eyes widened at the sight of the glowing pentacle. They hurriedly shut the doors behind them and joined me.

"What did you do?" Raye whispered.

"No idea. The light woke me up."

"The hum woke me up." Raye glanced at Becca. "You too?"

She nodded.

"It never did this when you wore it?" I asked.

"Never."

"I think it's ready," I said.

"For what?"

"The spell. When I lifted the chalice at the factory, the energy made my hand vibrate."

"Mine too," Becca said.

"Mine three," Raye agreed. "What about the pentacle?"

"There was nothing then. We need to do the spell again now."

"Now?" Raye repeated.

"What if the thing stops glowing? I have no idea why it started."

"She has a point." Becca picked up her athame from the kitchen table.

"Let's get 'er done." Raye wrapped her fingers around her wand, which sat on the counter.

They'd learned that they couldn't put the objects too closely together or they vibrated so much it seemed like an earthquake was imminent.

"Just the three of us," I said.

"The guys aren't going to like it."

I thought of Sebastian's battered face and broken ribs. "I can't put him in danger again."

Becca and Raye exchanged glances, nodded. I could tell by their expressions they didn't want the men they loved anywhere near demon Roland again either.

"What about Henry?" Raye asked.

"Is he here?"

She shook her head. "Probably with Pru."

"He might be handy to have along."

"Henry?" Raye said just above a whisper, then waited. She repeated his name and the waiting, then shook her head. "I could summon him, but it'll take time, and he doesn't like it. If he can come when I call his name, he will. If he doesn't, he's busy with ghostly, witchy things."

"He'll be able to find you, right?"

"Right. But how are we going to find Roland?"

"Think of him," I said. "His face, his voice."

"His smell," Raye muttered.

"Touch me," I ordered, and they did.

# Chapter 25

Sebastian came awake with a gasp, his heart thundering.

A wolf was howling. From the volume, it was howling in the yard. Pru? Becca? Elise? It didn't matter. The way she was howling, something wasn't right.

"Willow?" he called. She didn't answer. The watery gray light filling the room signaled that dawn had recently arrived.

He tugged on his pants, headed for the closed door, sticking his head into the bathroom just to make sure the place was as empty as it felt. It was.

He reached the living room at the same time Bobby did. Owen was already at the front door. The instant he opened it, Pru shot inside. Her eyes were wide and wild. She ran from room to room.

Franklin and Elise came out of theirs.

"What's wrong?" Franklin asked.

"She's looking for something," Owen said.

"Someone," Elise corrected. "Where are the girls?"

"Not here." Bobby scrubbed his hand through his hair. "Are all the cars outside?"

"Yes," Owen answered. "But they don't need a car. All they need is Willow and the moon. Although the way their powers have been increasing they might not even need the moon anymore."

"They wouldn't," Sebastian murmured. "Would they?"

"The elemental items are gone." Elise pointed to the places where they'd been. "I'd say they would, have, did."

"Why?" Now Bobby yanked at his hair; Sebastian understood the sentiment. "The spell didn't work. They'll get kicked into next week."

"Calm down," Elise ordered. "They must have figured out what went wrong and decided to end this before anyone else got hurt."

"No one's gotten hurt," Sebastian said.

"Have you seen your face?" Owen asked.

Considering how it ached, he probably didn't want to.

"We have to find them." Sebastian picked up his shoes. "The guy's a demon, with minions."

"Never thought I'd hear those words come out of your mouth," Bobby said. "But he is and we do. How?"

Pru yipped. The wolf stared at the empty corner, head tilted.

"Henry," Bobby said. "He'll know where Raye is."

"That's swell." Owen tried to yank on his hair but he didn't have enough of it to grab. "What good will that do us? We can't see Henry or understand Pru."

Pru spun and raced for the still-open door. Owen kicked it shut and she nearly ate wood. The great black wolf turned her emerald-green eyes on him and snarled.

"I'm not letting you out until you agree that we follow you in the Suburban."

The door started to open on its own. Owen set his big hand on it and held it shut. "Knock that off, Henry. Time's a-wastin'."

Pru dipped her head.

Everyone with two legs got in the SUV.

One minute we were at the cabin—warm and safe. The next we stood on the edge of a cliff staring down at a body of water big enough to be an ocean.

Lake Superior. We hadn't gone far.

The moon hovered on the horizon, spreading silver across the roiling waves. Soon it would disappear and the golden rays of the sun would burst free.

"This is where I died," Becca said.

She looked a little pale. I didn't blame her.

"Also where you came back to life." Raye moved to a low, flat rock nearly obscured by long, dry grass. "We can use this as the altar."

"It *is* an altar." Becca inched back. "I was sacrificed on it."

"And now we'll use it to end the one who had that really, really bad idea." Raye met Becca's eyes. "Okay?"

Becca nodded but she stayed where she was. I took her hand. She seemed to need it. Together we joined Raye and set our items on the stone. The pentacle stopped glowing the instant I took it off.

"Shit," I said. "Now what?"

Raye gestured at the necklace. "Put it back on."

I did, and the glow returned. All three of us released a breath.

"Start the chant," Raye ordered.

"Now?" I blurted. "We're alone."

"So were the crones when they started, remember? We need a head start."

"We need something," Becca agreed.

"All we have is each other," I said.

"Will it be enough?" She still seemed too pale.

"It has to be."

"Good always triumphs over evil." Raye's dark hair began to swirl in the chilly north wind. It blew toward Becca's red hair and the ends flowed together like they had before.

"You've been watching too many movies and not enough nighttime news." Becca's hair waved toward mine, and fire flowed into the sun. Our elemental items rattled and the pentacle around my neck lifted, tugging in their direction.

"Let's do this," Raye said. "Repeat the chant until we see him, then pick up the items and end him. Got it?"

Becca and I nodded.

"We join together the power of blood-linked elemental witches," we said.

Then we said it again, again, again. The wind continued to swirl. It brought the sound of voices. We turned toward the trees as nearly a hundred minions stepped out.

"He comes?" Raye asked.

"Eventually," I answered.

They caught sight of us and began to run across the grass in our direction. The lead minions flew sideways as if . . .

"Henry's here," Raye said. "Which means the others will be soon. I should have shielded us, but I was out of rosemary. Either of you have any?"

Becca and I shook our heads and Raye cursed. "We'd have to have a buttload to do the job right anyway. We need to hurry."

"Roland needs to hurry. If he doesn't come, then how can we make him go?"

"We could summon him again." Becca frowned at the wall of minions that flowed in our direction.

"Because that worked so well last time," Raye said. "They'll be on us before we get that spell done."

"I don't think so." Becca shot fire from her fingertips.

I held my breath, waiting for the shrieks of the dying. There were shrieks but more of surprise than anything else. A wall of fire went up all around them, trapping the minions in a flaming playpen.

"Nice," I said.

"Thanks," Becca said, but she was even paler. Shooting that much flame had drained her.

A movement at the edge of the forest drew my attention. Terrified the others had arrived ahead of Roland, I felt relief blossom at the sight of the demon himself.

"Showtime," I said.

He started toward us at a leisurely pace, as if he hadn't a care in the world. The glance he threw at the trapped minions was disdainful. The one he threw at us was feral. I couldn't help it. A lightning bolt zapped down in front of him. He ignored it. The next one hit him in the head. He staggered, but he didn't fall.

"I hate this guy," I muttered.

"Stop," Raye said. "Save your juice for the spell."

Roland pulled out a knife. The blade sparkled bright and shiny in the just-born sun. "Go ahead," he said. "Your spell will not work."

He levitated, flying ten feet into the air, then free-falling and smashing into the ground. A grunt was the only indication that he'd hit pretty hard. He stood up. He still held the knife.

"Should have brought a gun," he said. "But I do so like the sound a knife makes when it goes in."

Henry lifted him again. This time he kept the guy in the air. Unfortunately, he could still talk.

"If you allow me to kill you without any more fuss, your lovers can live. Keep this up and they die." He waggled the knife. "They die ugly. The wolf too."

He dipped as if the final sentence had shocked Henry enough to make him lose focus. I glanced at Raye, who was now as pale as Becca. Considering the numbness of my lips, I had a feeling I was too.

We'd come here alone to protect the ones we loved. If our deaths could guarantee that—

"We can't trust him," Raye said. "He's a demon. If we're dead, so are they. Along with every witch in the world."

"Which is nothing less than they deserve." His fingers tightened on the hilt of the knife. "My wife died screaming. My child never drew breath. Because of a witch."

"You're delusional," Raye snapped. "My mother tried to help your wife, to save your child."

"She did not. She used their deaths to give life to the three of you, and I will take those lives back."

"Don't bother," I said. "You can't reason with cuckoo." That much I knew.

"What is your answer? Think, lassies. You cannot kill me, and you cannot send me back."

"He wouldn't be making the deal if he truly believed the spell wouldn't work," Becca said.

"It *won't* work. You're one witch short. The power of blood-linked *elemental* witches. There are four elements and only three of you. You be short an earth witch."

I felt a chill. He was right. Except—

"There were only three crones."

"Were there now?" Roland murmured.

I didn't know what that meant, but I didn't like his smirk, or his confidence, or his seeming knowledge of what I'd seen.

"Finish this," Raye said.

"But—" Becca's gaze went to the tree line as Bobby, Owen, Sebastian, Franklin, Elise, and Pru emerged.

I could barely breathe. I didn't know what to do. If dying would save him, I would.

"If you try it," Roland said, "you will be sorry."

My sisters were as uncertain and terrified as I was. A tear trickled down Becca's cheek.

Reality shimmied, and in that teardrop, I saw the truth. Three crones, but not really. The one who had held the chalice and the pentacle was more than a crone. I suddenly understood what had been different about her.

"Do it," I said.

Together we spoke. "Go back from whence you came. Banished. Now and forever."

We picked up our items. As soon as we did, the pentacle around my neck lifted on its own. I leaned forward so we could touch the four of them together.

The next instant *zzzt* happened. Roland hovered in the air, but the entire world seemed to have paused—waiting, listening. The demon's gaze met mine. I smirked. His eyes widened. I gave him the finger an instant before he started screaming.

He flew backward through the air, clutching at nothing. Then he dropped to the ground with a solid thud. His fingernails drew furrows in the earth as he continued to pick up speed toward the edge of the cliff.

The three of us jumped up, ran after. The lake parted like the Red Sea, began to bubble and boil like a cauldron. Screaming, he dropped. The water closed over him, ending the sound, then flipped a single red-tinged wave up, smoothing out as if both Roland and the cauldron had never been.

"Wow," Raye said. "That was—"

"Fricking fantastic," I finished.

"He's really gone?" Becca asked.

"Yeah," I said.

"You're sure?" Raye still looked worried.

"Definitely."

"Why?" Raye said at the same time Becca said, "How?"

I took both their hands in mine, then drew them to my stomach. "Hello, my little earth witch."

# Chapter 26

Sebastian and the others arrived at the edge of the cliff just as the girls joined hands and touched Willow's stomach. Sebastian remembered what he'd forgotten the night before in a sudden burst of clarity, even before he heard her say, "Hello, my little earth witch."

"Dude." Owen slapped him on the back.

"Nice job." Bobby shook his hand.

Willow spun, eyes wide. "Sorry."

"I'm not." Sebastian reached for her, and she came into his arms.

"I told you you'd be the one to save me, to save us all."

"I thought you meant with my fists, my feet, a gun, my wits."

"Penis works," Owen said.

Sebastian shot him a glance, and Owen lifted his hands in surrender.

"We were missing an earth witch," Willow continued. "You gave her to me. To us. And now we're safe." She pressed her lips to the hollow of his throat and whispered, "Thank you."

"My pleasure."

"Would someone like to inform me just what is going on here?"

A very tall, thin, old, once-blond man stood between them and the still flaming ring of fire that hemmed in the minions. His German accent and plethora of guns and ammo revealed his identity even before Owen blurted, "Edward," at the same time Nic straightened as if he'd been goosed and said, "Sir!"

"Where did he come from?" Sebastian asked.

"Germany," Elise said.

"Today?"

"Today I came from New Orleans, but I was already on the ground when Elise called."

He continued to peer at the people beyond the flames, who called out for help, even tried to reach out, only to snatch their hands back when they were singed.

"Who did this?" Edward asked.

Becca tentatively raised her hand. Owen drew it back down. "Do *not* tell him what else you can do."

Considering the man was a werewolf hunter, probably a good idea.

"I will need you to put out the flames so I can deal with them."

"How's he gonna deal with them?" Sebastian eyed the pistols on the old man's hips and the rifle in his hand.

"They're killers," Bobby said. "Do you care?"

Sebastian released Willow from his embrace, but he kept his arm around her. "Roland whispered to them in their heads. That's kind of hard to ignore."

"My mom heard him," Owen said. "Maybe all her life."

"Your mom stopped listening to him." Becca took Owen's hand. "If she could do it they could too."

"Maybe." Sebastian lifted a shoulder. "Maybe not. Everyone's different."

"They're different, all right," Raye agreed.

Edward scowled at the minions. "I suppose that means I cannot kill them."

"Yes," Elise said. "That's exactly what it means.

We've had this talk. You can't just go around shooting people."

"I can, but it does cause so many more problems than it used to."

"We'll take them to our compound and evaluate them." Elise waved at the fire, which still burned hot, bright, and eight feet high. "You mind?"

"I—uh—" Becca bit her lip. "I know how to start a fire. No idea how to stop one."

"That's because you're the fire witch." Willow pointed at a stray cloud with one finger. "I'm the water witch."

She fired her finger gun, and rain toppled from the sunny sky directly onto both the minions and the fire. A hiss rose as the fire died. As soon as the flames fell, those who'd been confined tried to run.

A line of people with guns materialized out of the trees. The *Venatores-Mali* froze without even being told.

"I also have minions," Edward said. "Put them in the conveyance."

"They're soaked," shouted a petite blond woman with nearly as many guns as Edward. "And don't call me a minion."

He sighed. "You'd think a water witch could control that better."

"I could." Willow's gaze settled on one particular minion. "I just didn't want to."

Zoe saw Sebastian at the same time he saw her. "That's him," she shouted. "He kidnapped a patient."

"What patient would that be?" Edward asked.

"The one he's got his hands all over."

Deux pushed his way to her side. "He should be in jail."

"I should have tossed them farther," Raye said.

"Much," Becca agreed.

"I'm going to have to deal with this." Sebastian sighed. "Technically they're right."

"Not anymore," Edward said. "As of yesterday, Willow was never a patient."

"But I . . . was."

"You were never crazy," Edward continued. "You were magic. Therefore, no need to be a patient."

"Just because it shouldn't have happened doesn't mean it didn't." Sebastian rubbed Willow's back. He wanted to touch her stomach, like her sisters had, but it would have to wait. Maybe a long time if he wound up in jail.

"According to every record in the system, Willow Black not only didn't reside at the psychiatric facility, but she no longer exists. Once all this is settled, we'll give her a past that won't cause any problems."

"My boss knows differently." And Dr. Tronsted wasn't the type to let things go.

"You'd be surprised what people forget about when there's no evidence to support it."

"What does that mean?"

"Your superior has been told by *her* superiors that the situation has been dealt with higher up. If she continues to push the issue, if she tries to prove what there's no longer any proof of . . ." Edward shifted one shoulder.

"She'll seem crazier than I was," Willow said.

Sebastian pulled her closer. "You weren't crazy."

"You know what I mean."

"I broke a lot of rules." Maybe all of them.

"The rules of a world without magic don't apply to those who live in a world full of it," the old man said.

Edward sounded pretty certain of that. Sebastian wished that he could be. Perhaps it just took some getting used to.

"I have done this many, many times before," Edward continued, "and it has worked every time. Those in authority actually follow orders with a lot less questions than you'd think."

"And if they don't," Elise said, affecting a very convincing German accent, "we have ways of making them."

Sebastian wasn't sure if she was joking or not. He decided to behave like someone in authority and not ask.

"What about them?" Sebastian lifted his chin to indicate Zoe and Deux, who weren't going to shut up.

"From the appearance of your face, Doctor, I think you were abducted. I think they did it. How does that work for you?"

He thought of Zoe trying to smother Willow and Deux helping her do all sorts of other nasty stuff, including smacking him in the face while he was powerless to stop the blows. "I like it."

"Can he do all that?" Willow asked.

Good question. The old man might be crazier than any of the minions—his or Roland's.

"*I'm* going to have to do all that," Elise said. "But, yeah, consider it done."

Things moved so fast I got dizzy. Edward, Elise, and Nic left with the other *Jäger-Suchers* and Roland's minions, some of whom seemed to have woken from a trance with little memory of the past few weeks. Others, like Zoe and Deux, remembered everything and didn't care what they'd done.

I wasn't sure which was worse—being possessed by evil, or actually being evil.

"Is it really over?" I asked.

"I think s—" Becca began, then frowned and glanced right, left. "Where's Pru?"

Raye caught her breath. Her eyes filled with tears.

"What is it?" Bobby rushed to her, but she held out a trembling finger toward a space that appeared empty but must not be.

"Look." She beckoned for us all to join hands as we had before.

As soon as we did, I saw Henry, his arms wrapped around the woman I'd seen in a vision, dying on a pyre for the sake of her children. The two only had eyes for each other, and why not? They hadn't been together on the same plane for centuries.

"I think it's over," Becca said.

Henry's gaze fell on each of us in turn. "*Mo chlann,* it has just begun."

Then he kissed his wife as his children watched. It was one of the most beautiful things I'd ever seen.

"Mom." Owen's voice trembled.

Mary stood between us and our parents, who continued to make out.

"Baby boy," she replied.

"That's what you called the dog."

"Not anymore."

She glanced at me. "Hi, sweetie."

"Mary—" My voice broke. She sounded so lucid, like the woman she could have been if not for . . . so many things.

"You were the only friend I ever had, Willow. I'll never forget that."

I nodded, but I still couldn't speak.

"Are you okay, Mom?"

"Better than okay. Roland's voice is gone. I feel more myself than I ever have."

"Then why are you still here?"

"Same reason she is."

A young, thin girl, with long dark hair and Sebastian's

eyes materialized. From the familiar earrings—one of which still shone in Sebastian's ear—I knew who she was even before Sebastian whispered, "Emma."

"You need to let me go, Bass."

"I—I can't. I failed you."

"I failed me. You did everything you could."

"You were too young to die."

"I was. But it's over. Let it be over. Please. There are better places for me." She reached for Mary's hand. "For us."

He swallowed, nodded. The two remained.

"Aren't they supposed to fade?" I asked. "Vanish? Something?"

"We will," Mary said.

"After the wedding," Emma agreed.

# Epilogue

"It's fitting that we're getting married on Halloween," I said.

"Samhain," Raye corrected. "Henry keeps saying Old Hallowmas, which is what the Scots call it. The veil is thin tonight. The spirits can cross over more easily."

I hoped so. Sebastian's sister and Mary needed to go on. It bothered both Sebastian and Owen to have them here, even though they couldn't see them unless we were all connected. And Bobby—who'd felt spirits even before he met Raye—had gotten kind of twitchy.

"Samhain is the witches' new year," Raye continued. "Perfect time to start a new life."

"This is a time of magic," I said. "Can you feel it?"

Raye and Becca smiled. Of course they did.

We stood in front of the floor-length mirror in the largest bedroom of the cabin. We wore the same dresses—mermaid style—which flattered all of us and seemed apropos considering where our wedding would take place, as well as the otherworldliness of our lives. Right now they were a bland cream, but that wasn't going to last.

We each held a red rose. Around the stems we'd tied a strand of our hair. Three candles sat on the floor in front of us—yellow, red, and white, representing mind, heart, and soul. Raye lit the yellow, Becca the red, and I put a match to the white. We began to pluck the petals from our roses, outside to in, as we chanted.

"Show yourself. Your own true heart will be revealed for all to see. So shall it be."

We tossed the petals into the air, and as they cascaded over us, our dresses reflected our true colors.

Raye's shifted to an icy blue-white. A crown of baby's breath appeared atop her flowing black hair.

Becca's dress became brilliant yellow, her crown fashioned of orange irises, which should clash with her red hair but didn't.

My dress now reflected the depths of a tropical ocean, the circlet of flowers a twist of bluebells.

"Ready?" I offered my hands.

The instant we touched, we disappeared from the cabin and reappeared on the hill above Lake Superior. Our soon-to-be-husbands stood with their backs to the water. The sun hovered at the edge of night; the entire sky had gone pink and blue. Stars sprang up like diamonds as the moon began to rise.

A triple wedding. Seemed like the best way to go.

The stone altar held our magical instruments. A low hum emanated from them. To do what we wanted to for this wedding we'd need all the power we could get.

The three men wore identical black suits—Bobby with a white shirt and tie, Owen's shirt was red, his tie yellow, and Sebastian . . .

My gaze met his and my stomach danced. "Hush, little one," I murmured.

Silly, I couldn't feel her move yet. Except I did.

Sebastian wore an aquamarine shirt and a bluebell-shaded tie. Becca had healed his face. Even if she hadn't, he'd be beautiful. He'd tucked his curling dark hair behind his ears so the firelight turned Emma's earring from gold, to bronze, to silver.

I loved that earring. Always had. Always would.

Together, my sisters and I joined hands with our men,

creating a circle of six—or was it seven?—around the altar, our ghost guests and our parents. The moon blazed silver, and the spirits appeared as corporeal as we were.

At least for tonight.

Henry stood behind the altar, our mother at his side. Now that Roland was dead, the brands on their necks had vanished. That absence had convinced us more than anything that the horror was really, truly over.

Our father would marry us tonight as witches should be. In the air, beneath the moon, near the water, warmed by flame, our bare feet touching the earth.

In the coming weeks, Raye and Becca would take part in a second ceremony for their other families, who knew nothing of this, of us, of tonight. They wouldn't understand.

Sebastian tightened his fingers around mine. He and I had no one but each other and the people in this clearing. It was enough.

"We ask for the blessings of nature's elements," Henry began. "Air, fire, water, and earth."

He stood in front of Raye and Bobby. "We ask the spirits of Air to keep the lines of communication open between this couple. May their future be as bright as the sun on the horizon. As Air flows freely to and from and through us all, may their hearts and minds and souls come to know each other the same."

He turned to Becca and Owen. "Spirits of Fire, we ask that their passion for each other and for life remain ever strong, fortifying them each day with vibrancy, boldness, and courage. Fire clears the way for new growth. This power is theirs, to bring about the quality that comes from true love."

Henry stepped in front of Sebastian and me. "We ask the spirits of Water that their love for each other will be like the serenity of the ocean, an oasis that forever surrounds them, letting the surety with which Water makes its journey, flowing over rocks, and around trees, becoming vapor and riding the clouds, serve as a reminder that love endures."

Henry stepped to the center of the circle where Pru, Mary, and Emma stood—joy in their eyes, happy tears on their cheeks.

"Spirits of the Earth," he continued. "Give those who are here before you a rock-solid place to stand and fulfill their destinies. May their journeys mirror the vast planes and fertile lands, may they find the right seeds to sow to ensure a bountiful harvest."

Sebastian flushed. He'd sown a seed and it had definitely become bountiful. I suppose having his soon-to-be-father-in-law point that out during the wedding *was* embarrassing. Then again, if Sebastian hadn't done so, we'd all be dead. Some of us would be dead-er.

Henry lifted his gaze to the star that blazed over the water. "When they look at the Northern Star, may they know it is as brilliant and constant as their love for each other."

The star seemed to blink—bright, brighter, brightest—as if it knew we were watching. Was one of us doing that? Or was it all of us—together?

"Father, Mother, Divine Spirit, we ask your blessing upon these couples. May they become one in truth and forever revel in the magic that is love."

Several stars fell, leaving trails like silver fireworks across the night.

"Kiss the brides."

It wasn't easy to do holding hands in a circle, but we managed.

When I returned my gaze to my parents, Pru held a naked baby in her arms.

"Is that—" I began.

"Our granddaughter," Henry said. "We'll spend the next several months getting to know her. But I can already tell you're going to have your hands full."

"Swell," Sebastian muttered, but the gaze he turned on our girl revealed he was already in love.

"We'll return every year at Samhain," Pru said. "When the veil is thin."

"Just you two?" I asked.

"Whoever you like," Pru answered. "All you have to do is come together and ask."

The baby lifted a chubby arm and opened, closed, then opened her hand. Everyone in the center of the circle did the same.

The rest of us released our hold on each other, and they were gone—but not for good. There was comfort in that.

After a kiss on each wife's brow, the new husbands moved off so we three sisters could say good-bye.

"Right here, same time next year?" Raye asked.

We did a group hug.

"It's a date," I said.

Not that we wouldn't see each other before that. We wouldn't be very far apart.

Raye and Bobby were returning to her hometown of New Bergin, where she was a kindergarten teacher and he was the police chief. They had a black cat named Samhain, which was also fitting.

Becca and Owen would head for their hometown of Three Harbors nearby. Becca had a veterinary practice, and Owen planned to raise and train military working dogs for the Marines. His former MWD, Reggie, would be retiring soon and coming to live with them and their calico kitten, Grenade.

"Maybe we should get a cat," I said as the others drove away, leaving us alone beneath the stars.

"I think a baby is enough for now." Sebastian laid his palm on my stomach.

"Okay." I covered his hand with my own.

Elise and Edward had been as good as their word, and Sebastian hadn't lost his license or his job at the facility, though he had taken a leave of absence from the latter. There'd been hints he could have Dr. Tronsted's job, as she'd accepted one in Fairbanks, Alaska.

I had a new identity—Willow Frasier—complete with a shiny new passport. Sebastian and I had decided to try it out with a honeymoon in Scotland. There would be time enough to decide what to do with the rest of our lives when we returned.

Sebastian kissed me quick; then with our hands atop the earth witch to come, he murmured, "It's going to be magic."

One final star fell to the earth and burst open like a shower of flame across the water.

How could it not be?

Look for these other Sisters of the Craft novels by
*New York Times* Bestselling Author

**LORI HANDELAND**

HEAT OF THE MOMENT
IN THE AIR TONIGHT

Available from St. Martin's Paperbacks